To

Revenge is a deadly game.

Ray Wenck

Live To Die Again

Copyright © 2016 Ray Wenck
Editor: Jodi McDermitt
Cover: Tyler Bertrand
Published by Glory Days Press

1

"I expect you boys to help put the groceries away before you go running off to whatever you plan on doing," Margo Kelly said to her sons.

As usual, there was no response.

"Did you hear me?" she said. This time her voice hit the tone she used when she demanded an answer.

"Yeah, Mom, we heard you," fourteen-year-old Sean answered.

"You don't have to yell," said JT, mimicking his mother's voice.

Margo saw the two boys laugh and fist bump through the rearview mirror. The two boys always sat in the back to watch movies or play video games.

"Very funny, wise guy." Despite her tone, Margo smiled.

JT watched over the seat as his mother steered the minivan toward the ascending garage door, waited and then pulled in. The sixteen-year-old would be taking drivers' ed soon and watched often. When his mother was satisfied with her park, she shut down the engine and leaned toward the passenger seat to grab her purse.

JT looked down to undo the seat belt. In a sudden burst of motion, a young white man with stringy brown hair and wielding a knife, ripped open the front door and confronted Margo. A taller, white guy, hair shaved on both sides, leaving a tuft of hair standing straight up in the middle, tried to open the locked passenger side.

The suddenness of the assault startled them all. Margo screamed. The boys jumped and froze. Margo clung to her purse. The white man reached in to snatch it from her, but she jerked away.

The taller man pounded on the window. "Open this door!"

"Come on, bitch," the knife wielder said. "Don't make me cut you. Give it up."

"Mom?" JT said. The fear registered in his voice.

Sean, always the more aggressive of the two boys and the quickest to anger, flung back the sliding side door and launched out onto the thief. JT sat frozen in place afraid to move. He slid to the open door and sat on the edge of the seat, trying to decide what to do. His fear immobilized him.

JT watched as Sean drove the assailant into the side wall of the garage and began wailing on him. The man covered up to block some of the blows, evidently forgetting he was the one with the knife. The taller man came around the car. He also now held a knife. When he lined it up to drive it into Sean's back, JT forgot his fear. He yelled and jumped on the man's back. Reaching around the assailant's head JT clawed wildly at his face. The man screamed as JT raked an eye. The knife fell from his hand.

JT shouted, "Mom, call 911!"

JT clung to his opponent's back, one arm around his neck, while the other threw punches at the side of his head. The man struggled to break free, slamming JT against the wall, but the boy held fast and pulled harder against the man's throat.

With phone in hand, his mother jumped out of the minivan. Yelling into the phone to the 911 operator, Margo struck Sean's opponent repeatedly with her purse.

They were winning. Sean was pounding solid blows onto the first man's head. JT continued his chokehold around his opponent, but then caught a glimpse of a third man entering the garage. The new attacker, a more muscled black man, picked up an aluminum baseball bat that was leaning against the wall and advanced on JT. As JT's opponent spun to dislodge him, the third man swung the bat and connected with his back. The blow caused JT to release his hold and drop to the floor, writhing in pain.

Now free, the man JT had been strangling spun around and delivered a savage kick to his stomach. Then he turned to help the man Sean battled. JT looked to his brother for help. Sean had his man down on the floor and was pounding on him. His mother was still yelling into the phone and standing over her son.

JT saw his opponent bend to pick up the dropped knife and step toward Sean. JT pushed up from the floor and shouted, "Sean!" but he was too late to save his brother. The man drove the blade into Sean's back. Sean arched backward, trying to clutch the knife. Margo dropped her purse and the phone, bringing both hands to her face.

"Sean!" She screamed and flung herself at the man, flailing her arms at him.

All JT could think about was saving his mother. The frenzied man landed a punch on Margo as JT leaped on his back. With all his strength, JT yanked his mother's attacker backwards, causing the man to stumble away from her.

Sean toppled forward, face-first onto the cement floor. The sight of his brother falling to the ground sent JT into a rage. He went berserk, screaming and swinging his fists in long, wild arcs. Gripping the man's head, JT flung it against a wooden stud. The man buckled and went down.

The man Sean had beaten stood up behind JT's mother. "Mom!" JT shouted. She turned and charged the knife wielder, swinging wildly. The last thing JT saw before the explosion in his head was the knife plunging into his mother's chest.

2

The call came at an inconvenient time, as did all calls for Ian Kelly that came during the dinner rush.

"I told you to take a message, Connie."

"I'm sorry, Boss, but the guy is insisting I put you on."

"What d'ya mean, 'insisting'? If he's being an asshole, hang up."

"No; he's being a cop and he says it's an emergency."

That stopped Ian cold. He left the lasagna for someone else to plate, wiped his hands on the towel that hung at his belt, and took the phone from his hostess.

"This is Ian Kelly. What's this about?"

"Sir, this is Detective Mario Robinson. There's been an incident at your house. It's urgent that you get here as soon as possible."

A hard fist gripped Ian's heart and wouldn't let it beat. His mouth went dry and he had to swallow several times before he could form words.

"Is it someone in my family?"

"Sir, I'd rather not talk about this over the phone."

"Please," Ian pleaded. "Are they all right?"

"No, sir, they're not."

Ian felt the gorge rising in his throat. His mind went blank. He froze, unable to speak.

"Mr. Kelly?"

The detective's voice snapped him from his fugue. Ian's voice was barely audible when he said, "I-I'll be right there."

Ian's mind flooded with worst-case scenarios. Sean broke his leg. JT had a tooth knocked out. Sean got in a fight. JT crashed the car when Margo was letting him drive. Margo got in an accident. With each variation, Ian's conclusions became worse. "Please God; please let them be all right," Ian prayed over and over, his grip growing tighter on the wheel with each mile that he drew closer to home.

Ian drove like a madman. His fear overpowered his judgment. Running through a red light, Ian barely missed a pickup truck.

Veering wildly around slower moving vehicles and changing lanes in quick, sharp cuts, he left a multitude of angry drivers behind him. Arriving home, he could hardly draw air into his lungs. Police and rescue vehicles lined the suburban residential block. His neighbors were out in full force. At this point, they knew more than he did.

Home was a place he paid for, but somewhere he didn't really live. Certainly, he showed up there late each night to use the facilities and take rest in his bed. Recently though, more times than not, he fell asleep on the couch. Six, sometimes seven days a week, he refreshed himself each morning in the shower, said his hellos and goodbyes, then went off to work another sixteen-hour day, which only added to his guilt now. He should have been there. What had all the long hours been for in the end?

By the time he arrived, the police had pieced the story together from the scene, which was a combination of a neighbor's account, and what they got from Sean before he died.

A tall, light-skinned black man in a suit coat came down to meet Ian as he ran up the driveway.

"Mr. Kelly, I'm Detective Robinson." He put an arm out as Ian moved to go around him. Ian slapped the arm away and tried to keep going, but Robinson was ready for him. He grabbed Kelly by the shoulders and spun him around to face him.

"Stop!"

Ian fought to get away. "I want to see my family."

"Kelly, listen to me. No matter what you think, no matter how you feel, you do not want to go in there. It will be no way to remember your family."

Ian stopped. He struggled to breathe before saying, "What are you telling me? What's happened?"

"Mr. Kelly, I don't even know how to tell you this, but your family were victims of a mugging gone bad."

"Who-who got hurt?" Ian swallowed hard, dreading the answer.

Robinson struggled to raise the courage to tell this poor man, knowing his answer would destroy Kelly's life. "I'm afraid all of them."

"What?" Ian couldn't comprehend what Robinson was saying. "They were all hurt?"

"Mr. Kelly, your wife and youngest son are dead. Your older son has sustained serious injuries and is already on his way to the hospital. I'm sorry, sir. I truly am."

Ian couldn't keep the emotions from overwhelming him. His legs would no longer hold him upright. As he started to fall, Robinson grabbed him but was unable to hold the weight. As easy as he could, Robinson lowered Kelly to the ground.

The tears flowed and sobs wracked his body. There was no way this could be happening. This wasn't real. Couldn't be real.

"No. No." Through tear-filled eyes, Ian looked into the garage. A man squatting inside stood and moved, revealing Sean's lifeless body. "Oh God! Sean!" Ian pushed to his feet and ran toward the garage. Robinson caught him from behind, but Ian swatted at his arms and drove closer to his son.

"Let me go. My son needs me. Let me go." A policeman ran over and helped Robinson try to subdue Kelly.

"Kelly, stop. You can't help him. You have to let the crime scene techs do their job. Don't you want the people who did this to be caught?"

Ian's efforts began to fade.

"If you go in there now, you might destroy evidence we'll need to catch these killers."

Ian could take no more. He wanted the pain in his heart to end. He stopped and tried to see past the officer into the garage, but someone had covered Sean's body.

His mind whirled in continuous motion, not allowing thoughts to settle. His stomach roiled, threatening an upheaval. The bile burned the back of his throat. He struggled to swallow for relief but couldn't create enough saliva to manage the deed.

"Listen, Mr. Kelly." The detective's voice cut through the haze, helping him to focus. "I know how—no, I can't even imagine how you must feel. I promise I will do everything possible to catch the people who did this. But if you really want to help your son, go to the one who still has a chance."

Ian looked at Robinson.

"JT needs your prayers. If you can handle it, I'll have Officer Anders here take you to the hospital now. You and I can talk later. Can you do that?"

Ian nodded. "Yes, please, take me to my son."

Robinson motioned to Anders, who took Ian by the arm. "This way, sir." As Ian was led away, he glanced back over his shoulder. A black bag was being lifted off the floor. Ian closed his eyes. *My Sean. My little Sean. This can't be real.*

3

"Okay, what do we have?" Robinson looked down at his notes. Gathered around him were two other detectives, a police sergeant, and a crime scene tech.

The first detective, a ten-year vet named Morales, swept a hand around inside his jacket and hoisted his pants. Letting the jacket fall back in place, he pulled out a notepad and checked his notes. "The witness, a Mrs. Fulton, lives across the street. She says she heard screaming. She looked out her kitchen window and saw a black man and a white man helping another white man into a small blue car parked in the driveway. The one white man appeared to be hurt; she said he was holding his head. They got in and drove off. She doesn't remember anything beyond that."

The second detective, Jackson, a massive black man with a whisper soft voice, picked up the discourse. "Timetable goes something like this: about four-fifteen, the Kellys came home from grocery shopping. I'm guessing they were followed. They were attacked by two, maybe three unknown assailants. One of the assailants was a black man of unknown height, weight, or distinguishing features. The other was a white man with long brown hair. There's some confusion about whether a third person, another black man was involved."

Jackson flipped pages.

"Mrs. Kelly's purse and cell phone were on the floor near her body. She was the one who called 911. There was a knife on the floor and blood on an aluminum baseball bat. Looks like the boys put up a good fight."

"Yeah, but if they would have just let the muggers have what they wanted, they might all still be alive right now," Sergeant Kirkman said. "It changed armed robbery into murder."

"What about you, Sam?"

The crime scene tech pushed his glasses up. "There's plenty of trace. Hair, blood, fingerprints. If the killers are in the system, we'll get a match. I'm leaving now. I should have a report for you soon."

"All right. Let me know." The tech walked down the driveway.

"Medical examiner says the younger son died of a stab wound to his back. He'll give me more after his autopsy. Mrs. Kelly was stabbed once in the chest. Looks like it pierced her heart. The other boy, JT, sustained a blow to the back of the head with the baseball bat. You'll know more about his condition when you get to the hospital."

Jackson said, "Any reason to be looking at the husband in connection?"

Robinson stared down the driveway, playing over the facts in his mind. He turned to Jackson. "He obviously wasn't involved in the actual assault." He shook his head. "It doesn't feel right, but we need to take a look anyway. Stranger things have happened."

Robinson put a hand on his face and rubbed his jaw. "Okay, Jackson, I need you to check the grocery store's security footage. Find the Kelly car and see if a blue car pulls out after them. Check all the street cameras and see if you can find the car leaving.

"Morales, check the hospitals. See if this injured guy shows up anywhere. Oh, I'll do Mercy since I'm going there. When you get done, start a background check, including finances, on the Kellys.

"Kirkman, get some of the guys to canvass this street and the houses along the path back to the main road. Have one of the techs drop the garage door when they leave so the house and crime scene aren't open to the curious and the looters.

"I'm gonna head to the hospital and see how the survivor's doing." The thought of having to face the distraught father made him cringe. "Man, some days I really hate this job."

***

At the hospital, Robinson flashed his shield at the emergency room desk and asked about Jason Kelly's condition. A harried young black nurse with red streaks through her hair pounded on the keyboard and squinted at the screen, before informing him the boy was still in surgery.

"Hey, can you tell me what kinda cases have come through the door in the past two hours?"

The nurse hesitated and Robinson said, "Look, I'm not asking for any personal info here. One of the people who put the Kelly boy in surgery was injured. We're trying to find him. You can understand that. He's a tall white man with long hair. Possibly has a head injury."

Again, the nurse did not reply. She sucked in her lower lip and gnawed on it. Abruptly she stood up. "I'll be right back." Her short round form disappeared into an enclosed area behind her. Minutes later, she returned with a much taller Hispanic woman.

"Detective, I'm Betty Lopez. I'm the supervisor in charge. You understand that we have rules governing the information we disclose."

"Look, I don't need a name or even the extent of the injury. I need to know if someone matching the description came through that door. If I know that, then I can take the necessary steps to protect everyone. If that was your child in surgery, fighting for his life, wouldn't you want the police to do everything in their power to find who put him there?"

Lopez stiffened. "You don't need to resort to guilt, Detective. I understand what's at stake. There was a young man who may match that very vague description that came in about a half hour before Mr. Kelly did."

Robinson got very excited. "He still here?"

"He's in an exam room now."

Robinson snatched the phone from his pocket and made a call. "We may have one of them here at Mercy. Send me a squad and take care of any paperwork we might need for the hospital." Ending the call, he returned his attention to the nurse. The adrenaline was pumping now. "This is very important, Ms. Lopez. I need to know when he leaves that examination room. Please."

"He'll come out this direction when he's released."

"Okay." Robinson's hand wandered to the gun he wore in a hip holster. If this guy had anything to do with the murders, he was not getting away.

4

After what seemed an eternity of pacing, Ian collapsed on a small couch in the surgery waiting room. He curled up his legs and lay on his side. Tears fell, hitting the vinyl seat and trailed downward to soak into his hair. His eyes locked on a spot near the door and lost their focus. His mind, for the moment, had gone blank; perhaps as a self-preservation measure to protect his sanity. Ian couldn't cope with the magnitude of his loss.

The waiting room door opened. Ian sat up and tripped over the table in front of the couch. He almost fell on top of the nurse that entered the room.

"Is he-is he all right?" The tears streamed anew.

"I don't know anything yet. I'm sorry. I saw you lying there and wanted to know if I could get you anything."

Dejected, Ian's eye level dropped to the floor. He couldn't take the not knowing. JT had to be all right. He just had to be.

"Can I get you something? Some water? Coffee? I can call a counselor to come up and talk to you, if you wish."

"No. No, thank you. I just need someone to tell me how my son is."

"I promise, as soon as there is any news, someone will come in and tell you, okay? I'm sorry."

Ian nodded absently and turned away from the nurse. He vaguely heard the door close as she left. Ian's body began to shake. He slapped his face and his grief burst forth with such force that his legs gave out and he collapsed to the floor. He rolled, clutching his body and cried loudly. Through his tears, Ian looked to the heavens for help, praying like he had never prayed before. His prayers remained constant for hours. Then the door opened again.

It was after eleven o'clock that evening when the surgeon finally came in. Ian crawled across the floor toward him, begging for good news. He grabbed the doctor's pant leg and sobbed his plea. "Please tell me he's all right. Please!"

The doctor helped Ian to his feet and led him back to the couch. Taking off his operating cap, he sighed. "We've done all that we can at this point. It's in God's hands now. He is alive and stable. His skull was fractured. We have relieved the pressure on his brain, but at this time, we have no idea if there has been any irreversible damage or if he will recover. I know this is not easy for you, but keep up the prayers. Hopefully, we will see some response in the next twenty-four hours."

"Can I see him?" Ian pleaded.

The doctor took a long time in forming his answer as he studied the emotionally broken man in front of him. He shook his head and said, "Not at this time."

"Please. I need to see him," Ian said. "I have to see him. He's all I have left," he sobbed.

"I understand that. I truly do. But I don't think you are emotionally ready to see your son. Right now, he needs undisturbed rest. The condition you are in can only serve as a detriment to his recovery." Cutting him off with a raised hand before Ian could object further, the doctor quickly added, "I'll make a deal with you, though. Let him get a couple of hours' rest and you get yourself cleaned up and under control. I'll let you stay with him as long as you don't touch him or cause a scene that might hinder his recovery. He might be your son, but he is my patient. I will not let anything stand in the way of his possible recovery. Do you understand?"

"Yes. Please. I promise. Just don't let my son," he choked on the word, "die. Please." Ian sucked in a breath. "I've already lost so much. I can't lose him, too."

"Okay. I'll come for you in a little while. Let me check the charts and I'll be back. You pull yourself together and remember that your son is depending on you. I'm going to send a nurse down here with a mild sedative. There will be no argument on this. Take it. Let it calm you and I'll be back." He patted Ian's leg and stood up to leave.

"I know this is hard for you, but I promise we are doing everything humanly possible to see that your son recovers. That may not be much to offer, but for now it's the best we have. I wish I could give you more hope, but I'd rather be honest with you. Keep the faith, Mr. Kelly." He left, leaving Ian feeling numb. Despite JT's injuries, the doctor's words had given him some hope. Ian had to believe that was good. It was all he had. His prayers resumed.

5

The door opened again a few minutes later, but Ian didn't look up.

"Excuse me, Mr. Kelly. I'm Detective Robinson." He was holding two cups of coffee.

Glancing up, it took a moment for recognition to register. "We talked for a few minutes this afternoon at your house."

Robinson offered him one of the coffees. "I thought you might need this."

Ian hesitated, then reached up and accepted it. "Thank you." His voice was hoarse.

Robinson sat down on the sofa next to him and said, "Look, I know there is never going to be a good time to talk, but if you feel up to it, let's try to get this over with. I just need to ask you a few questions."

Ian didn't speak but nodded his consent, sipping at the coffee. He answered the basic questions posed: Where was he? What did he do for a living? Was there anyone that had a grudge? etc.

Then he had a question of his own. "Can you tell me what happened?"

"Here's what we know right now. It looks as though there were three men who followed your family home from the grocery store. They must have tried to rob your wife as she exited the van. Your family fought with the attackers and…well, you know the rest."

"How did they die?" Ian looked the detective in the eyes. "How did those bastards kill my wife and son?"

Robinson studied Kelly for a few seconds before responding. "Knife. They were both stabbed. JT was hit on the head with a baseball bat. Your wife called 911 during the fight, so units were on the scene fast. Sean lived for about a minute and told the police that there were three attackers."

Ian thought he was angry enough to hear the details but he was wrong. His head began to spin and nausea swept over him. He put the coffee cup down and leaned forward, trying to breathe. Ian felt Robinson's hand on the back of his head, guiding it lower. "Put your head between your knees. Try to breathe as normally as possible."

The nausea passed a few minutes later and Ian sat back. He rested his head on the back of the couch and stared up at the ceiling.

Robinson watched the grieving man, his own heart heavy. How would he react if it were any of his children? Robinson sipped his coffee and left Ian alone with his thoughts for a while, then tried to bring him back into focus.

"I know it's no consolation, but your family put up a good fight. There was a lot of evidence that shows the attackers took some damage."

"And look what it cost them," Ian said, more to himself than the detective. "I should have been there."

To which Robinson thought, *Then, there'd be another victim.* What he said was, "This is not your fault, Mr. Kelly. There was no way to be prepared for something like this. We'll catch the animals who did this. The evidence collected will lead us to the killers. We have units out now searching for the car they drove. One of your neighbors heard screaming and came out to investigate. She's been very helpful. I promise to keep you updated as things develop."

Then Robinson let out his surprise. "I thought you would want to know we have a suspect in custody right now."

Kelly's head shot up. A strange look crossed his eyes. His face became distorted with anger. "Where is he?"

Robinson had seen that expression before: The anger. The hatred. The hard emotion in a man's eyes. All signs that a man might cross lines he would never think to approach with thoughts of violence and hopes for revenge controlling his actions.

"He's in custody and I think he'll be giving up his two friends soon. We found him here at the hospital. He was seeking medical attention for an injured eye; evidently one of your family members gouged it. His friends must have dropped him off here and fled. Some of my colleagues are working on him now. Hopefully he'll give up his partners."

Ian exploded to his feet, taking Robinson by surprise. He began pacing excitedly. "I want this bastard to pay. I want them all to fry for what they did to my family." Ian put his hands to his face and continued moving back and forth across the small room.

Robinson watched. Kelly was angry. *Was he thinking of revenge?* That was always a thought in the grieving process of a murder victim's family.

"I understand that, but it will be up to the courts to decide. Let's just hope we can find the other two before they get away. You stay here and look after your son. I'll keep in touch and let you know what happens." He stood to leave and said, "Mr. Kelly, I know that look on your face. Do not do anything that will jeopardize this case. Do not let your son, who needs you, lose his father over this. There is no way for you to get to the suspect anyway. He is no longer here."

Robinson stood and put a hand on Kelly's shoulder to stop his pacing. Robinson looked him in the eyes. "I hope you're listening. You want justice, not revenge." Robinson saw he wasn't getting through, but then, what did he expect? If it were him in this situation, he'd react the same way. The difference was that as a cop, he might actually be able to follow through with assassinating his family's killers. There was no way Kelly could do that. Besides, he really didn't seem like the type to put those kinds of violent thoughts into deeds. Still, Kelly would bear watching over the next few days as the investigation played out.

***

When Ian was alone, his mind raced with wild plans to avenge his family. The hatred gave him a new resolve and strangely was the catalyst that helped him gain control over his rampant emotions. He now had something to focus on. Somehow, Ian would make them pay for what they did.

A picture of Sean flashed before his mind's eye. His heart tore open. Next, an image of Margo's face displayed so vividly that Ian tried to touch her; to caress her cheek and brush back the hair from her face.

She was so beautiful. They had been so much in love and so happy, at least until he opened the restaurant. That had put a good deal of distance between them.

"Forgive me, Margo, for never being there for you. I should have been. I'm sorry for putting my needs in front of our family's and for neglecting you and the boys. I apologize for not being a better husband and father." The tears rolled nonstop. It was too late to make it up to her and Sean. Through all his words and prayers, he knew he would never be able to forgive himself for abandoning his family in their time of need.

He wiped away his tears with an angry swipe and redirected his prayers toward the suspect in custody and the prospect of the police capturing the other two murderers. If he could find them first, would he have the courage to avenge his family? It might not be very realistic, but at this point, the thought gave him what he needed to get through the coming weeks: hope and revenge.

6

Ian sat in his car and stared at the house. So many wonderful memories still lived there, but since the murders, the images had begun to fade. The house was closed up and anything he thought he might need, which wasn't much, was packed in the car.

It had been a long and miserable ten months since the funerals. Ian's relatives and friends told him he needed to move past the tragedy, but how did anyone ever really do that? At any rate, Ian hadn't been able to and the depths of his depression had grown, bringing him to where he was today.

His thoughts returned to the days of the trial and the hopeless, helpless feeling his anger left him with. Darryle Lawson refused to roll on the others. The police, in checking Lawson's known associates, had some suspects, but nothing solid to tie them to the crime. To date they had managed to elude capture. The police speculated they were hiding somewhere out of town and still had not released their names. Ian couldn't understand that logic. If the names were released to the media as persons of interest, they might stand a better chance of finding them, but Robinson said his hands were tied until they found the two men or until evidence turned up connecting them to the murder.

Ian could barely stand seeing the Lawson each day as he was paraded into the courtroom. The boy looked pathetic with a patch over his damaged eye. His attorney argued there was no proof that his client had done the killing. In fact, his testimony was that the others were responsible, arguing Lawson had no idea what his partners had planned.

However, more than enough evidence was found at the crime scene to seal his conviction. His blood was in several places, and his skin and some of his eye were under JT's fingernails. No way was this killer getting off, but even that could not quell the deep-seeded hatred Ian had developed for the boy. Prison time was not enough punishment. He wanted Lawson dead.

The boy cried when the verdict came in, begging for forgiveness. He cried for his mother to help him and she cried, too.

But they at least could do that; Ian's wife and son would never share tears again. The boy's attorney had actually tried to blame Sean and JT for the deaths, saying that if they wouldn't have tried to defend themselves, none of it would have happened.

That was all Ian could take. He was on his feet, moving toward the lawyer before he realized it. Ian made it through the gate but was hauled back and restrained by deputy sheriffs. They physically dragged him from the court while he screamed that the lawyer as well as the murderer deserved to die. When Ian was released, he discovered Robinson had been one of those who grabbed him from behind.

Robinson shoved Ian in the chest and pushed him against the wall.

"That's not going to bring your family back. You need to calm down before your behavior causes a mistrial. You want to be the reason that killer gets put back on the streets?"

Still flushed with rage, Ian answered, "I wish they would release him. I'd hunt him down and kill him myself."

Robinson's eyes had softened a bit then. "No, you wouldn't. You think you would, but taking another person's life is not in you. It's your hurt, anger, and frustration talking. Killing would make you exactly like that animal in there. Then you'd be in jail and who would look after your son?"

Ian felt helpless. He wiped the tears from his eyes. The detective was right and was only trying to help, but something inside Ian had changed. He blamed himself for everything that happened to his family. He felt worthless and defeated. Though his heart wanted revenge, his mind understood he would never be able to handle those punks like he once could have. He was a far cry from the college athlete he had once been. Now he was just a fat old man who had failed to defend his family. A poor excuse for a husband, a father, a man.

Ian walked away from the courthouse that day and did not return for the sentencing. He went to the private care facility to see JT who was still in a coma since the surgery. He begged his son to come back and help him get through the pain, but as always, there was no response. Almost a year of no response and the pain still had not receded.

An emptiness existed where once he had a heart. His head hung in defeat; his mind a haze of loss and pain. His life held a hollowness of purpose.

As Ian sat in the driveway thinking back, a red pickup truck pulled up to the house. A short, stocky man climbed out and pulled a real estate sign from the bed. Walking across the front lawn, he stopped and shoved the two legs of the sign into the ground. He moved it to make sure it was firmly in place, waved to Ian, and drove away. The sale price of the house would hopefully see JT through another three to five years of care.

With one last glance, Ian started the car and backed down the driveway. As he drove away, Ian was surprised to feel the moisture on his cheeks. He wiped the tears with his hand and looked at the wetness, confused how there were any left to shed after everything he had been through.

Lost in thought, Ian had no memory of the drive as if the car had driven itself. When Ian stopped in the downtown parking structure, he had no recollection of the trip there, as if he had just awakened from a dream. Oh, how he wished it were only a dream.

Ian looked into the rearview mirror, studying the features of the stranger who looked back. The dark, sunken sockets; the haunted, perpetually red-streaked eyes; the once round and rosy cheeks, now gaunt and colorless; the skin from the weight loss that hung loose under his neck made Ian look like a droopy-faced, sad-eyed cartoon dog.

He forced his eyes away from the mirror and stepped out of the car. He leaned against it and tried to focus. *Was he really going to go through with this?* The answer was really no answer; it was just reality. He couldn't go on the way he was, so what other option was there? His entire life had become an endless, emotionless void. He pushed off the car, walked across the garage, and entered the elevator.

The shiny stainless steel inside the car reflected a caricature of him. His clothes hung on him like a child who wore his big brother's hand-me-downs. He really had lost weight. The paunch was gone. At another time in his life, he might have been proud of this accomplishment. Losing your family was not a diet plan he would recommend.

The elevator doors opened onto a lush foyer. A graphic design logo and sign read: *Leslie Stern, Attorney-at-Law.*

7

An attractive middle-aged woman greeted Ian from behind a large reception desk.

"Good morning, Mr. Kelly. Mr. Stern is waiting for you in his office. Go right in. Can I get you anything? Coffee? Water?"

"No, thank you."

Ian walked down a short hallway and entered the room at the end. It was large with an oversize desk in the middle of the floor and two cushioned chairs in front of it. Massive bookshelves ran the entire wall behind the desk. To the left, a wall of windows offered a scenic view over the downtown area and the river beyond. To the right was a small round table with four dark wood chairs.

***

Leslie Stern had not been looking forward to this meeting. Ian Kelly refused to listen to his counsel. The man was making a mistake, but Stern could not seem to get through the thick wall of grief for him to listen to reason.

"Ah, Ian, it's good to see you."

The short, dark-haired man stood and moved out from behind the desk with his hand extended. Ian's grip was weak and he avoided the attorney's gaze.

Ian sat where Stern motioned.

"How are you?" The voice was touched with concern.

"I'm, ah, I'm doing okay."

"You've lost a lot of weight. I know the deaths of your wife and son have taken their toll, as one would expect, but it's time to move past that. You have to start looking after yourself." Stern sat on the edge of the desk. "This is not what your family would want for you."

"I'm all right, Les. Do you have everything ready for me?"

Leslie Stern stared at Ian for a long moment. His client was in trouble. Not legal or financial trouble, but one born from the internal struggle of a man giving up. Stern had a good idea he would not be seeing Ian Kelly again after today. That would be a shame. There had been enough tragedy in the poor man's life already. But in the end, it was Kelly's choice. Stern couldn't babysit him. If the man wouldn't listen to reason, what could he do?

He sighed and walked around his desk. He slid on a pair of glasses as he sat down. "Everything is as you have asked. Do you want to go over it?"

"No, not really. As long as it provides for JT's care in case something happens to me, that's all I'm concerned about."

"All of your assets have been set up in an account, and you and I are the only authorized signers on it. However, you cannot draw out funds without my approval. The balance right now, after selling the restaurant and liquidating your portfolio and other assets, stands at more than seven-hundred-fifty-thousand dollars. When the house sells, that should add another quarter million to the pot."

Stern slipped the glasses off and looked at Ian. "I have your Power of Attorney for all decisions concerning JT, which will take effect while you are away in case something should happen to you."

This was wrong. Kelly wasn't coming back. Stern could see the signs of defeat and resignation on the man's face. Stern decided to try a different tactic.

"Tell me again what the doctors say about JT."

Ian frowned, obviously seeing through the ploy and not wanting to go into the story again. He looked down at his hands folded in his lap, then raised his head to look at the lawyer. His eyes lost focus for a moment. Stern imagined Kelly was visualizing his son. Good. The boy was Stern's last hope.

"The doctors don't really hold out much hope for JT's recovery. They don't come right out and say that, but I can tell. They say that JT could remain in a coma for the rest of his life. Of course, they also say he could come out of it at any time. Even if he did wake up, the doctors suspect he will have some brain damage, although to what extent, they can't say. The private care facility where he is at has good people. He will be well looked after there, especially if the staff knows JT is being watched over by an attorney.

"I'll be going there right after I leave here, and I will let them know you will be calling about JT's care. They already have you listed as a contact person. If they can't get hold of me, they will call you." The words tumbled out in a robotic, unemotional fashion.

Stern nodded but did not respond. He let the silence continue to the point of being uncomfortable before saying, "But where there is hope, there is life. What will happen if your son wakes up and finds his father is, ah, gone?"

Ian gazed at Stern. "That's why he has you."

"I'm no replacement for his father. *When* he wakes up, JT is going to be confused. He may be haunted by the memories of his ordeal. He will want a familiar, comforting face in front of him to get through the traumatic times ahead." *If only there was the chance that he would wake up.* Then, perhaps, Ian might alter his course.

"In the off-chance that JT does awaken, you and the care facility both have my number." Ian's face contorted for a moment, a slip of emotion trying to fight its way to the surface. He lowered his head, swallowed to regain his composure, and looked at Stern. "I won't be gone that long. I just really need to get away. I need to make the memories fade. I can't do that here."

Stern nodded. He had seen the mask on Ian's face crumble, if only for an instant. He wasn't fooled. Ian was a man driven by never-ending mental anguish. The man must have determined there was only one way to make the pain end permanently. Stern didn't know what to do to help him. He slid the glasses back on his face.

"It would be easy to make serious errors in judgment with your mind so clouded with grief. I hope you have taken that into consideration before you continue with whatever your plan is. It would be a tragedy upon a tragedy if you were unable to undo your actions."

"I appreciate your words, but you don't live in my mind. You can't understand what I feel." Ian turned his head. When he looked back, his eyes were moist. "I just need some time away to think and clear my mind."

"I understand, Ian. But please make sure your mind is clear before making any permanent decisions. I will handle things here until you return. But make sure you *do* return. Your son deserves to have his father near."

The two men locked eyes for a long moment. Past the vacant look, through the grief, Stern thought he caught a glimpse into his client's soul. The man's decision had been made.

Stern stood. Picking up the file, he said, "Let's move over to the table where I can lay this all out for you."

8

Thirty minutes later, the meeting was over. Stern shook Ian's hand and held it for a few extra seconds. He looked into Ian's eyes and said, "You call me anytime. I will keep you abreast of what happens here with the house and with JT. I'll see you soon."

Ian smiled but had trouble holding the older man's intense gaze. "I'll see you again."

With that, Ian left the office. As Stern watched him leave, no doubt existed in his mind that Ian Kelly was a man who had given up on life.

***

Leslie Stern had not become successful because he didn't care about his clients. Many of his colleagues tried to tell him he needed to keep a cold, more business-like distance between himself and those he represented; that he couldn't serve them to the best of his abilities if he was too friendly with them. Unfortunately, Stern could not be dispassionate the way his attorney friends were. Sometimes you had to get involved for the good of the client. That was what made him different, and in the end, very successful.

If ever there was a time to get involved, it was now. Stern walked back to his desk, sat down and hit speed dial. A gruff voice answered. "Seriously dude? I was up all night playing poker."

"Well, then you must have won enough that you can afford to pass up a job, huh?"

Silence greeted that statement. A smile spread across Stern's face. He could picture the expression on the face of the of the man he spoke to.

"Yeah, I'm ready to retire today."

"Okay, I'll call someone else."

"Whoa, now. I said I was ready to retire, not that I was capable of doing so. Whatcha got?"

Stern's smile grew.

***

Ian drove to the care facility where JT was a resident. For the longest time, he visited twice every day; sometimes talking to his son, sometimes reading to him, and sometimes just sitting and staring, lost in his own form of coma. As of late, his visits had become less often and of shorter duration.

It was on days like those when Ian had come to his decision, realizing what it would take to get out from under the pain of the constant hell he lived in. It took him two months to sell the restaurant. Most of the money had been placed in an account to cover JT's expenses. He sold all his investments and added those to the fund as well. According to Stern, the amount was substantial enough to see JT through at least ten years and the sale of the house would add three more. Knowing that brought some comfort to Ian.

He entered the private room and stood looking down at his son's inert, atrophied form. Each day before Ian entered the room, he said a quick prayer that he would see his son sitting up. Each moment he stayed there, he dreamed of seeing JT's eyes flutter open. He had come every day for almost a year with the same hopes, whispering the same prayers, but there was no change.

As he sank deeper into despair, Ian found it more difficult to visit his son. His stays became shorter. Because of that, Ian's guilt grew. The more the guilt spread, the less he wanted to make the trip to see his son. It created a cycle that only darkened his depression. Visitation had become a chore; one he could no longer face.

Ian moved to the bed and took his son's hand. Despite his near-deathlike appearance, the hand was still warm. He squeezed, lifting the lifeless limb to his lips. The gentle kiss started the tears flowing.

"I'm sorry, JT. I just can't do this anymore. I've tried. I really have. I-I'm going away today. I won't be coming back. I'm sorry. I can't live with this—this pain—this guilt anymore. Please forgive me."

Ian pulled a chair closer to the bed and sat, still clutching his son's hand. "I can't stand seeing you waste away in that bed. I failed you. I failed your mother and Sean." His face contorted in agony. "I can't take the constant pain in my heart and the endless nightmares." A sob choked off his next words. He started again. "I don't want to face life alone without you guys. I'm so sorry, JT."

Ian stood and leaned over the bed. He planted a kiss on JT's forehead, brushed his hair with his fingers, and studied the boy's face. Whispering a final apology, Ian turned to leave.

As he reached the door, it pushed open and a woman entered. "Oh, I'm sorry, Mr. Kelly. I didn't know you were in here. Would you like me to come back later?'

Ian turned his head and wiped his face with his hands. "Ah, no, that's all right, ah, nurse, ah… I was just leaving." He couldn't recall her name. Ian glanced at the name tag. There were double Ks on the plastic badge.

"I'm Nurse Brogan, Mr. Kelly. Or Kay or even KeKe. I answer to them all." She gave a nervous laugh. "Can I get you something? A glass of water or some Kleenex?"

"Huh? Oh, no. Thanks anyways."

She stepped away from the door. As Ian exited, he heard, "See you tomorrow. I know JT looks forward to your visits."

Ian said, "Yeah. Tomorrow." Then he left the facility for the last time.

9

Stern's phone rang. "Yes, Pamela?"

"Your beloved investigator is on line one."

Pamela's message took a moment to register. Currently, Leslie had no cases that required an investigator. Then the request he had made of the man came back to him. "Thank you, Pamela." He picked up the phone. "Elvin, what have you got for me?"

"Aw, Boss, you didn't say anything about this being an out-of-town job."

"Where is he?"

"He's on the turnpike heading west. We just crossed the border. If your man's gonna do what you think he is, it's gonna be in another state. You still want me to pursue?"

Stern reflected on the options. That was a lot to ask his investigator to do, especially since they weren't getting paid. Still, Stern perceived the threat to be real. Could he turn away now?

"Stay with him for now, but keep me posted."

"Aw, man, I was afraid you were gonna say that. Well, you're gonna call Gloria and tell her, 'cause I know she won't believe me if I tell her."

Stern laughed. Gloria, Elvin's diminutive wife, was half his size but inspired fear in the big man. "I'll call her as soon as I hang up with you. I promise."

"You'd better, 'cause I won't be much good to you in the hospital after she kicks my ass."

The line went dead. Stern replaced the receiver, steepled his fingers, and leaned his chin on them. *Where are you going, Ian?*

***

The drive to Colorado was long. Ian chose the Rocky Mountains because it was where they had spent their last family vacation. They had gone up into Rocky Mountain National Park and camped for a week. Ian was surprised when he realized the trip had been nearly three years ago. Where had the time gone? Clearly, Ian was at fault for the whole family not going on another vacation since. His efforts to get his new restaurant off the ground had consumed his days. That had been a constant struggle and demanded long hours. He always thought that once the business became successful he could afford to take some time off, but the demands of a busy restaurant had required even more time and effort to maintain. The hours, days, weeks, and months evaporated before his eyes. There no longer seemed to be enough time for him to break away for a vacation.

Margo had taken JT and Sean on the last two vacations alone because Ian had not been able to find the time to join them. He regretted that deeply now. There would never be another family vacation. Death didn't offer second chances.

The drive gave Ian ample time to let his mind fill with wonderful memories. His journey through the past helped pass the time and keep his mind from the course of action he had set upon.

He drove eighteen hours, long into the next morning, and stopped only for gas, to eat, and relieve himself. Around three-thirty, with his eyes far too heavy to keep open, Ian pulled into a rest stop near the Colorado-Nebraska border. He stopped in the dimly-lit parking lot, away from the building that housed the bathrooms.

With tired, numbed fingers from the extended time wrapped around the wheel, Ian pulled a bottle of Jameson's Irish Whiskey from a brown paper bag. Once darkness fell, Ian began taking quick hits from the bottle. The effects added to his exhaustion.

Lifting the bottle to his lips, Ian sipped the amber liquid, feeling the warmth trickle down his throat. As it hit bottom and threatened to rise again, Ian put his hand to his lips and waited out the rebellion. When his stomach once more settled, Ian sipped again. If he could stay in a constant state of inebriation, his decision might be different, but drunk would be a worse condition than he was already in. And if he ever sobered, the pain would return.

After several larger slugs of whiskey, the threat of vomiting became so strong that Ian decided he'd better go to the bathroom or have to face the putrid smell all the way to the mountains. That thought hastened the rise of his stomach's contents. Ian exited the car and ran.

The rest stop was almost deserted except for the two men in his path that Ian almost ran over as he was bursting into the bathroom. He tried to issue an apology, but was afraid to open his mouth. He just made it into a stall when the explosion occurred. His body convulsed and Ian heaved loudly. Amid his retching, Ian could hear the two men laughing.

When his body finally quit its expulsion, he was exhausted. He wiped off using the single-ply toilet paper and went to the sink. To his relief, the two men were no longer there. Ian splashed cold water on his face. There were no paper towels but only hand driers mounted to the wall, so he used his sleeve to wipe his face and bumped into a burly man with a wild, full beard as he turned to leave. Ian avoided eye contact and issued an apology.

"No problem, friend. You all right?"

"Yeah, just a little—yeah, I'm fine. Thanks."

Ian staggered from the building. The cool night air hit him like a fist. He rubbed his temples in an effort to alleviate the throbbing. *This is why I don't drink.*

As Ian neared his car, rushing footsteps from behind set off an internal alarm. Through his tired and alcohol-fuzzed mind, Ian was slow to react. A blow to the back of his head rocked him, shooting a bolt of white light behind his eyes.

His legs went wobbly. Dazed, the second blow drove the air from his lungs and sent him to his knees. The convulsions came back, this time in the form of dry heaves. Someone shoved him to the ground and kept him pinned there. Hands began pulling at his pockets. He was defenseless; unable to move. Through the fear, somewhere in his mind, a voice said, *Maybe they'll do the job for you.*

More movement announced that another mugger had arrived. Then there came the sound of solid skin on skin contact and the weight was lifted from his back. Ian attempted to rise, but could not get his feet to respond. Instead, he dragged his knees under him and began to crawl.

Sounds of an all-out brawl registered behind him, but he dared not look. Another wave of nausea swept over Ian and his arms gave out. His chin struck the pavement. He yelped in pain, lay his head down, and fought to stay conscious. Try as he might, he could neither lift his head nor open his eyes.

10

Ian was awakened by a strange grunting sound. He fought to open his eyes, struggling against the daylight. A foul smell assaulted his nose and grunts drew his attention to a livestock hauler loaded with pigs, parked next to his car.

He looked around, confused. What had happened? Memories fought to come to the surface of his throbbing head and aching body. He remembered being attacked but could not recall what happened next. How had he gotten back to his car? Ian looked around the interior. Nothing seemed to be missing. Well, except for his bottle of Jameson's, but after last night, that was no loss. Had that been what the mugging was about: stealing a bottle of whiskey?

Ian reached underneath him and felt for his wallet. It was gone. He *had* been robbed. No wait; there it was, on the floor beneath his feet. With great effort, he bent enough to pick the wallet up. To his amazement, everything seemed to be there, including his money and charge cards.

What the hell had happened? Was it a bad dream induced by exhaustion...and the Jameson's, of course?

Ian stretched. His body rebelled. His stomach and chest hurt from the heaving. The back of his head hurt, though, too, like he had been punched. Maybe the assault hadn't been a dream. On the other hand, maybe he was falling-down drunk and had hit his head.

He was tempted to return to the bathroom to wash his face, but the smell of what he assumed was the pigs was too overwhelming. Ian started the car and got back onto the highway. The smell, however, seemed to follow him. After a few sniffs, he realized the odor was coming from him. He reeked. Groggy and confused, Ian drove on for an hour before stopping at a truck stop.

Taking a clean shirt from his bag with him, Ian washed up in the bathroom and changed. He smelled and felt better. Throwing his dirty shirt in the garbage, Ian went out to the diner and ordered breakfast.

While he was eating, a large bearded man wearing a black leather motorcycle vest entered. He looked at Ian for a long second and then turned the other way. He sat at the counter.

There was something vaguely familiar about the man, although Ian couldn't imagine where he might have met him. He shrugged the feeling off and went back to shoveling eggs and hash browns into his mouth. Though he didn't taste it, the food helped to clean the disgusting vomit from Ian's tongue.

Later that day, when the mountains first came into view, Ian's spirits were lifted.

A few hours later, Ian got a room at a hotel just outside Estes Park, the start of the climb into the National Park. After settling into his room, he walked around town, taking in the spectacle of the mountains and the lake. The vista almost gave him pause to reconsider his decision. Even the air had an invigorating effect, threatening for a time to heal his dying soul. But as the reminders of the purpose for the trip began to filter back into his mind, he became confused. His decision walked a fine line between life and death. He decided to sleep on the decision and take care of things tomorrow.

Ian stopped at a restaurant and ordered a large steak for dinner, washing the meal down with four beers. If this was to be his last meal, he wanted it to be worthwhile. Then in his room, he polished off a six pack he purchased at a carryout. He drank himself to sleep and woke only when housekeeping banged on his door the next morning. Pushing the steady throbbing headache to the background, he showered, packed, and started his drive.

Ian wanted to retrace the previous route his family had taken. The car struggled at times in the thinner air. He had the pedal pressed flat to the floor, but the car barely made it to the top of the inclined road doing thirty. Fortunately, there weren't many cars on the road to get bogged down behind him.

As Ian neared the peak, he began looking for the right place to pull over. It was time. The scenery and the memories had been a nice distraction for a while, but they could never erase pain that ruled his thoughts. A short time later he found what he was looking for. He parked at a scenic overlook. Popping the trunk, he locked the door and left the key on the front seat. He remembered this spot. Margo had insisted on stopping here to have a picnic lunch.

He stood for a while, enjoying the beauty and sucking in large breaths with the scent of pine that filled the air. As the last happy moment of his life left his eyes, Ian opened the trunk and grabbed a cloth bag containing the only equipment he would need and a bottle of water. Drawing in a deep breath, Ian began the hike to his final resting place.

The trail to the top of the mountain was farther than it looked from the road. The climb took more than two hours and, from what he could see he was only about halfway up. With his breathing coming in gasps, Ian stopped and put his hands on his knees, wondering about the irony of having a heart attack while on his way to kill himself.

Deciding he didn't need to reach the top to accomplish his mission, Ian ventured off the trail and worked his way through the trees until he came to a clearing that overlooked the picturesque valley below. Trees surrounded him on three sides. Ian stopped and sat against an enormous boulder. Mountains stretched further than he could see. Fifty feet below him, a brook meandered along, bubbling and clear. He could sit there forever, and in fact, he would.

No one was around. He was too far off the road and nowhere near any trail where a hiker might accidentally stumble across him. Alone and for the first time in a long time, relaxed, he leaned against the boulder and scanned the horizon. The view was indeed as beautiful as he remembered.

He wanted so much for there to be beauty in his life again, even if only for a while. Ian craved the serenity. He finished the remaining water and slipped the bottle inside the bag. When his hand reappeared, it was wrapped around the butt of the .45 caliber handgun. He set the weapon down on his lap and crumpled the bag up tight. He didn't want it blowing away, littering the natural landscape.

Ian toyed with the gun for a minute. He'd bought it new from a local sporting goods store going through the standard background check, but had never fired it. Staring down the dark muzzle, reservations crept up as survival's natural defense mechanism kicked in. He had fear, but knew he would overcome that obstacle and do what had to be done.

A sudden rustling startled him. He lowered the gun and looked to his left. The noise came again. Ian waited. When the sound did not return, he lifted the gun. Taking several deep breaths to psych himself up, he placed the barrel to the side of his head just as a deer bounded out from the trees and scampered in front of him. The intrusion happened so fast it startled him and caused his heart to race.

How silly that a deer should scare him at this point. Ian laughed. As the deer disappeared from view, so did the smile from Ian's face. It was time.

Picturing Margo, JT, and Sean once more, Ian took three quick breaths and again placed the gun to the side of his head. Even as the tears fell, he knew relief from the memories in his tortured mind was but a heartbeat away. As he steeled his nerves for the final pull, the noise returned. The deer would bear witness to his end.

He closed his eyes and smiled before he pulled the trigger.

11

They were grouped in rows, kneeling on prayer rugs. Seventeen men, the leader, his staff and the twelve men chosen for the mission, who had made an extreme commitment to a cause greater than themselves, bowed their heads as the final prayers were offered. The Imam stood and blessed each man once more and left the small, barren room.

The others remained kneeling, awaiting their final instructions. After nearly a year of preparation and training, the mission was about to begin. The three men in front stood and faced the others. A fourth man stood, went to a stack of large shipping envelopes and began distributing them to the chosen thirteen. The plan only called for twelve, but that would be addressed shortly. No one opened the envelopes. They knew better. There would be time allowed for that after the final instructions. The men would move to a location where they alone could peruse the materials. When they each had been given their assignments, the leader spoke.

"You know what is expected of you. You have been chosen for this great honor because of your skills and your commitment. Everything you need to know is in your envelope. Study your files. Memorize them. They will not leave the compound. When it is time to go, you will leave the packets." He nodded toward the two other men standing.

He looked around at the men he had hand-selected. They were good men; religious, strong, smart, and most importantly, deadly. Even if only half of them succeeded, they would make the world fear what might yet come.

"I will see each of you before you leave. Your teams and equipment are all in place, awaiting your arrival. You will leave at different times and from different locations. You will not vary from those routes. You have an emergency number to call should a problem arise. Your training is complete; only the mission remains. Now go."

The men rose and drifted off with their packets.

The leader, a man respected and feared and whose name was

only whispered in dark corners throughout the Middle East, motioned for one of the men to follow him. No names were ever used, but although the other two men were unknown to the group, everyone recognized Wafik Masselmeiny. His exploits were legendary. He was responsible for hundreds of deaths via raids and bombings. With each successful operation, his fame grew along with the number of followers.

They entered a room and Wafik gestured for the one he had chosen to close the door. The leader paced around the room and circled his minion, then walked toward a barred window. After several moments, he turned and spoke.

"What is your name?" He barked it out like a demand.

"David Greenberg," the man replied.

Wafik let a smile touch his rugged face. He had not known the man's cover name. This soldier—this believer—was already in his role. He had chosen well. This was a man he could count on to fulfill his mission and more.

"Your nationality?"

"I am Israeli."

The terrorist's smile grew bigger.

"Does that bother you, Ahmed?" He said, for the first time using the man's real name. "Playing the role of a hated enemy?"

"It matters not. I have a mission to fulfill, whether I play the role of an Arab, an American, or a Jew. The mission will be achieved because of who I am, not what I appear to be."

Yes, the leader thought. *This is the right man.*

"What do you think your chances are?"

"With Allah's blessing, we cannot—"

"No!" Wafik shouted at him.

The man jumped.

"Do not put this on Allah. Allah watches. Allah smiles at our successes, but Allah will not be standing shoulder to shoulder with you on this mission. I asked you what *you* thought your chance of success was."

Ahmed took a breath before he spoke. In truth, he did have some reservations about their chances. He feared not for his own life, for he knew that by accepting this assignment he had already forfeited his life. He was an intelligent man and saw several places where the plan was weak.

The leader saw the hesitation. "You may speak freely and

honestly with me."

Ahmed nodded. "Overall, the plan is sound and has great potential to cause damage and fear, but I am only one soldier. I do not know my cell members and do not know what they are capable of."

"Yes, that could be a problem. If anyone of them gives you trouble, kill them as an example. The rest will follow." He walked to a table and sat down. "Come. I must discuss something important with you."

Ahmed sat across from the great man, his curiosity piqued. Why had he been singled out?

"Ahmed, there is a more immediate problem. Several problems, in fact. What do you think of the other cell leaders we have selected?"

"They seem capable soldiers."

"Yes, yes; that is a given. What about their leadership abilities?"

"That is hard to say. I have not seen them in a leadership situation. If they accepted this assignment, they should be qualified or you would not have selected them."

"What would you say if I told you I believe most of them will fail?"

"I wouldn't know what to say."

"The planners of this mission believe that only four of you will be strong enough to get beyond the first day. Of those four, I believe you to be the strongest."

Ahmed did not respond.

"That is why I have a second assignment for you after yours is completed."

"Excuse me, but I thought the completion of my mission would also be the completion of my life."

"No, you must survive. Regardless if the entire plan is complete or not, you will end it and escape if the authorities are too close to you. If there are any other members of your cell alive, kill them. Then I want you to go to the other cities. I will give you a list that you must protect with your life. Go to the other cells and help them if they need it, then eliminate anyone left alive. We can have no survivors who could give up information to the enemy's agencies. You are too valuable to us. Your orders are to survive, eliminate any other survivors, and return here to us to fight bigger and better wars. You will start your assignment days before the others so you will be ready to assist them. I have selected you for a reason. If you are successful, your future will be set. Do you understand?"

"Yes, it shall be as you wish."

"We have one more problem. In our midst is a traitor."

Just then, the door opened and one of the other trainers came in quickly. He leaned into Wafik and whispered in his ear. The man's head jerked up.

"Find him and kill him," Wafik ordered.

The other man rushed out. The leader stood and bade Ahmed to follow him. Outside the door, a soldier handed Wafik an AK-47. He passed it to Ahmed.

"You only know each other as numbers. Find number nine and kill him."

Ahmed gave one quick nod, then without question or hesitation, rushed off to begin the hunt.

The leader accepted another gun and instructed his two assistants, "Send the guards to gather the cell leaders together in one room. Keep them there. No one leaves. If anyone tries, they are to be killed." The two men sped away. Wafik left the room and made for the roof. Moments later The Imam joined him. The entire mission relied on stopping the traitor.

12

In a remote corner of the compound, Michael Jalal, known to the others as number nine, hid while talking on his cell phone to his contact.

"They're on to me. You must get word out quickly."

"How do you know they're on to you?" his CIA handler asked.

"Because we've all been given our assignments and my envelope was empty."

Without hesitation, the agent said, "Get out of there now." He knew his spy was made.

"But I have some information to pass."

"Talk on the run. Go now."

Jalal looked around and hopped the short porch wall. It was a good twelve-foot drop to the sloping ground below. He hit hard, sending a sharp pain through his left ankle and hip. He began an uncontrolled roll down the tree-filled slope, stopping when he smacked into a small tree. Grabbing on to a branch, he righted himself and started running, aware of a stabbing pain in his side.

Gunfire erupted behind him, tearing through the leaves and branches close by. His escape had been discovered already. Michael picked up his speed but he knew there was nowhere for him to escape. He put the phone to his ear and in gasps, relayed as much as he knew.

"There are twelve men, all highly trained. That means twelve independent targets because I'm sure they'll replace me. They were only given their targets today. I assume all the targets are American, but I don't know if it's only on U.S. soil or also in worldwide assets. I just know it's big and the emphasis is always on maximum death toll. The operation is supposed to commence in two months. All support personnel and equipment are already in place…" The words came out unevenly as he gulped for air. "That's all I've got."

More bullets began raining down around him. He could hear pursuit in the distance.

"Tell my mother I love her." He closed the connection and pitched the phone as far as he could. He didn't want them to know word had gotten out.

Bullets began to hit closer. Michael risked a glance over his shoulder but could see nothing. Before him, the land cleared onto a dirt road. A sliver of hope began to build at the possibility of catching a ride but was quickly snatched away. His eyes bulged in shock as the figure of a man moved into view. Standing in front of him was number three with an AK-47 pointed at him. Michael didn't even have time to slow down before the first bullet ripped through him. He was dead by the third shot and never felt the next ten.

Ahmed stood over the man as the others caught up. Two guards arrived and hoisted the body back up the hill.

On the roof, the Imam said, "We must find out who he talked to. Whoever it is must be close by."

Wafik answered, "I already have people on it. They think they have found him. As soon as we suspected a traitor, we began searching. Do you wish him dead or do you want to learn what he knows?"

"Not necessary. The traitor was fed false information about when the operation begins. Even if the information was passed on, they will think they have time when they do not. Kill him, but make sure he feels pain."

***

Mark Reynolds stared at the phone with rising panic. Had that been gunfire he heard before the connection went dead? He feared Michael was burned and most likely dead, and that meant he could be in danger, too. He rushed around his small hotel room, grabbing his things and tossing them into his getaway bag. He made one final quick scan of the room and walked out. In the hallway, he called his contact and gave the emergency extraction code.

He exited through a back door, avoiding the front desk. If he was blown, he didn't want them to know he was leaving. They had his passport, but whoever came to extract him would be able to handle that.

Outside he hailed a taxi, telling the driver to take him to a local market. On the way, there, he sent several texts explaining what he knew. Hopefully, someone would be able to understand his code and figure out what was happening.

Reynolds was a career agent with almost twenty years' worth of experience. He had been in a few close calls and tight situations before, but this one unnerved him. The timeline for an escape was narrow here. If Michael had just been burned, he wouldn't have felt so anxious, but since his packet was empty, then they had known he was a traitor for some time.

Knowing he shouldn't even look, Mark glanced nervously over his shoulder. No one was following him that he could see, but it didn't make him feel any safer. Turning back, he was suddenly aware that the cab had passed the market. He looked at the driver's reflection in the mirror, but the driver, who had been watching him, averted his gaze. Mark realized then it was already too late. Still, he didn't have to make it easy for them.

He calmly placed the duffel bag on his lap. As the driver made a turn, Mark opened the door and dove out, using the bag to help break his fall. The cabbie didn't respond immediately, but as Mark rolled over and over he could see the brake lights blink on.

Ignoring the pain radiating throughout his body, he jumped to his feet and ran down a nearby alley. He might not make it far, but he was going to make them work to capture him.

13

The explosion threw Ian sideways. A searing pain shot through his head, followed by severe pounding. He lay on his side, looking at the trees through blurry vision. Stunned, Ian had difficulty focusing his thoughts. *Was this death?* But if he was dead, why was he in so much pain? Maybe he wasn't completely dead yet.

Something warm trickled down his face. Ian didn't understand why he could feel it. A sound like leaves rustling drew his attention. Perhaps the deer had come to investigate, or maybe it was some other wild animal that would start to eat him before his life faded. The thought both scared and repulsed him. It would be just like him to botch the job and die from some animal having him for dinner. The shock brought clarity to Ian's vision. He struggled to see what approached.

Instead of an animal, Ian saw a blurred large and hairy form step into his line of sight. Ian's first thought was that Big Foot had found him, but then the being spoke. "What kinda fool thing you trying to do?"

The being bent and grabbed Ian, lifting him from the ground. Ian's eyesight began to clear. A brief bolt of recognition shot through his mind. He'd seen that face someplace. Before he could make a connection, Ian's body was slammed backward into the rock face.

Ian grunted as a fresh wave of pain ran through him. Strangely, it helped clear his mind. The bear of a man was growling at him, crazed eyes glared at Ian.

"So, you want to die?" The man released Ian with one hand. Reaching behind him, the large man pulled out a gun and pressed it hard against Ian's forehead. "Here, let me help you with that."

Ian felt his breath catch in his throat. His heart pounded in his chest. With weakened hands, he reached out, attempting to pull the man's arm away. Desperate little whimpering sounds escaped his lips.

"What's that I see in your eyes? Fear? How can that be? How can someone who was going to kill himself anyway be afraid that I'm about to blow his brains out for him? Look at you. You're struggling to survive. Does that sound like the efforts of a man ready to die?"

The gunman swatted Ian's hands away with the weapon. "Stop." The gun came down on Ian's head. He let out a yelp. "I said stop."

Ian put his hands on his head and felt the wetness.

The big man pressed in close, mere inches away from Ian's face. "You look me in the eyes and tell me you want to die." He pushed Ian against the rock, causing still more pain. "Look at me, you coward."

Ian did. Tears welled in his eyes, blurring his vision. Ian became angry.

"What do you want from me?"

"The truth. Are you ready to die?"

Ian renewed his efforts to break free. "Yes, damn you. Yes, I'm ready to die."

He kicked the man in the shin.

"Ow! You little fucker." He released Ian, but before he could move away from his attacker, the man punched Ian in the gut, doubling him over and dropping him to his knees. Ian clutched his stomach and retched. When he could speak, he shouted, "What do you want? If you're going to kill me, just do it! Stop torturing me!"

The feet backed away from Ian's view, but no reply came. After several minutes, Ian looked up. The man was just standing there, staring down at him. The gun hung at his side.

"You may think you're ready to die, but you're not. Get up."

Ian rolled to a sitting position. "Why are you following me?"

The man looked away for a moment, as if searching the forest for an answer.

"You had the look of a man who needed help."

Ian lifted a hand to the side of his head and winced as he discovered a painful graze of torn wet flesh next to a large bump.

About ten feet down the slope, Ian caught sight of a motorcycle helmet. "Is that what you hit me with?"

"Seemed like the thing to do. You want to talk about it?"

Ian pushed to his feet and brushed off his pants. "No. You did your good deed for the day. You can go."

"Let me rephrase that." He raised the gun and stepped forward. "You *want* to talk about it."

"Oh, and if I don't, what? You're going to shoot me? Go ahead."

A bullet ricocheted off the rock, sending stone chips flying over

Ian's head. Despite his words, Ian jumped and fell back to the ground, covering his head. This situation was beyond his control. That made him nervous, which was ironic, since his intent was to do exactly what this madman was threatening.

"There are worse things than death. I will shoot you in both legs and then in both arms. Is your silence worth the pain?"

"Why are you doing this? What difference does my living or dying make to you?"

"None whatsoever, but it's clear you're willing to fight to live under certain situations. If that's the case, perhaps you just need your death fixations directed towards another goal. So do us both a favor and talk. I don't want to shoot you, but I will."

"I don't understand this. Why can't you just leave me alone? If I choose to end my life, that's my business, not yours."

"I'm making it mine. If you want me to leave, convince me what you are doing is the only option available to you."

Ian shook his head. "I can't believe this," he muttered. "I can't even do this right."

The sound of the gun being cocked drew Ian's attention. As he watched, the gunman lowered the barrel and sited on Ian's left leg. Ian pulled both legs under him and curled in a ball.

"Last chance. This doesn't end until you talk."

The words raced out. "My entire family was killed and I can't take living anymore."

Silence greeted his statement.

"How did your family die?"

Ian closed his eyes. He didn't want to relive this story again. He opened his eyes and studied his inquisitor. "Why do you want to know?"

"I just want to understand what drives a man to this type of extreme behavior."

"They were killed in a mugging."

"How many in your family?"

"My two sons and my wife."

"And these muggers killed them during a robbery?"

"Yes. Well, one son, my oldest, is still in a coma."

"So you have one son who's still alive?"

"He's been in a coma for almost a year. The doctors see no reason to believe he will ever come out of it."

"But he's not dead. As long as he lives, there's hope. My God, man. You were gonna give up on your only surviving child?"

Ian said nothing, but the man's words struck home, causing him to sink a little lower.

The big man changed tactics. "What happened to the muggers? Did they catch them?"

"They caught one of the three, but they can't find the other two."

"So, let me get this straight: you have not only left your son to face the world alone once he wakes up, but you are going to let the two remaining men responsible for killing your family walk the earth without punishment? Man, you are pathetic. Maybe you should die. I should do you a favor and kill you now. But you don't deserve an easy end."

The man walked over and retrieved his helmet. "You're taking the easy way out, you chicken shit. You've got unfinished business. How can you meet your maker, knowing you haven't done everything in your power to avenge your family?"

The gun disappeared behind the man's back.

Ian looked at him, confused.

"Dude, if it were me, I'd go back and hunt those bastards down. I'd make 'em pay for what they did. Your family deserves justice. You sure as hell ain't gonna get it from the police. They got other shit to do. And if it was a year ago, they've forgotten all about it by now. Other cases have taken their place."

He started walking away.

"Go ahead and kill yourself if you want. It seems like your dead inside already, anyway. You're not worth my efforts to save you. But how you gonna justify your death to your wife when you see her in the afterlife? Hey, I'm just saying. If you were gonna kill yourself anyway, why not make it count for something? Go after those other two killers. If you get them, you'll at least have closure here on earth and can move on in peace. If you die trying, well, at least you made the effort and you aren't any worse off than you would have been, had I not come along.

"Huh, what've you got to lose, dude? Your life? Hell, you already gave up on that. Think about it. But if I were you, the next time I pulled that trigger, it would count for something. You need to live to die again."

The big man walked around the boulder, leaving Ian sitting there, confused but with a growing revelation. The stranger's words had affected him. They made him angry. His rage grew and ran the gamut of wanting to blame the man for ruining his plans to wanting to follow him and kill him for being forced to relive his misery.

Ian stared at the gun lying not four feet away. But this time he saw it in a different light. He focused on what the man had said about avenging his family. The idea gave him new direction and a purpose that his life had lacked since the day he received the phone call from Robinson.

Could he do it? Could he hunt his family's killers down and execute them? He had no experience with that sort of thing. Was he capable of killing someone in cold blood? Ian thought about the funerals of his wife and son. He saw an image of JT in his bed. *Yes, I could kill those bastards.*

Ian stood and reached for boulder as a sudden wave of nausea hit him. He closed his eyes until the vertigo ceased. A red stain decorated his shirt as blood dripped from his head. He looked for the gun, but unable to find it, assumed his savior had taken it with him. He started the long, slow process of descending the mountain, now happy he hadn't made it to the summit.

One thing the stranger had said came back to Ian. What difference did it make if he died hunting those men, as long as he tried? This was going to take some thought and a lot of planning. Fortunately, Ian had a long drive home to begin the process. First he had to stop the bleeding, then he had to call AAA to unlock the car.

14

Ahmed was next. When the customs official at Hartsfield-Jackson Atlanta International Airport motioned him forward, he placed his passport on the counter and waited. They chose the Atlanta airport because of how busy it was. An internal battle brewed between his fears and his training, but Ahmed's outward appearance remained calm.

"Mr. Greenberg, have you been to the States before?"

"No, sir. This is my first visit." His voice displayed only a hint of an accent.

"Are you here for business or pleasure?"

The standard question brought a smile to Ahmed's face. "I'm here on business, but I certainly hope to have enough downtime to see some sights."

The man flashed a fake smile as he continued to tap on a computer and look from the passport photo to Ahmed's face. He studied the computer screen hard for several nerve-wracking seconds, before handing his passport back. "Enjoy your stay." Ahmed attempted to smile, but his facial muscles didn't want to comply. He took the passport, nodded and just like that, was passed through and his mission was underway. After collecting his lone bag, he waited outside for a cab. When he was seated, he instructed the driver to take him into Atlanta. He was dropped at the Renaissance Atlanta Midtown Hotel, where he walked straight through the elegant lobby to the opposite doors, where another cab waited for him.

Ahmed slid his bag into the back seat and sat in front. This new driver was his first contact. They exchanged nods and the driver pulled into traffic. A few minutes later they were on the expressway heading north.

Ahmed closed his eyes. He was exhausted from his flight but far too excited to sleep. He would have to force himself, though, because he couldn't afford to make mistakes. The rhythm of the car eventually took him under. By the time he woke, they were midway through Tennessee. He glanced out the window, angling his head so he could see the sun. Though he wore a watch he was used to telling time by the sun's position. It was an hour short of midday.

Ahmed said, "Find somewhere to pull over."

Without a word, the driver drove into a rest stop. Ahmed got out and walked to the bathroom. When he came back, he found that the driver had laid out a spread of food and drink for him to choose from; some choices were American, some Mediterranean. He ate and invited the driver to join him. Ahmed unfolded a map. He would not allow the use of GPS for fear of being tracked. "Show me where we are," he said in English.

The driver leaned forward, ran a finger along the route, and then stopped. "Here."

"How much more time before we get there?" he asked.

"Eight, maybe nine hours."

"Have you made contact with the others?"

"Yes. They will all arrive within the next two days. They were told to arrive separately and at different times."

Ahmed nodded his approval. He popped another olive into his mouth. Folding the U.S. map, he pulled out his target city's map. Toledo, Ohio, an unsuspecting Midwestern city where the people would line up like lambs for the slaughter. The corner of his lip twitched in anticipation.

"Has everything been arranged?"

"Yes. The weapons, clothing, and supplies are all in place. The information that was requested has been compiled and is there as well."

"Very well. Let's be on our way. We have history to make."

They arrived ten hours later. Ahmed's impatience had worn thin by then. He cursed the driver for not knowing more precisely how long the drive was.

A man greeted them at the secluded rural house they were using as their base. It was a large two-story home with four bedrooms, located on a half-acre lot surrounded by trees on three sides. A detached three-car garage sat behind the house.

"Welcome, my friend. I hope your journey was peaceful."

Ahmed scowled at the driver. "Peaceful, yes, just longer than I thought it would be. Has anyone else arrived?"

"It is just the three of us. I am called Al. I am your expediter and aide." Al turned to the driver. "Move the cab into the garage. It will be suspicious if it is sitting out where people can see it." When the driver had gone, Al said, "He is a good man. Do not take your anger out on him. In the end, we will need everyone." It was his subtle way of asking Ahmed not to kill the driver.

"Very well. I will trust your judgment. Do you have the information?"

"Yes. I thought we could go over it and plan our attacks before the others arrive."

"Yes, of course. It is best that we make our plans behind closed doors. The less they know until it is time, the better chance of overall success."

"My thoughts, too. Come. I have set up a table in one of the bedrooms. We can lock the door and plan in private."

The two men poured over the maps, sketches, photos, and notes Al had collected over the past month. There was much information to decipher. By the end of the evening, they had a rough idea of what their targets would be. The two terrorists slept then with the idea of finalizing the details later that day when Ahmed could physically view the selected sites.

***

"I need to know. Do we raise the terror alert level or not?" Martin Chapman, Secretary of State, asked, pacing the room.

The four men sitting around the large wooden table looked at each other, but no one spoke. No one wanted to be responsible for crying wolf.

"Gentlemen, make a decision. If I'm going to have to take this to the president, I need something solid to place it on. Is it a yes or no?"

The man seated across from the secretary of state's empty chair said, "According to our man, the attacks are not supposed to take place for another month or more." He was Jordan Foster, Director of the CIA. "Let's heighten airport security for now. Tell our computer geeks to look hard at all cyber-mail. Maybe we can gather more information before a decision has to be made."

"Look, gentlemen," FBI Director Richard Knight said. "I understand your reluctance to raise the cry. I do. But think about this: isn't it better to err on the side of caution rather than to suffer through another 9/11? If we're going to get called on the carpet with our jobs at stake, wouldn't it be better to have cried wolf than to have to explain why a terrorist attack occurred when we might have been able to prevent it?"

Chapman said, "If we're talking prevention, this should have been brought forward immediately. Now it's well after the fact."

"Have you had any further contact with your agent?" queried Arthur Penn, head of Homeland Security.

"No," replied Foster, "and I have a bad feeling he will not be heard from again. He knew they were on to him. He's an experienced agent and would've known the importance of getting this information to us. I trust his judgment, but we've received nothing new for weeks. He missed his evac. If he were able, he would've at least contacted us, so I'm assuming he's no longer able. We have no other assets in the area."

"And he said the timeline was two months?" Penn asked.

"Yes, and that was a week ago. We've been working to verify the information ever since."

"And?"

"We were unable to come up with anything, which in itself may be verification. There is always some tidbit of data that leads us somewhere. It's when things dry up that we suspect something is brewing."

"We need to move on this now. They could already be in the country, preparing," the FBI head said. "This should have come to us on day one," he accused, looking at the head CIA man.

Chapman frowned. The fools were already positioning for alibis. He held up a hand to stop Knight from further verbal assault and addressed Foster. "Is this actionable intel?"

"There is a very high probability. The loss of contact with our man and the absence of chatter has raised suspicions. You see now why, even without corroborating evidence, I had to bring this forward."

Department of Defense Director Wesley Yates shook his head. "Alert all airports. Give us all two more days to try to verify what we have and uncover something new. Regardless, after that, we go to the president. He will expect us to corroborate the information anyway. Let's try and do that first."

Chapman took charge. "If whatever they have planned is not scheduled for six more weeks, we have a little time, but it will go fast. Have someone check to see what major events are scheduled for that week. Two days and we report. Get me something, gentlemen."

15

Ian returned home two days later. The drive back was less leisurely than the one to the Rockies. It was a trip he never expected to make. The solitude gave him a chance to think things through. Ian was now determined to hunt down and kill those responsible for the deaths of his wife and son. But the question was, how? If the police couldn't find these men, how did he think he was going to?

The first thing Ian did after arriving home was call the realtor and lower the price on the four-hundred-and-fifty-thousand-dollar house. He would need capital if he was going to go hunting.

Next, Ian called Stern. The man sounded surprised to hear from him. Ian arranged for some of JT's money to be transferred into his account so he would have some accessible funds.

After Ian settled back into the house, he went to see JT. The thinness of his son surprised Ian. In less than a week, JT looked even smaller. The sight of his once active, well-built boy looking so frail was enough to make Ian weep. He sat down and took JT's hand.

Using his sleeve, Ian wiped his eyes. Thinking of how best to divulge his plan, Ian stared at JT's face. To reveal his goals to his son out loud was to give them reality. Ian wanted his son to have a connection to his plans.

"JT, I—I... hell, I didn't expect to see you again. I'm sorry. I was wrong. But my time away was worthwhile. I know what needs to be done now." He paused. Excitement grew inside him as he spoke. "I'm going to find the bastards that put you in this bed. I'm not sure how yet, but I'm going to hunt them down and kill them." He left out the part about most likely getting himself killed in the process.

For the first time since the deaths, Ian had a real goal and the motivation to see it through. *Was he actually going to do this?* Ian looked at his son. "I promise you, JT, I will see you avenged." And he would. With the vow spoken, he would have his revenge. Like in the old Marvel comic books, he would become an Avenger.

As Ian fantasized the outcome, one of the nurses entered.

"Oh, hi, Mr. Kelly," she said cheerfully. "I haven't seen you in a while. How've you been?" She stopped short and put a hand to her lips. Her eyes widened in shock. "Are you all right?"

Ian's hand went to the bandage wrapped around his head. He hadn't given much thought to his appearance. "Ah, yeah, I'm-I'm fine. I was in an accident, but I'm okay now."

She started to say something else, but stopped herself. She checked on JT. "I'm sorry." Her face reddened. "I didn't mean to react like that."

Ian's lips tightened and he tried to form a smile. "It's all right. I'm sure I must look a fright."

"Oh, no," she said in haste. "You look fine. I mean you… ah, the bandages just took me by surprise." She began turning JT on his side.

Ian recognized her but couldn't remember her name. Seeing she was having some difficulty coordinating her efforts, he jumped up and held JT so she could prop pillows along his back to keep him up.

"Why, thank you, sir." She smiled to cover her awkwardness.

"No problem."

He watched her as she worked. She was not very tall and had a slim, athletic body. Her short brown hair curved around her face, framing it. A sprinkling of freckles across her nose made him think she was more cute than beautiful. Lost in his depression, Ian had barely paid attention to any of the nurses before. Maybe having something to focus on now made him more aware of his surroundings.

KeKe was flustered. She hadn't meant to react like she had, but the sudden sight of the bandages covering much of Mr. Kelly's head caught her by surprise and she was unable to prevent it. She busied herself, avoiding eye contact to gain composure.

"How's he doing?" Ian asked.

His question startled her, breaking her away from her thoughts. "About the same, I guess. You'd have to ask the doctor about that. I'm not allowed to give opinions or advice." She avoided looking at him, not wanting to make another mistake by staring at his injuries.

"I understand, but you see him on a daily basis. The doctor sees him, what? Once every two weeks?"

She smiled. "Unfortunately, there's nothing new to tell you. I'm sorry." The light in Mr. Kelly's eyes faded a bit and the sadness that had been there so often before returned.

The staff was aware of the circumstances surrounding JT's

condition and the death of his mother and brother. In a place like this, they were used to seeing pain and suffering. KeKe herself had lost her husband to a hit-and-run driver three years earlier. She still had not recovered, but at least she had moved on. Mr. Kelly's pain was still too fresh.

"Well, I give him a workout once a day. I'm keeping him lean and fit for when he wakes up." She relaxed the more she talked. "And I know he loves to listen to me sing to him."

She looked up then, smiling until her eyes locked with his. She tried hard to maintain a casual expression, but flushed again and had to look away. The poor man, having to bear such internal pain and now physical injury as well. Her heart ached for his burdens. Strangely, though, the thought warmed her and allowed her smile to beam again.

Ian smiled almost before he knew it. He couldn't stop watching her as she moved around the room. He listened to her talk. Her voice had a melodic tone. She was clearly unsettled by his appearance, though she tried hard not to show it. He would have to do something about that. The self-wrapped bandages not only made him look monstrous, but would be too memorable once he went hunting.

Then their eyes met for just the briefest of moments. The smile faded from her eyes first and it saddened him. Though it did return to her lips, the smile never quite reached her eyes. He wanted to speak, but not sure what to say, he averted his gaze. Then a question came to him.

"I'm sorry, but I've forgotten your name?"

"Kay or KeKe Brogan. I'm the daytime nurse in this section."

"Thank you, Ms. Brogan, for singing to my boy."

KeKe stopped and looked at Ian, her smile sincere and warm. "My pleasure."

"Can you think of anything JT might need?"

"Not really. Just his father visiting him as often as possible. I'm sure that's all he would want."

Ian lowered his eyes, his guilt overwhelming him. Her words, even unintended, hurt deeply. Without thought, he lifted his hand toward the wound, but placed it back in his lap before she noticed. If she only knew how close he'd come to never being there for JT again.

Instinctively, KeKe knew she had hit a nerve and possibly crossed a line best left alone.

"I'm sorry, Mr. Kelly. I didn't mean to insinuate you weren't being there for him. My mouth sometimes makes sounds before my brain can regulate it. I know it's hard to be here all the time, but don't you ever worry. If you can't make it, you know I'll be here to take good care of him."

Ian lifted his head and a lone tear tracked down his cheek. He wiped it away before looking at her.

The involuntary mothering instinct in KeKe made her want to take a step toward the pained man, but she stopped before she made another mistake. They looked at each other for an awkward second before turning away.

"It's good to know someone will be here to take care of him in case…" But he couldn't finish the sentence.

A chill ran up KeKe's spine, although she wasn't sure why. "In case what, Mr. Kelly?"

The words were hard for him to push out. Suddenly, she was afraid to hear the answer.

"You know. In case, I, ah…can't be here for him."

"We're just talking about an occasional miss though, right?"

Ian wiped his sleeve across his eyes and stood up. "Yeah, just occasionally. That's all. I have to go." He reached the door.

"Mr. Kelly, I'm glad you're all right. I'm sorry for your pain. But think about how JT's world is. He's relying on you to be strong for him."

When Ian turned back toward her, his face was hard, like another person was occupying his body. The look made KeKe snap her head back in alarm. "You don't need to worry about that, Ms. Brogan. I've already promised him I am gonna be." Then, as if his normal personality gained control again, he said in a softer voice, "Thank you." And he was gone.

16

Back in the car, Ian pounded on the steering wheel. He promised his son he would get his revenge and now it was time to start preparing. He had a list of things to do, people to contact, and items to buy. Some of it was even legal.

His first call went to Detective Robinson. "Detective, it's Ian Kelly. I want to know if there's been any progress in the case."

"Mr. Kelly, I'm glad you called. We've been tracking our suspect's known associates. We have names and a few leads. We're just trying to find them. I'm pretty sure they've left town, but the word is at least one of them might be back. We're still searching for him."

"What are the names?"

Robinson hesitated, then said, "I'll let you know when we find them, sir. Until then, it's best we keep that information to ourselves. I'm sure you can understand that. We wouldn't want anything to leak out that could jeopardize the case."

"Okay, but please keep me informed when you find them."

Before Robinson could respond, Ian hung up. He thought it was very strange they were holding the names so close. By now they should've been all over the news. But he'd find out. He'd find a way, if only because he had a right to know.

Ian's second call went to an old customer from the restaurant. He and two of his buddies were members of a motorcycle club and looked every bit the part. All three were huge men with long wild hair, a variety of tattoos, and black leather everything. They were loud and scared some of the customers, but they had always been respectful to him and his restaurant. Over the years he had come to know them and developed a friendly relationship. When the motorcycle club had a fundraiser for the children of a member who was killed in a bike accident, Ian donated a lot of food. He was a friend to them from then on.

"Bonzo?"

"Who's calling?" The voice was harsh and suspicious.

"It's Ian from Kelly's Restaurant."

The voice changed instantly. "Oh. Hey man, how's it going? The guys all miss you over there. We don't go in there much anymore."

"Sorry to hear that." Suddenly, he couldn't think of what to say.

Bonzo picked up on it. "So, Ian, what's up, man?"

"I, ah, I... you heard about my family, right?"

"Yeah man, that was a real shitty deal. We were real sorry to hear about it. Is that why you're calling, man? You need some help?"

"In a way. I need to buy a gun." The big man who had brained him with his helmet had taken the .45. "I was hoping you might know who to send me to."

Silence filled his ear. For a moment, Ian thought Bonzo had hung up on him.

"You know, man, since you been closed, me and the boys've been hanging at that new place down the street from you. You know the place I mean?"

Ian was confused by the abrupt change of subject. "I think so."

"We eat there all the time, usually breakfast, but we go there for dinner, too. You should drop by. I think the guys would be happy to see you again."

"Ah, okay, I'll do that."

"Good. Well, it's been nice talking to you. Take care."

With that, the phone went dead, leaving Ian wondering what had just happened.

While he thought about the conversation with Bonzo, Ian drove to a chain sporting goods store where he picked up a list of items he might need. He filled a cart. He could have bought a gun there, but it would be registered and he would have to wait to get it. Squeezing his purchases into the trunk, Ian grabbed a few things from the packages and sat in the car. Looking in the rearview mirror, he unwrapped the bandage and tossed it in the back seat. The wound was still raw. He applied a triple antibiotic ointment and pushed a gauze pad down on the affected area. After taping it in place, he slid a ball cap gingerly on his head.

Ian checked his watch. It was dinner time. Hoping he had Bonzo's message worked out, he drove toward a diner he had never been in, located four blocks from where his restaurant had been.

He drove the parking lot but saw no bikes anywhere. In fact, there were only three other cars. Ian wondered if he had misunderstood the location, but parked and went in anyway.

A waitress with her hair pinned up and a sleeve of tattoos covering her left arm from shoulder to wrist led Ian to a table. She handed him a menu and walked away.

Ian stared at the menu, not sure what he should do. He hadn't been eating much lately, figuring it wasn't going to matter in his suicide plan, but if he was going hunting, he'd better start building his strength back up. It took quite a while for the waitress to return, even though most of the time she just stood behind the counter, reading the paper. She collected money from the only other customer before she returned to his table. Ian ordered a burger with fries and an iced tea.

Ian passed the time staring out the window, reviewing his purchases and thinking about what he still might need. When he finally refocused on the diner, he realized it had been close to half an hour and his food still hadn't arrived. He looked around for the waitress but didn't see her. She was probably outside, wrestling the cow to the ground.

Finally, she appeared through the swinging doors carrying a tray full of food. She set the burger down in front of him and then placed various other plates around the table. Ian tried to find words but was too confused to get them out. She landed the last plate, winked at him, and left.

"But-but…" was all he managed. The waitress went behind the counter again and stood. Ian stared at her and followed her gaze when she turned her head toward the outside door. At that moment, Bonzo, Tex, and Big Jim walked through the door and straight for Ian's table. Ian felt his jaw fall open and hang. Bonzo and Tex took chairs across from him while Big Jim diverted toward the counter where he planted a kiss on the waitress.

"Hi, honey. How's your day been?"

"Just fine, stud. How 'bout yours?"

"I think it's just about to get interesting."

Big Jim came over and sat down next to Ian.

All three men shook hands with Ian and said how nice it was to see him again. Their behavior and was so strange and so different from what he was used to that he wondered if he'd made a mistake. They dove into their food hungrily. With a mouthful of turkey and gravy, Bonzo explained, "When you closed up and we found we didn't much like the new owner, Big Jim bought this place for his wife to run." Bonzo was the smallest of the three men, but that was like comparing offensive linemen on a pro football team.

"Oh," Ian said, not sure if he was more surprised that Big Jim owned the diner or that he was married.

"Yeah," Big Jim said. "Missy's awesome, but she doesn't like us coming in too much. She's afraid we'll scare away the customers." He laughed loudly.

"Not so, you big oaf," his wife yelled from the counter. "You eat here so much, you're getting fat."

The guys laughed. Big Jim stood well over six foot and had to be pushing three hundred pounds.

"Fatter, more like," added Bonzo.

The talk was light. They kept far away from any subject relating to guns. It was just four guys having dinner. When they were almost finished, Bonzo got a call. He listened for a few seconds. "Maybe fifteen. Cover us."

A few minutes later, Missy picked up the plates and laid down the bill. The others, as if on cue, looked from the bill to Ian. He got their message and smiled as he picked it up.

Then Bonzo leaned over the table and said in a hushed voice, "We're gonna leave now. You follow us. If at any time you see us speed up and try to lose you, it'd be better for you if you don't follow and never contact us again. We would be very disappointed if that should occur."

His words were spoken softly, but their meaning carried a huge threat. A chill crept down his spine. It took a moment for Ian to realize they were afraid he was setting them up. As one, the three bikers stood and moved toward the door. Ian walked to the counter and paid the bill, adding a very generous tip.

"Thanks, sweetie," Missy said. "Be safe now."

When Ian got to the parking lot, a red Dodge pickup truck was pulling away. Not wanting to get left behind, Ian jogged to his car and hurried out of the lot. In the distance, the roar of bikes coming to life caught his attention. In his rearview mirror, he saw two Harleys pull out from a lot two buildings down. He assumed they were Bonzo's people.

The bikes moved up on either side of Ian's car. The biker on the right moved closer and looked inside the car as if searching for someone hiding on the floor. After a moment, he dropped back behind the car. The man on the driver's side glanced at Ian. When Ian met his gaze, the biker lifted a finger and pulled the trigger on his imaginary gun. The symbolic gesture turned the undigested food in Ian's stomach into a lead weight. The biker dropped back behind Ian as the other one had.

The bikers bracketed him, giving him a feeling of being trapped. He still had time to change his mind and go it alone. But without help, what chance did he have?

Ian looked in the rearview mirror at the two men following him. Had he made a mistake in seeking help here? The riders dropped back farther. Before Ian looked back at the road, he caught his reflection in the mirror. His gaze hardened. No. This was the course he had chosen. If he survived this meeting, he might actually stand a chance of avenging his family.

17

Ian stayed with the truck, but not too close. Twenty minutes later, it turned off the main street and onto a narrow, almost one-lane road. After another mile, they took another left down a dirt road. There were no other houses on the road. The path twisted a few times before ending at a locked gate.

Tex got out and unlocked it. The two bikes came up behind Ian and idled. Tex motioned his big hand at Ian to drive through. He followed the truck further until it came to a large cabin. Bonzo parked the truck and got out. One bike, with Tex hitching a ride, pulled up next to the truck. Ian got out and walked toward the group. He started to speak, but Bonzo held up his hand.

"Do you have a cell phone?" Bonzo asked.

"Ah, yeah."

Bonzo held out his open hand. Ian hesitated an instant, then pulled the phone from his pocket. He placed it in Bonzo's hand, and he passed it to one of his escorts. "We'll get it back to you when you leave."

The man with the phone snorted and said, "*If* you leave." He barked a harsh laugh. Bonzo smiled. "There's just one last thing." He motioned to Big Jim.

Big Jim stepped forward and frisked Ian, patting down his entire body. He winced when the big man pulled off his cap. "Whoa!" Big Jim said. "I'll bet that hurt." But even after saying that, he touched the wound to make sure nothing was concealed beneath the gauze pad. Ian flinched, but tried to not to move, closing his eyes against the pain.

Big Jim stood and nodded to Bonzo. "He's clean." He handed the hat back. Bonzo stepped forward and embraced Ian.

"Brother, we're all sorry about your family," he said into his ear. "If there is anything we can do to help you, all you have to do is ask." He let go and stepped back. "You understand?"

Ian nodded and tried hard to fight back tears. Standing there in front of these men, ready to ask them for help, was no time to appear weak.

Bonzo put an arm around Ian's shoulders and guided him into the cabin. "I'm sorry for all the spy stuff. We had to be sure we weren't being set up."

The inside of the cabin was much larger and cleaner than Ian expected. They walked through a kitchen and dining area into a family room with a large stone fireplace. Bonzo left him there for a moment as the bikers huddled in the dining room.

Ian took the opportunity to look around. The large room looked like a hunter's cabin. Windows lined the rear wall and looked out onto a scenic ravine. To the left was a small, plain cabin with no windows; to the right was a barn converted into a garage. Ian guessed the little cabin was for storage.

Bonzo called him over and motioned to a large wood plank table that had seats enough for twelve. One of the bike riders he did not know joined them. When all five men were seated, Bonzo began. "What is it you want to do, and I'll be better able to tell you how we might help."

In a rush, Ian blurted, "I want to hunt down the men responsible for killing my wife and son."

The words came out easy, but what surprised Ian was the force with which they were delivered.

"I respect that," said Bonzo. "I do. I'd feel the same way if it were me. But you're talking about taking another man's life. Are you sure you're capable of doing that?"

"Yes."

"Wouldn't it just be easier to hire it done? We know people who would do it for a price. That would take the heat off you."

"No. This is something I have to do myself."

The man Ian didn't know stared at him. Tex and Big Jim nodded as if approving Ian's words.

"I don't think you understand that killing a man changes you forever. You can't take it back or say, 'Oops! Sorry'."

"How do you think my life has changed now? You think I give a shit anymore about my life changing?" Ian spit the words out. "I need to do this. I'll do it with or without your help. I'll find a way. It'll be a lot easier if you help, though."

The unknown man leaned forward and snarled. "What makes you think we can help you with this? You think because we're bikers, we're all criminals and can get you what you want? And even if that were true, why should we help you? You're not one of us. Hell, you're not even a biker. I doubt you could sit a real bike."

Ian was taken aback by the venomous verbal onslaught. Doubt flooded through him. This had been a mistake. It was stupid to think these men could or would help him. But could he blame them? They didn't really know him. *I should go now.* He was about to slide his chair back and do just that when something ignited within him. His spine seemed to stiffen and he sat up straighter. He put his hands flat on the table and leaned forward, facing the man.

Working hard not to let his voice crack and keeping his tone level, he said, "If that's the impression I've given, I apologize. If I have acted on a stereotype, forgive me. The only reason I am here is because I need help. Whether you can give that help or not, I don't know, but I was hoping you could at least guide me in the right direction."

He turned his gaze to Bonzo. "I have great respect for you and meant no insult. I appreciate your time. I will look elsewhere for the help I need." He stood. "At any rate, it was good seeing you all again."

"Hold up a sec, brother," Bonzo said.

He paused a beat, then looked to the others. "Excuse us a minute."

The five men walked outside and huddled on the large deck with their backs to him. Ian stared down at the table and tried to think of what else he could say to help his cause. No matter what Bonzo's decision, Ian would carry on with his plans. In truth, he had no idea where to begin, but he was determined, even though he knew no one else to ask for the type of help he needed. However, if they said no, he would find a way somehow.

A few minutes later, Bonzo came back in, but the others went to the storage cabin and disappeared inside. Bonzo sat down.

"I respect what you're telling me about avenging your family. I'm not sure you have killing in you, but we'll help you. I have some very important things to say to you and I need you to understand them. They are not meant to be personal, it's just business.

"Normally, we would not bring a customer here. We felt we had to handle you differently, if not completely out of trust, then at least out of respect. You can never mention us, this place, or our club to anyone. This you must vow or we cannot help you."

Ian nodded. "Absolutely. I'm not looking to take anyone else down with me."

"If you're caught with these guns, they are not traceable. But if you give us up, we'll be forced to come after you. The Brotherhood is always first. We protect our own at all costs."

Ian smiled, but not from mirth. "I don't plan on getting caught, but if I do, I don't plan on being taken alive. I want to finish this and I'm willing to die to see it done. That gives me an edge."

"It's obvious you've given the possibilities some thought. It's easy to say the words, but when it comes down to the actual deeds, though, dying can seem extreme."

Ian looked away. "I'm not afraid to do this. I'm not a fool." Ian turned and held Bonzo's eyes. "I know it won't be easy. But if I find the two animals that killed my family, I won't hesitate to pull the trigger."

"I sincerely hope it works out for you, brother. Follow me."

They got up from the table and went outside, stopping on the deck. It took several minutes before Bonzo spoke again.

"If we go any further, there is no turning back. You understand that?"

"Yes."

"Let me hear you say it."

Ian looked at the large man and held his eyes with no fear. "There *is* no going back. Not for my family. Not for my son. Not for me. Let's do this."

18

Bonzo led Ian toward the smaller, windowless cabin. "You do realize this is business. The items are for sale, right?"

"Yes, I have money."

"With you?"

"Some. If I run over, I'll have to go get more, but it'll be covered."

Bonzo opened the door and entered with Ian behind him. When they were both inside, Bonzo closed and locked the door. The room was full of various pieces of landscaping equipment. Two riding mowers and two snow blowers lined one wall, while assorted other items for the upkeep of the property hung from pegs over a large workbench. In the far right-hand corner, a portion of the floor had been cleared and a trap door lay up against the back wall. Below, a wooden ladder led to a hidden, lit space.

Bonzo descended and Ian followed. The thought struck him, surprisingly for the first time, that he did not know these men very well. Admitting he had money on him and then climbing into an underground hole with them was not the smartest thing he'd ever done.

As he touched the ground, he noticed Big Jim and Tex standing around a long table covered with firearms. The unnamed fourth man was leaning against the wall, watching Ian as if he expected him to pull out a gun and rob the bikers.

The room was about the same size as the cabin above, sixteen by twenty feet. The floor was hard-packed dirt.

Ian approached the table. The assortment was vast. Ian knew next to nothing about guns. He had only shot a gun twice and one of those times was at himself, and he missed. As he scanned the weapons, Ian recognized an AK-47 from the movies. He knew the difference between a revolver and a semi-automatic. He was fairly certain one weapon was an Uzi. There had to be close to fifty guns and rifles there. Other than to be amazed that they had enough weapons to start a small war, Ian wasn't sure what to do.

Not wanting to appear stupid, he turned to Bonzo. Pointing at the table he asked, "May I?"

Bonzo smiled. "Oh, absolutely. Feel free to examine all of them."

Ian picked up a squared off black semi-automatic and hefted it. He didn't know what else to do. He tried to jack back the slide, but it wouldn't budge. His cheeks reddened with embarrassment.

Tex stepped forward and took the gun, pushed down a little lever, and racked the slide back. He then handed the gun back to Ian for inspection.

Bonzo moved next to him. "Ian, I don't mean to be rude or anything, but have you ever shot a gun before?"

Ian frowned. "Yeah; a little. I've shot a rifle a few times hunting, but never really a handgun." He set the gun down. "What do you recommend?"

Bonzo studied Ian for a few seconds, perhaps thinking this was a bad idea.

"Let's find out what you can handle." He picked up three different handguns and nodded toward the fourth man. He turned and pushed a button and the wall he had been leaning against slid back, revealing a long, narrow corridor set up as a firing range. Three partitioned shooting booths had been built there. The range stretched out about forty feet further from the booths. Wire lines had been hung to hold paper targets.

Bonzo moved to the middle stall and set the guns down on the bench that ran in front of all three booths. Tex came up from behind with several boxes of bullets. Bonzo showed Ian how to load the magazines and insert them into the handles.

"This is a 9mm, this one's a .40 caliber, and this one is a .45."

He handed Ian an electronic headset.

"Put that on and the shots will be quieter than one of Big Jim's farts."

Over the next hour, the three men took turns showing Ian how to handle, aim, and shoot. With the 9mm, each one of his shots was pretty much on target. The .40 was about seventy-thirty, and the .45 had too much kick to be effective.

"I think the 9mm's gonna be your best bet at hitting something," said Big Jim.

"Yeah. You did good with that," added Tex.

Ian nodded. "Yeah, that one for sure. What else you got?"

Bonzo raised an eyebrow.

"Well, let me ask you this. How close you gonna be to your target?"

"I haven't thought much about it. I've gotta find them first."

"Do you just want them dead, or do you want them to see your face first and know why they're dying?"

Ian thought about it. The flare of hatred sparked up again.

"I want them to see my face, but I want them dead. So if I can't have one, I definitely want the other."

"Tex, bring the .22 here, would ya?"

Tex handed Bonzo a long-barreled handgun. Then Ian saw Bonzo unscrewing a portion and realized it had a silencer.

"This might be a perfect weapon for you if you can get up close. It's silenced for stealth work, but it doesn't have much stopping power. So unless you can get close, it's not a good choice." He handed it to Ian. "Take a few shots. See what you think."

Ian checked the magazine to make sure it was loaded, then jacked a round into the chamber. He lined it up as he was taught and fired two rounds. Both were hits, center circle.

He looked at it and nodded.

"That'll work, too. What else ya got?"

Bonzo looked at the other two men and shook his head. "I think we created a monster." They laughed and went to get more guns.

Ian looked down range at the paper target and pictured blank-faced men. Could he be monster enough to finish this? Then he thought about JT lying in a hospital bed, perhaps for the rest of his life. He felt his anger flare. He could kill. He no longer had any doubt.

Ian turned to see that the boys had brought out the big stuff. A savage smile took over his face.

19

An hour and half later, Ian was packed and driving back down the long dirt road. He had purchased three handguns, a rifle, a cleaning kit, and three hundred rounds of ammo for the assorted weapons. He also picked up ammo pouches, an old-style pair of night vision goggles, and a worn leather trench coat with extra interior pockets and a shooting hole cut in the right-hand outer pocket. His purchases also included one old pineapple grenade that came with no guarantees and two burner cell phones. Along with the other items purchased from the sporting goods store, Ian felt he was ready to start hunting. Hell, he was ready to start a small war.

Before Ian left, Bonzo said, "I know you don't have any experience with this type of thing, but you should never go into a fight without backup or backup hardware. Let me show you some things that might save your life." By the time he left, Ian felt more confident, the extra information Bonzo had offered was both eye-opening and sobering.

Ian flashed back to Bonzo's parting words. "I hope your hunt is successful and that you survive it. But even if you do, a part of you will die. I'll pray for you, brother." He embraced Ian then. Without another word, Bonzo walked back inside the cabin. Their business was over.

Ian drove to his house and sat in the driveway. A flood of memories hit him like a bullet. It took a long time before he was able to raise the garage door and drive inside. He pushed the pain away by telling himself it would all be over soon. Ian prayed that God, if He existed, would understand his actions and reunite him with his wife and son.

Lowering the garage door behind him, Ian unloaded the car and spread his new purchases out on the family room floor. He looked them over then began arranging them into three groups. One for his daily patrols, one for longer ranges and the last as a backup.

After loading all three guns and the extra magazines, he set each in one of the groups. A knife was placed with each gun. An expanding baton was set off to the side. He would carry that with him. It took him well into the night to get the packs filled the way he thought best. Ian lay down on the sofa, not wanting to sleep alone in the bed he had shared with Margo. His final thoughts were of pulling a trigger over and over at faceless villains.

Ian slept later than he wanted. He took a quick shower, flung some clothes on, and headed to see JT. Ian planned on starting his search later that evening, although he hadn't decided on a starting point as of yet. If something bad was going to happen, he wanted to be with JT one more time.

When Ian entered his son's room, it was dark. JT was lying there peacefully; so much so he appeared to be dead. If not for the monitor and machines making their steady clacking sounds, no one would think he was alive. His chest still rose and fell in a regular breath, but for how much longer? Was there really any hope? Ian sat down and shook the negative thoughts from his head. He had to believe that one day his son would regain consciousness and live a normal life. Otherwise, what he was about to do would have meaning, but serve no purpose. JT had to know he was avenged.

Ian scooted his chair close and in a low conspiratorial voice, explained his plan to JT as if he were an active contributor. Ian knew the name of the killer now in jail: Darryle Lawson. He had lived in an area known as the North End at 524 E. Park. Ian's plan was simple. He was going to walk the neighborhood and ask anyone he saw if they knew Lawson. He would then ask about people Lawson hung around with and where he might find them. Somebody knew something. He would offer money for information, but decided that could work against him too much. For one, he could never trust the information and two, if people knew he was carrying money, he would attract more attention than he wanted.

Granted, it wasn't a great plan, but it was the only one he had. Eventually, word would get back to those he sought. They would either run or they would send people to find out who he was and deal with him, if necessary. He didn't really care. Ian wanted them to come, to make their move. He would be ready, or so he told himself. He could see the altercations in his mind and he always came out on top. It gave him a false sense of security to think he could handle anything that arose.

It was about lunchtime when Nurse Brogan came into the room.

"Well, hi there. It's good to see you here again. I'm sure your son appreciates it."

"I hope so. Tell me, have you ever seen someone in a coma

come out of it?"

She paused, as if contemplating how best to answer. "No, I can't say that I have, but I know for a fact that it does happen. Just don't give up on him. He's been through a severe trauma, both physically and mentally. He's healing and not ready to wake up yet. Give him time."

"Thank you. I needed to hear something positive."

She flashed a brilliant smile. "Anytime. That's what I'm here for."

KeKe performed the same move she did the day before, but this time she turned JT on the opposite side. Ian stood and helped again. It made him feel good to be doing something for his son. At one point, they both reached for the same pillow and their hands touched. Ian pulled his hand back as if it had been stung. "Sorry."

"Oh, don't be silly. It's not like you were trying to hold my hand," KeKe joked. She had a nice laugh.

Ian felt the heat from the blush that crept across his face and he was surprised by his reaction. The touch scared him. Not because of any ill intent, but because it had sent an electric reaction through him that was once solely reserved for his wife. Guilt attacked him. He tried to rationalize the feeling by reminding himself his wife was gone, but Margo would never be out of his heart. Besides, what was the point of wasting time on silly feelings when he wasn't going to be around long enough to develop them?

Ian went back to his seat and avoided her eyes. KeKe busied herself doing whatever it was she did, humming joyfully the whole time. When she left, she tried to keep her voice upbeat, but clearly something had changed.

"Have a good day, Mr. Kelly. I'll check back in later."

While Ian watched his son, he was saddened by his thoughts as they wandered back in time, reliving the golden moments of his relationship with Margo: how they met; their first kiss; the first time they made love; the wedding; the births of their sons.

"Mr. Kelly, are you all right?"

He never heard her enter. Startled by the voice, Ian looked up, embarrassed to find he had been crying. He wiped his face on his sleeve while KeKe pretended not to notice.

"Ah, yes, I'm fine. I'm just having an emotional moment. What time is it?" he asked to change the subject.

"It's a little after two," KeKe said.

Ian was shocked. Two hours had passed. He had been so immersed in memories he had lost track of time. Not that he had anywhere else to go, but he needed to get out and walk for a while to clear his head and focus on what he needed to do.

As he approached JT, a hand gently touched his arm.

"Mr. Kelly, are you sure you're okay?"

Ian looked into KeKe's concerned eyes and thought about what a good person she was. JT would be in good hands with her. He forced a smile.

"Yeah, I'm okay."

"We do have professional, ah, assistance available if you need someone to talk to."

"No, that's all right. I'll be fine."

She dropped her hand from his arm.

"Well, if you ever need to talk to someone, I'm here. Okay?"

"Yes, thank you. Just please, no matter what, take good care of my boy."

"Ah, sure, I always do, but 'no matter what'? You're still going to be here for him, aren't you? He needs your support." She appeared worried. "That's the second time you've said that. Are you going away?"

Ian smiled again, but he knew it wasn't fooling anyone. "I just meant on days I can't be here."

"Oh," she said, but clearly wasn't convinced.

Ian bent to JT and kissed his forehead. Staring at the boy's face, Ian had a premonition it might be the last time he saw him. Before the tears started flowing again, he stood and walked toward the door.

"Thank you for all you do."

"You come back now, Mr. Kelly." It sounded like a demand. "You hear me?"

Without looking back for fear that she could read the truth in his eyes, Ian waved and left. He walked briskly to his car. It was time to clear his mind and put his plan into action. He still had much to do before he started his hunt.

20

If Ian expected to have any success finding the killers and taking his revenge, he needed to relocate to make it more difficult for the police to find him. He couldn't accept a partial success. If he got one of killers but not the other, the police would be searching for him. When they arrived at his house, they would find it empty.

Ian drove several miles west of his house until he was in a more rural area. Ian wanted to be close to his son, so he decided to stay on the west side of the city. He picked up a real estate magazine and searched for local rental properties. There were only two listings that drew his interest.

He drove past both locations and then called the listed number of the first one he liked. The owners lived next door to the property, so he was able to see it right away. The small ranch house was close to the road. It was sufficient for his needs, but he didn't like that it was so close to the owners. He didn't need anyone dipping into his business, so even though Ian told the woman he would get back to her, he hoped there were better options open to him.

The second appointment wasn't until six. He had nearly two hours to kill. Ian decided to drive the area to see if there were any other options. He turned off the main road and drove over a small bridge that covered a creek that was lined on both sides by large trees. Fifty yards farther on the right was an old run-down, two-story home that looked as though it needed plenty of work.

A *For Sale* sign was attached to one of the front windows. Ian turned into the driveway and got out of the car. The house looked as though it leaned slightly. He wasn't too concerned about that; he wouldn't need it for long. Trees lined the property, though the land behind the house was open for quite a ways before ending at a small copse. The nearest neighbor was barely within sight. Trees concealed the house from the main road. About forty yards to the rear of the house stood an old barn that looked to be in worse shape than the house.

Ian went up on the porch and pressed his hands on the dirty window to look inside. The room was empty. Hardwood floors and bare walls were all that he could see, but it appeared to be livable. Stepping off the porch, Ian walked the perimeter. The side windows were too high up to see through, but off the back was a small enclosed porch. The screen door hung at an angle across the frame. Ian pulled it open and it fell off the hinges. He stepped back as it hit the ground. Looking up, he saw that the four-by-six-foot room was covered in spider webs. He felt an involuntary chill run up his spine.

Ian found a stick and swatted at the strands, wrapping them around the wood. When enough of the webbing had been cleared away to pass through, he stepped up on the porch. Through the window in the back door, he could see the kitchen. A hand pump was attached to the sink. An ancient stove and refrigerator stood against one wall. It was sparse, but it would work for the safe haven he needed. He went to the front and punched the number on the sign into one of the two burner phones.

An old man answered. When Ian explained he wanted to see the house, the man responded with, "What? You serious? What the hell's wrong with you?" He laughed. After Ian assured him he was interested, the man agreed to meet at the property.

An hour later, an old red and rust colored International pickup truck that had seen better days, pulled up in the driveway. Harley Jackson stepped out of the truck and limped toward Ian.

"I guess you're the fella that called me, eh?"

"Yep." Ian held out his hand and the man shook it.

"Well, let's take a look at the house. See if you still want it."

"Why? What's wrong with it?"

"Well, for one, it's older than me."

"It doesn't look too bad from outside."

Jackson made it up the steps with some effort and produced a skeleton key for the door.

"Oh, it's in good enough shape. It just needs lots of updates. There's no running water. The banks get kinda fussy about things like that. However, there is an indoor toilet; that much got updated. There's two wells for your water. One's outside and there's a small pump in the sink. You'll have to have the water checked to make sure you can drink it. There's a septic system, but that'll have to be checked, too. The electric is only sixty amps. No one will loan you money on this place unless you update that. There's only a few outlets in the house, too."

He pushed the door open and stepped inside.

"Ain't been lived in in nearly ten years. Got old lead pipes; those'll have to be replaced, too, if you want safe water. I sure wouldn't trust them."

"Mr. Jackson, it sounds to me like you're trying not to sell this place."

"Oh, I want to sell. I'm just a realist. Besides, I wouldn't feel right if I didn't give you the lowdown on the place."

Ian walked around the house. There were two bedrooms, a living room, dining room, and kitchen. Two more bedrooms were upstairs. The bathroom was covered in old-fashioned yellow ceramic tiles.

"Mr. Jackson, how much are you asking?"

"Well," he scratched his chin. "I was asking fifty thousand, mostly because of the land that it sits on. But I suppose if you're interested, I'd be willing to listen to offers."

"Well, here's the thing. I was just transferred back to town. I'm not sure how long I'll be here. I know I'm here for six months for sure. If it's longer than that, then I'll be here permanently. How about this? I'll take it for six months, cash. I'll fix it up a bit and make some repairs. If I'm here after six months, I'll buy it. If not, you walk away with the money and get a slightly updated property that might be easier to sell."

"I don't know. Is that even legal?"

Ian laughed. "Yes. It's called a land contract. You and I will sign an agreement. I'll pay you, say, five hundred a month in advance."

"Five hundred dollars?" The man seemed shocked.

Ian laughed again. "Yes, five hundred dollars. I'll pay you six months' rent up front. That's three thousand dollars. You got any use for that kind of money?"

"I sure as hell do. But how do I know you're legit? You could be trying to scam me."

Ian took out his wallet and counted out three thousand dollars. "Well, here's the money. If you're not happy with the deal, you can kick me out after six months."

Jackson still seemed to be hesitant. "How do I know you're not a terrorist or something? I read the papers about things like this."

"Huh. Well, I guess there's no way of proving I'm not. If the deal makes you feel that uncomfortable, let's just forget it." Ian put the money back in his pocket. "Wasn't about to turn the money over to you without a receipt anyway, so you would have that. I mean, trust is a two-way street here. You could take my money and call the cops and say I was a freeloader or something." Ian started for the door. "Well, thanks for your time."

"Ah, wait. What you said about this land contract. We're gonna draw it up so it's legal, right?"

"Of course. I wouldn't have it any other way."

Ian went to the car and found some paper and a pen. They negotiated a price and the terms of the contract. Ian drew it up and explained each part so Jackson felt secure about it. When they both had signed, Ian handed over the money. Jackson's face lit up at the touch of it. He handed over the key.

"You take the document so you know it's safe. I would appreciate it if you would make me a copy when you get a chance."

"Sure, I can do that." He looked at the signature and said, "Mr. Clark. I'll get it to you by tomorrow."

"That's great." He locked the door and the two men shook hands and drove off in opposite directions.

Ian went back to his house and packed up everything he thought he might need. The list grew longer as he thought of the house and what it lacked. He took lamps, a sleeping bag, blankets and a pillow, bottled water, food, and cleaning supplies. It took longer than he thought it would. If possible, after tonight he didn't want to return.

When Ian was done, he stood in the doorway and looked around. Too many great memories had been destroyed in one day. Hopefully, he would soon make it right. He closed the door, drove down the driveway, and didn't look back.

21

By the end of the next day, all plans had been outlined and the remaining four team members arrived one by one, carrying duffel bags. Each man had his hair cut short and was clean shaven. They wore American jeans and t-shirts. The only thing they couldn't alter was that they all looked like soldiers.

Once the cell members settled into bedrooms and had eaten, Ahmed held a general meeting. "You know why you are here. The mission will be explained to you soon. Until then, no one is to leave this house unless I give an assignment. Your cell phones are to be passed forward now." The men complied without hesitation. "There will be no contact with anyone outside this house." Ahmed looked from face to face. He had no need to know their names. Few of them, if any, would survive the week anyway. No one would survive after the final mission.

"The weapons are in the basement. You will each be responsible for making sure they are operational. You should carry backup weapons, extra ammunition, and a knife. Other items we may need will be stored in the vehicles. The list of targets has been selected. I will drive by them today and decide the order and feasibility of success." Ahmed's voice was impassioned, growing in volume as he said, "With Allah's help, we will deliver such fear into the hearts of our enemies that they will never again doubt our power and resolve."

He scanned their faces as he spoke. None showed any reaction to his words. No emotion, no fire. Ahmed smiled to himself. *Good.* These men were too professional to get lost in religious hype. No fanatics with false courage. They would do their jobs without losing their nerve. He began to believe the mission actually stood a chance.

"We will begin in two days. Make yourselves ready, but remember: no one is to leave this house."

As the men stomped down the basement steps to find their weapons, Ahmed turned to Al. Ahmed's unofficial second-in-command had done well so far. The man was well organized. "Get the car. I want to check the targets in case we have to make any changes."

The drive took thirty minutes. The house was just the right distance from the city; far enough away to be hidden, yet close enough to get there in a reasonable amount of time before pursuit could be mounted. Each assault was designed to be quick but devastating. The first one, since it would be the only one people would be unprepared for, would take the longest. The death toll would depend on the numbers inside each building. Each day's attack was designed to escalate in severity of destruction and increased loss of life.

The two men drove to the northern outskirts of the city as the sun was setting. The street the targets were located on ran almost the entire length of the city's northern boundary. Ahmed looked at his notes and commanded Al to stop several times along the route. They sat in the parking lot of the first target and watched the activity around the building. He looked for patterns and traffic flow from both cars and patrons. Ahmed also wanted to see how many of the surrounding businesses would be open at the hour of attack and if any would pose a potential problem. Since the plan called for entry into each building from front and back, checking that each had a rear exit was a priority.

When satisfied, Ahmed instructed his assistant to move to the next target. The ritual was the same at each site. He studied the floor plans of the interiors Al had provided. Each location had been examined weeks before and detailed diagrams drawn out. Ahmed wanted to make sure the men would know what to expect upon entry.

Through Ahmed's trained eye, he saw problems and mentally worked out possible solutions. He jotted notes on each target's page. By the time they finished at the last site, Ahmed felt more confident about what they faced and their chances for success.

It was late into the night before they returned. Ahmed was pleased to see the men had taken it upon themselves to set up a watch schedule. The man at the front window nodded but otherwise made no comment. Another man stood at the back.

Ahmed went upstairs to the workroom to go over his notes and finalize his plans. Seeing the targets allowed him to make the necessary adjustments to the assaults. A picture of each location became clear in his mind. He visualized and followed the flow of the attack to its predicted conclusion. *Yes, it was a good plan.* Of course, no plan was foolproof. Unexpected problems always arose, however, his men were hand-picked, not only because of their combat skills, but also for their adaptability. They would handle whatever came up with deadly efficiency. If they could get through the first few days, Ahmed felt nothing could stop them. He reviewed the plans once more, then went to bed. Anticipation swelled, making sleep difficult. He knew he had to keep it contained for the good of the mission. Ahmed closed his eyes and willed sleep to come, but he dared not dream of his glory.

22

Ian parked his car on a residential street, blocks away from where he planned to start his search. He hoped the car would be safe, especially considering what was in the trunk. He needed it in the proximity should the need arise to flee for his life. The car had been one part of the plan he hadn't thought through. He should not be using his own vehicle. If he survived the night, he would deal with it tomorrow.

A nervous pulse of excitement filled Ian as he walked down the street. The long leather coat was too warm and conspicuous, like a stereotype from some slasher movie. He felt out of place. He wore dark pants, dark rubber soled shoes, a black t-shirt, and a ball cap with no insignia. Thin leather gloves covered his hands, which were buried deep inside the coat's pockets, nervously fingering the weapons within.

Ian walked through an older area of town where the houses sat close to the streets and had little space between them. Street lights, placed at too great a distance to be effective, fought for space to shine through the branches of the many trees below them.

After only a block, sweat was already pouring down his face; a combination of the heavy coat and nerves. Fear gave him second thoughts. Maybe he should reconsider. He could still turn back and hire some of Bonzo's connections to deal with the killers. There needn't be any guilt. The job would still get done, but regardless of who did the deed, he had to find the killers first.

Even with doubts playing constantly in his brain, Ian's stride never faltered. He traveled two more blocks along deserted dark streets. Though it was late, Ian didn't think he'd be the only person wandering the streets. Gravel and two-track dirt alleys ran behind the houses on almost every block in this section of town. Ian had just passed one before he realized he had company.

"Hey, boy. You walking in bad territory."

The voice startled him. He turned his head but kept walking, fighting hard not to increase his pace and show fear. Hell, he was trying hard not to run screaming down the street as fast as he could.

Two tall, but not very large men, one black, one white, were less than ten feet behind him. Ian got the feeling they were barely out of their teens, if at all.

"You could get hurt walking these streets alone. Maybe you should let us protect you."

"Yeah," the white man added. "We protect you real good for all your money." They thought that was hilarious, speaking with the cool confidence that came from being on home turf and having the enemy outnumbered.

"Hey man, you can't outrun us. Best thing to do is to stop and pay up. Don't make us hurt you, now."

Well, Ian thought, *this is what you wanted; now what?* He took a deep breath and spun on the two men. His hand wrapped tightly around the silenced .22 in his pocket. Ian fumbled to put the weapon through the shooting hole. Building panic made his efforts more clumsy. *Why hadn't he practiced the move?* He stopped so suddenly that the two men almost ran into him. It probably never entered their minds that he might be a threat. To them, Ian was a sure thing and was gonna pay one way or another.

They stopped short, their expressions changing to concern. Backing up, they prepared to defend themselves. Now they didn't seem so sure about this strange white man in the long black coat.

Ian tried to remain calm and keep his voice from giving away his nervousness.

"You want to earn some money without getting hurt? I'm looking for friends of Darryle Lawson. Give up some names and I might be willing to pay you."

"Man, you crazy. Ain't nobody in this neighborhood by that name," the white man said.

"Wait, wait, bro." His partner held up a hand. "How much you talking, friend?"

Ian smiled. So, it was 'friend' now?

"Give me the name of someone I can talk to and I'll make it worth your while."

"And you can pay now?" The black man gave a friendly smile.

"If the name pans out, you'll get the money."

The second man caught on to his partner's train of thought. He walked wider, trying to outflank Ian.

Ian stepped back. "Don't be thinking something stupid, now. No one needs to get hurt, here.

The man to the right stopped, flashing a big innocent smile. "Hey man, we cool," he raised his hands to show he was harmless and took a step backward.

At that moment, with Ian distracted, the front man lunged for him. Ian backpedaled, his movements awkward, but he managed to catch a glimpse of the knife that stopped inches from his belly. He pulled the knife back, having just missed with his first attempt and stepped forward, ready to plunge the blade deep into Ian's gut. Ian kept going backwards, feeling panic begin to choke his breath. The action he thought he craved was happening a lot faster than it did in his fantasy simulations.

He fumbled with the gun as he tried to drag it from his pocket, forgetting that he could shoot through the opening in the coat. The second man was working around behind him to stop his escape. The man with the knife lunged again; this time, swiping laterally and trying to score a cut across his abdomen.

Ian used his free hand to knock the mugger's arm to the side as the blade caught the edge of the coat. The white man managed to get behind Ian and wrap him in a bear hug. Without thought, Ian reacted, snapping his head back into the man's face. Ian felt a jolt of electricity shoot down his body. The pain was severe, but evidently more so to the man behind him, because he released his hold. At that same instant, the knife man took a big step forward drove the blade straight at Ian.

The knife seemed to slow down as it approached. Ian stumbled sideways. The knife wielder followed Ian's body with his eyes, but could not stop his momentum. The blade passed Ian and bit deep into his partner. The wounded man let out a scream and clutched at his stomach, wrapping his hands around the blade lodged deep inside him. The knife man reached for his friend as he fell to the ground. The shock on his face turned to anger. He turned to Ian with his hands up as if he wanted to choke the life from him. He took one step forward as Ian managed to clear the .22. The man continued as if he didn't see the gun.

"Stop!" Ian shouted.

"Fuck that."

The man continued, either unaware of the gun or not believing Ian would use it. He dove for Ian but before he reached him, like a nervous twitch, his finger contracted and two shots exploded like cannon fire. Struck twice, the man landed hard on Ian, knocking him down and driving the air from his lungs.

Ian rolled the attacker off him and scrambled to his feet. He shook so badly he couldn't hold the gun still. He looked from the man he shot to the stabbed man, not knowing what to do, swinging the gun back and forth. The man Ian shot wasn't moving. The man with the knife still sticking in him moaned and then cried.

His mind careened from thought to thought like a pinball in an arcade game. Ian's first instinct was to run before someone saw him. He lowered the gun and looked at it. What had he just done? Cold fingers of dread clutched at his chest. It wasn't supposed to feel like this. He looked at the crying man. Ian's body began to shake. He couldn't just stand there.

Taking two fast steps away from the attackers, an image of JT flashed before him. Remembering why he was there, Ian shook off the desire to flee and pushed aside his urge to vomit.

Instead, Ian went to the wounded man and knelt next to him. The man looked up through teary eyes. "Help me, please."

"I'll call an ambulance if you tell me who Darryle Lawson's friends are."

"It hurts real bad. Please, man."

Ian pulled out his cell phone. "Give me a name."

"Call, please. I need help."

"Why should I care? You just tried to kill me. I'm giving you a chance." Ian put a hand on the knife. The man's eyes went bright with the fear of more pain. "Tell me or I'll push it in deeper and end your miserable life."

"Look for Jervis, man. Jervis be running with Darryle. Now, please, call an ambulance. I don't wanna die." His crying became louder his pleas more desperate.

"Jervis? Jervis who?"

"I don't know his last name. Please. I swear I don't know. Call an ambulance."

Ian stood and stared at his hand like it had a mind of its own. He was disgusted with what he had done. He backed away, looking at the dead man then back to the one he could still save. Was he as big a monster as they were? He lifted the phone to his ear and started to walk away.

The cops wouldn't know what to make of the scene they found. He felt an urge to explain. On an irrational whim, Ian stopped and pulled out a small note pad and a pen from an interior pocket. With a shaky hand, he wrote, *They shouldn't have tried to kill me.* He stared at the note, thinking it was stupid to leave a clue for the police, but for some strange reason--whether from guilt or as justification-- Ian wanted whoever investigated the crime to know he hadn't started the fight. He'd merely finished it.

With an angry flare, he signed it *A*. After all, wasn't he an Avenger? Ian walked back to the body, tore out the paper, and dropped it on the dead man. Then he searched the man until he found his phone. He didn't want the call he was about to make to be traced back to him. The wounded man's phone was a nicer, more expensive one than Ian had. The call also couldn't be traced back to him.

Ian walked away at a fast pace, not wanting to run. He'd read once in an old crime novel that running man drew attention. The injured man called after him. "Please! Help me!"

Ian could barely breathe. He punched in 911. Before the operator could speak, Ian said, "Two bodies. Corner of Hudson and Park." He hung up and pitched the phone down an alley.

As hard as it was to resist the urge to run, Ian kept walking, forcing his gaze straight ahead. When he came to the street where he had parked the car, he turned the corner and unable to control the urge, Ian looked behind him. No one was following, that he could see. When the corner house blocked his view of street the bodies lay, Ian sprinted for his car. He couldn't help his desire for speed and distance. He needed to get away from there and didn't care if someone saw him.

Ian beeped the lock open, pulled the door and jumped in, smacking the top of his head in his haste. He couldn't stop his hand from shaking, hindering his efforts to line the key up with the ignition. Using both hands, Ian finally slid the key in amidst a flurry of four letter words and their longer relatives. He gunned the engine to life, and with all the control he could muster, placed the shift in drive and slowly pulled away from the curb. He didn't turn the headlights on until he reached the main street, two blocks ahead.

Forcing himself to drive the speed limit, Ian realized his heart was racing faster than the car was. He couldn't get the images out of his mind. "I didn't have a choice," he said aloud. "They didn't give me a choice. They were going to kill me." He felt an irrational need to justify his actions, as if the guilt itself were an accusing entity.

Ian screamed and beat on the steering wheel. "My God, what have I done?" He made a turn and headed for the expressway, ranting out loud at himself. Nervous energy bubbled up from within, like he'd drank several large espressos. Pounding the wheel, he screamed. "AHHHHH!" He settled for a second, then said, "What did you think was going to happen, you dumb ass? You knew the possibilities. You planned on something happening, so don't try to pretend it wasn't your fault. You went there looking to kill someone—and now you have." Tears began to flow. He swallowed something acrid and wiped at his face. In a calmer voice, he said, "Now you're just as bad as the ones who killed Margo and Sean."

His thoughts kept going back to the bodies. Hopefully, the ambulance found the man before he died. Then, a blast of anger shot through him as if dual personalities battled for control of the host body. "No, let him die. He would have killed you and thought nothing of it."

The car climbed up the on-ramp. The battle raged inside him, escalating to the point Ian thought he was going to explode. The road began to spin before his teary eyes. Nausea swept over him, forcing him to pull over on the shoulder. Something gripped his throat. He gasped for air, jumped from the car, and ran to the guard rail where he vomited violently. After a while, there was nothing left to come up, yet still he retched. When he was through, he slumped to the ground, exhausted. His tears dripped; his body and mind were drained.

Ian had to move before a state trooper happened by. He struggled to find strength enough to stand. It took several attempts before he made it to his feet. Stumbling like a drunk, Ian made it back inside the car. The eyes that now looked back at him in the mirror were red-streaked and fearful.

Plopping open the glove box, he pulled out several napkins and wiped his mouth. He blew his nose, feeling the burn of vomit coming through his nostrils. He took several deep breaths to calm himself. With the window open, he sucked in air like he was drinking water. The breaths helped, but barely. Putting the car in gear, he pulled out onto the expressway and drove home in a robotic mode.

Before he realized it, Ian had turned up the driveway of his old house. He stopped for a moment and was about to reverse when he decided that staying there tonight was somehow appropriate. The Ian who once lived there with a loving family was dead now, too. The new Ian was a stranger in the old body. He'd become a killer. The night may not have gone the way he had hoped and he hadn't found the killers he was looking for, but now Ian had a name to work with.

He washed his face with cold water and stared in the mirror. Harder, calmer eyes returned the gaze. It was the face of a man who had taken the first step toward vengeance. He was blooded. He was one of them now. The face was determined.

"Toughen up and get used to it, asshole. The hunt has just begun."

23

"Hey Robinson, got two gangbangers here for ya." Stu Marsden, the ME, was a tall, heavyset man of near fifty. He took off his gloves, balling them up, and placing them in a plastic sandwich bag. He stuck the bag in a large leather case. He stretched his back and groaned.

"The world needs more of that," Robinson replied. "What've we got, Stu?" As he listened to the reply, Robinson looked at the two corner houses in hopes of finding a security camera. Nothing.

"One was shot. Looks like a small caliber, but won't know till I get into him. The other was stabbed. The knife is still in him."

"Okay, we've got one murder weapon. How 'bout a gun?"

"Have to ask the officers, but I haven't seen one."

"Okay, thanks." Robinson slid into gloves and bent down to examine the bodies. "Is it okay to move them?"

"Yeah, I've been all through them. Pictures have already been taken. It's all you now."

"This one looks like it took a while to die. He tried crawling."

"Yeah, I noticed. Looks like dirt under the nails, too."

Robinson went over both bodies then approached the first officers on the scene.

"Gentlemen, did either of you find a gun?"

"No, sir, and we looked."

"How far?"

"In the vicinity of the bodies. Since we didn't find one, we figured there must've been a third person on the scene. We wanted to wait for you before we widened the search."

"Oh, you did, huh?" Robinson smiled at the young officer. "Doing my thinking for me now, Grabow?"

"Ah, no, sir, I was just…"

"Relax, Rookie, he's just pulling your chain." Grabow's partner was a veteran of more than twenty years. His name was Born and he was good at his job.

"That's good thinking, though, Grabow. Get some of the guys to widen the search area for me."

"Sure thing, sir." He ran off as eagerly as a rookie would.

Born and Robinson watched him and laughed.

"He really is a good kid," Born said.

"Yeah, but I wish you'd get him to stop calling me 'sir.'"

"Hell, no. If it bothers you, I'm gonna get the whole department doing it."

"Bastard. You recognize either of them?"

"No. They must be new or low level thugs."

"I didn't recognize them, either, but I've been off the street a few years."

"You're doing good, Mario. The guys respect you and they appreciate the fact you haven't forgot where you came from."

"Most of those guys are responsible for the training I got to get me to this point. I respect them." He pointed at the bodies. "I think we got a third person here; maybe more."

"I just hope it's not rival gangs or all hell might break loose."

"Can you check word on the street?"

"Yeah, I'll have the boys check their CIs."

"Man, I hope this doesn't end up a gang war."

"Personally, I'd just as soon let them duke it out. Clear an area and let them kill each other off. The whole city'd be better for it."

"Yeah, but you're being selfish. Think of all the paperwork I'd have."

"Better you than me."

They laughed and Robinson went back to the crime scene. A few minutes later, a uniformed officer trotted over.

"Detective, I found this down the street. It was blowing along and I kinda hate litter, so I picked it up, not realizing it might be important."

Gloves still in place, Robinson took the small piece of paper. It looked like a sheet torn from a small notebook like the one he carried.

"*'They shouldn't have tried to kill me'*," he read out loud. His brows furrowed. It was signed with a capital *A. What the hell? Was the criminal signing his confession, if this was indeed the killer?* It could also be meant to throw off the investigation. He reread the sentence. Robinson didn't think a gang member who wrote the note. They wouldn't have bothered, for one; and two, it was written properly, like someone who had actually benefitted from his education.

He looked around the neighborhood. The shooter could be someone who lived here and was tired of the daily threat of danger or living in fear of all the local gangs. Perhaps the resident had started carrying a gun for protection and now had to use it.

Robinson looked down the long tree-lined street, to a house, he could not see. The images rushed to him. The house he'd grown up in just the other side of Lagrange. His father was black, his mother Puerto Rican. His father drove a city bus, while his mother worked from home as a seamstress and volunteered at the local school. It had been a good home for him and his two brothers. He'd been one of the fortunate ones. He'd risen above and got out. Many of his friends never did. Every time he was called to a crime scene in this neighborhood he feared the body would be someone he once knew. He glanced at the bodies of the two young men. Not this time. He was thankful for that.

Between the lines of the note, Robinson read that the shooter felt guilty about what had happened and wanted the police to know the killing was justified. He had no trouble believing the two lying there were the instigators. But if that was the case, why not simply identify himself and wait for the police? Defending yourself against deadly violence was not illegal. Of course, maybe whoever killed the two muggers didn't want the scrutiny of an investigation, or just didn't want to get involved. The price might be that other gang members might come after the defender for revenge.

"So your prints are on this, right?"

"Yes, sir, sorry, I didn't…"

Robinson held up his hand to stop further explanation.

"It's all right. I just want to know to tell the crime scene techs. You did fine; no worries." He looked around again. The shootings occurred on the corner of a residential neighborhood. Someone had to have heard the shots. "Get some of the boys out knocking on doors in this area. It's late, but someone should have heard something. Canvass this intersection a block in each direction."

"You got it." The officer jogged away to pass the word.

Robinson fished out a baggie and slid the note in. He went back to the bodies to see if he missed anything.

Stu held up his own bag. "Got a .22 casing. Whatcha got?" asked Stu, pointing at the baggie.

"It appears the shooter might have had a conscience."

Stu read it through the plastic. "Huh? You think the A is the first letter of the guy's name?"

"Hell, I don't know. I mean, what killer is gonna sign his name to a note?"

Stu shrugged. "Could happen. It's not like we're dealing with the smartest and most sane people. Probably the same guy who called it in."

"Maybe he was trying to save the vic with the knife wound," Robinson said. "Regardless, it still goes down as a murder until we find out otherwise."

"That's a shame. Guy should get a medal for ridding the city of two more burdens to society."

"No doubt."

24

Ian slept fitfully, tossing and turning most of the night. He couldn't clear the images of the two dead men from his mind. Only in his sleep, they were more grotesque and the wounds bloodier. The entire scene was exaggerated. After several hours, he gave up. He rinsed his sweaty face with cold water and then went downstairs. With the TV playing an infomercial, Ian gradually drifted to sleep sitting in the lounge chair.

When he awoke, he put on a pot of coffee and went up to shower. Packing a suitcase with clothes, he filled a thermos with the coffee and drove off to visit JT. On the way, he listened to the morning news programs on the radio. There was a brief mention of two bodies found in the North End. The police had little to say other than they were treating it as a double homicide and the investigation was progressing.

Ian stopped at a gas station and sat for a while, trying to understand what 'progressing' meant. Had he left a clue to his identification? Had someone seen the car? Maybe he left DNA samples on one of the victims? His head had been full of chaos and he was unable to think. All sorts of evidence might have been left, but what could he do about it now?

Not knowing if the police were on their way was more devastating emotionally than the actual killing had been. He couldn't stand the anxiety. At any minute, Ian expected a SWAT team to pull up and surround him, their weapons all pointed at him.

His paranoia was driving him insane. He got out of the car and went into the convenience store. There he bought a pre-packaged breakfast sandwich and popped it into the microwave. While he waited for the food to heat, he scooped up a copy of the local newspaper. When the microwave dinged, Ian grabbed the sandwich, paid the cashier and went out to the car.

He forced the tasteless food down his throat while he searched through the pages for the story. He found the small paragraph on the first page of the second section.

The bodies of two unidentified men were found on the corners of Hudson and Park late last night. The police have labeled it a double homicide. Detective Mario Robinson said, "We are treating this as a homicide and have a few leads to follow. We ask if anyone has knowledge of what went on last night to please contact the police help line." Detective Robinson did not rule out the possibility that the deaths were gang and/or drug related.

Ian read and reread the paragraph, trying to discern any nuances within the report. He finally flung the paper in a heap in the backseat, not knowing what to think. The confrontation replayed in his mind. The entire fight couldn't have lasted more than two minutes. He was missing something. Then he remembered the note. He never should have left that stupid note.

What was wrong with him? Why had it been so important to explain his actions to the police? If he'd stayed and given a statement, he'd have been fine. It was a clear case of self-defense. Of course, making his presence known to the police would have hampered his efforts to track down the killers.

With the egg sandwich doing flips in his stomach and a sense of impending disaster, Ian continued on to see JT.

In his son's room, Ian paced, burning up nervous energy. A large black woman with very bright red hair was taking care of JT today. Ian was disappointed. He hadn't realized how much he had been looking forward to seeing KeKe. He berated himself for even having the barest inkling of interest in the girl. She was younger than he and very attractive. She wouldn't want anything to do with the father of one of her patients.

Again, he reminded himself about how stupid getting involved with someone would be when his life expectancy was so short. Still, Ian wished she were there to talk to. He wanted to feel the warmth her smile gave him. They didn't have to develop a relationship; didn't have to go anywhere. There didn't have to be anything at all, except maybe companionship. KeKe's presence filled a void, if only for the moment.

"Is KeKe, not working today?"

"KeKe? Oh, you mean Nurse Brogan. No, sweetie, she's got the day off. I'm afraid you're stuck with me. Is that okay?"

"Huh, oh, sure it is. I just, I, I just wanted to ask her something."

"I'm sure you did, sweetie. She is a pretty thing, isn't she?"

"Oh, it's nothing like that," Ian said, too emphatically. He felt his cheeks flush with heat while he waved his hands as if warding off the thought.

The woman let out a high-pitched squeal that evidently she used as a laugh. "Oh, honey, I'm just teasing you. The look on your face was precious, though. Wish I had a picture; I'd-a posted it on YouTube or something." She laughed again. The tone made Ian wince.

"Anyway, honey, we're taking good care of your sweet young man. He is a good-looking boy, isn't he? I pray for him every day, just like I pray for everyone in here."

Ian sat down. "He used to be," he motioned with his hand. "Before this."

"Oh, he very much still is. And trust me, honey, he will be again. Don't you give up on him. He hears you. I truly believe that. He may not be able to respond yet, but I truly do believe he can hear you. Isn't that right, you sweet boy?" Ian felt his eyes mist. "Thank you."

"No problem. I'll be back in a while. Can I get you something?"

"No, thank you."

She walked out, leaving Ian alone with his thoughts. He began pacing again. Then, in a rush, he leaned on the bed, placed his mouth near JT's ear and told him about his adventure.

"I know it's not the ones who did this to you, but it's a start. I've got a name to work with now." Ian hesitated. He looked toward the door to make sure no one was entering. He had become excited, explaining the previous night's events to JT. Gone was the regret and the guilt. That was past and the two would-be muggers had gotten what they deserved. At that moment, despite the police investigation and his sinner's remorse, Ian knew he would go out again that night.

"Can you really hear me, JT? I hope you can. I need you to understand that if one day I don't come back, it's not because I don't love you or care about you anymore, it's just because—I can't."

Ian sat and stared at his son for a long time. Eventually, his thoughts drifted from the memory of the killing to where to start his hunt tonight. Ian stayed with JT until noon. He had a plumber going out to the new house at one and then he needed to look for a car.

25

"I cannot believe this incompetence," Ahmed raged. "When he arrives, I shall kill him."

"It was certainly stupid, my friend, but we will need him. He most likely will die at the hands of the American law officers anyway. Why waste a bullet? He may yet prove useful."

The man in question had been sent to bring back one of the cars they would use for the attacks. On the way back, he had been stopped and given a ticket for speeding. The fact that the man spoke with a very thick Arabic accent made things more difficult. He hadn't brought any of his ID papers with him, so one of the others who spoke English more fluently had to go bail him out and show his documents.

The SUV and the man driving it were now in the system. They would need another vehicle. As for the man, his assistant was right. The fool would probably die in a hail of bullets. If not, Ahmed would take care of that himself.

The attacks would now be delayed a day. It was not the end of the plan, although, since he had been ready for so long, the delay felt like it was. They had a time schedule to adhere to, but it did allow for one day of heat when the police were too close and they needed to lie low. Now that extra day was gone. Heat or not, they had a mission to fulfill. It would have to be done straight through now. One attack each day until the end.

He slammed the table, sending papers fluttering to the floor. Al bent without a word and began picking them up.

***

Ian drove his new car, a blue 1998 Chevy Impala with less than forty thousand miles on it, to the opposite side of the North End this time. He found the car in the paper. An old lady was selling it. She had just bought a new Cadillac, though Ian wondered how she could possibly see over its steering wheel. He paid her cash and had her sign over the vehicle title, telling her he would take care of the transfer for her. He drove his eight-year-old Buick to the old house and parked in the garage and then called a cab to take him back for the Impala.

Sitting in the car, he watched a group of young teens walking down the middle of the street a half block from his location. He wanted to avoid any trouble tonight if at all possible-- that is until he found Jervis.

It took the teens twenty minutes to slowly meander past him. Ian ducked down on the seat, his long black coat covering him, until they went by. He pulled the cover from the dome light and took out the bulb and put it in the glove box.

Ian had no idea where to start looking for Jervis, but it was time to start asking. Again, he started his search in a residential neighborhood, perhaps a quarter mile east and two blocks south of where he left the bodies. It was also an hour earlier than the previous night. He went three blocks east without seeing anyone. Reaching the main street where small shops lined the road on both sides, Ian stopped, not wanting to be seen under any lights or by possible security cameras. He used a paved alley behind the commercial buildings on the west side of the street to cut to the next block. Midway, a dirt alley that ran behind the houses connected with the paved one. He slowed when he drew near to avoid being taken by surprise again.

At the next street, he paraded five blocks west then took a side street north to the next block and had yet to see anyone. Ian knew it was late, but that's when the type of people he was looking for came out of their holes.

By the time he made it east again and back to the main street, Ian was losing patience. Frustration tempted him to go into the convenience store on the corner and ask someone there if they knew Jervis.

Deciding to make one more sweep up and down the next two blocks, Ian cut through the paved alley that ran parallel to the main street. The businesses to the right blocked the view of any passing traffic. He made his move, staying near the buildings and watching the backyards and the dirt alley.

A muffled cry from down the paved alley caused him to halt and step into the shadows of a building's rear wall. His eyes attempted to pierce the darkness. No lights shone from the buildings or the poles above. Not that there weren't lights there, but they had long ago burned out or been broken.

Because of the blackness, Ian had to rely on his hearing. Seconds later, he heard what sounded like a scream being cut off. The momentary silence was broken by the very recognizable sound of skin meeting skin with force. The slap seemed to hang in the air.

Ian didn't want to get involved in anything that would delay his search, but he was drawn to the sounds anyway. He couldn't just turn his back if someone was in trouble. He just wanted to check, he told himself. He had no intention of getting involved or intervening.

With as much stealth as his fear would allow, Ian slid along the wall toward the middle of the alley. Keeping the brick to his back, Ian's hand slid into his pocket and once again began fingering the gun.

"No!" he heard; the voice, definitely feminine. She was crying.

"Shut up, bitch, or I'll slap you again."

The struggle continued and another slap filled the quiet. Two more hits that no longer sounded like slaps followed. The assailant had gotten serious.

Ian advanced closer. He now had an angle to see down the dirt alley. Halfway down, a lone light hanging from a utility pole let him see the alley was vacant. He stood straighter, confused. Maybe the sound had come from one of the houses. A frown touched his face. It was time to move on, and he started for the far end of the paved alley.

Then he heard the crying coming from behind him and froze. Turning slowly, his eyes as wide as they could go, Ian discovered a four-foot-wide space between two of the buildings. Ian poked his head around the corner. With some light filtering in from the street side of the buildings, Ian could make out a dark mass lying on the ground, rising and falling. The muffled crying came from beneath the mass. Instantly, he knew what was happening. The anger flared strong, but he tried to convince himself to walk away, he was too late to stop the assault anyway. Ian hesitated. He should leave it alone, but when he heard the girl crying and beg, 'Please, stop,' he knew he could not.

A flash of red clouded his vision. He was three steps down the alley before he was aware he was moving. He crept carefully toward the large, overweight man, who had started grunting. His bulk obscured the woman beneath him. Sliding the silenced .22 from his pocket, he started lining up his shot. Coming up behind the man would make the shot easy, but he had to take into account that should he miss, the woman would be in a direct line.

The man was too lost in his desires to notice Ian's approach. He might be too late to save the woman from the rape, but not too late to make sure the man would never do it again.

Stepping to the side of them, he noticed the woman's face was averted. With each step closer, Ian's rage grew.

Ian moved the gun to within inches of the man's head. "Hey."

The startled man turned his head, closing the gap between skull and barrel. Before the rapist could flinch away, Ian pulled the trigger. The body collapsed on the woman and she began screaming. "Shh!" Ian said. "I'm here to help you. Now be quiet and slide this way." Ian shoved the large man off the half-naked woman. Even in the dim light, Ian could make out the tear streaks running down the light brown face. Her eyes were wide with fear. She whimpered and tried to scurry backwards. She was small and young; not a woman, a girl. *My God, how old is she and why is she was out this late?*

"Please, please, don't hurt me." She started crying and her voice grew louder.

"Shh! Quiet now. I'm not here to hurt you. I just wanted to stop him from hurting you. I'm sorry I didn't get here sooner." He stepped closer, kicking something soft. When he bent down, his hands closed around a pile of clothes. He picked them up and tossed them to her.

"Get dressed and go home. And please don't tell anyone you saw me."

"I won't." But the way she said it, he knew she would agree to anything just to get away. She started fumbling her clothes on.

Ian stepped back. "You don't need to be afraid of me. If I was going to harm you, I would have shot you when I did him."

He reached into an interior pocket and pulled out the small notepad he had placed there earlier. On it he scribbled, *He got what a rapist deserves. A.* He bent down and stuck it in the man's slack mouth.

Ian stood up and looked down at the girl, who was almost dressed. When she saw him look at her, she froze. "I'm sorry this happened," he said. With that, he turned and walked back the way he came. He felt no guilt, no nausea, and no prayers for forgiveness. This time, Ian felt nothing. When he reached the corner, he glanced back in time to see the girl deliver a savage kick to the man's body.

Though he couldn't see, he guessed where the kick had landed. He smiled. The night hadn't been a complete loss.

26

On the drive home, Ian noticed he did not have the same physical and emotional response as he had the night before. H he become numb to taking a life already? Was this how a stone-cold killer felt? He compared the two events.

The previous night had not only been his first killing, but his life had been in danger. He was scared to the point of almost freezing with his life at stake. He understood his reaction after the fact. Even though the two punks would have killed him with no thought or remorse, Ian still felt guilt after killing them. Tonight, there had been none of that. He raged over what was happening to that girl and acted upon it. With detached emotion Ian realized he had no problem with the killing. The man deserved to die.

However, that brought new thoughts to light. In one short day, Ian had elevated himself to God status. Who was he to decide who deserved to die? Couldn't he have just subdued the man and called the cops? What right did he think he had to choose between life and death for another person?

He stopped at an all-night burger place and took food back to his new home, which was another difference from last night. Tonight he had an appetite, last night he was puking up his dinner. He pondered both killings while he ate. He was a lost soul now; there was no turning back. He thought for a moment of that poor girl and wondered if his actions meant anything to her. He was too late to prevent the rape, but judging by the way she kicked the body, he had given her a measure of revenge.

Searching deep for any emotions, all he found was a cold empty space where his conscience once resided. Had he lost his soul, and with it, any chance of seeing his wife and son in the afterlife? Did that matter now? If it did, he should have thought of that before he went looking for trouble. Now his eternal soul would be damned.

He should stop this drive for vengeance, but he knew he wouldn't. Other than ending the life of a rapist, he had made no progress finding Jervis. Ian vowed to try again the next night. However, leaving three bodies on the street in two days might make it more difficult to move around unseen. Ian would have to think of a good reason to be in that neighborhood at that time of night, in case he was stopped. Of course, there would be no explaining away the arsenal he carried.

He would have to give that scenario some thought. If he got caught, would he allow himself to be taken? Or would he choose death by cop?

With that thought playing through his mind, Ian curled up on his bedroll and went to sleep. He had no recollection of any dreams, haunted or otherwise.

The next morning, Ian snapped awake and listened to the sounds of the old house for several minutes. Despite the predicted warm weather, the house felt cold. *Is the cold I feel the house, or is it a carryover from the heartless killer I've become?*

He showered and shaved, then made his now-daily run to see JT. Unfortunately, he wouldn't have any good news to share with him about the hunt. He briefly thought about KeKe before pushing her from his mind. Those thoughts held no future.

Again, he stopped for a breakfast sandwich and a newspaper. This time, he ate while he drove. He could read the paper in JT's room.

As he entered the long one-story building, he found himself looking down the various hallways. When it dawned on him he was looking for KeKe, he stopped. He had to get over this budding interest. Those adolescent behaviors would do neither of them any good. Perhaps his interest in other areas was sparked by the feeling of purpose he now had in trying to hunt down his family's killers.

JT rested peacefully, or as peacefully as one could be in a coma. Ian leaned over the bed and kissed his son on the forehead and stared at the boy's features for a long while. He had been such a handsome boy; now he was gaunt and his eyes sockets were dark, sunken circles. How much longer would he survive? Ian prayed it was long enough for him to find the killer.

"It's me. I made little progress last night, but I promise I won't rest until I find them. I did manage to help someone, but it's not really worth talking about. It sidetracked me from my search. I'm sorry. I won't let that happen again. But you have to hang on for me. You have to stay with me long enough to see this through. Then both of us can join your mother and brother."

Ian heard a slight noise. He stood erect.

"Oh. I'm sorry I didn't know you were here."

Ian spun around to see KeKe—Nurse Brogan—standing in the doorway.

"I didn't mean to interrupt your visit. You go ahead. I'll come back later."

Before Ian could reply, she was gone. Had she heard him? The look on her face was one of surprise, but it also looked like fear. Ian couldn't tell which. If she did hear anything, would she pass it on to anyone else? He replayed his words to see if he'd said anything that could cause alarm. He didn't think so. His words might cause some worry or raise questions, but he didn't say anything that would have been an admission of guilt.

Ian squeezed JT's arm and sat back down. Picking up the paper, he scanned for any news of the body he left, but found nothing. Either the news had been reported too late to make the morning paper, or the body hadn't been discovered yet. Ian found himself thinking about the girl. Did she call the cops or maybe tell a friend or family member?

She was a witness to the shooting. She wouldn't be able to give a good description of him, but she would be able to report certain things like the color of his skin or what he had been wearing. He might actually have to put together a second outfit. But what would it be? His wardrobe needed to be nondescript. He certainly wasn't going to wear a Hawaiian shirt or anything white. He was going to have to be more careful when patrolling the streets. It might be smart to just take a few days off.

He got up and paced for a while. When he sat down, he realized KeKe hadn't been in to check on JT yet. Usually she'd be there by that time of day, sometimes stopping in twice. He wondered if she got sidetracked with another patient or if she was just avoiding him. Ian leaned his head back against the wall.

A noise brought his eyes slowly open. He had nodded off and had no idea of how long he had been out. KeKe, with her back to Ian, was leaning over JT's bed and whispering to him. As he watched, he saw her twice brush at her eyes. What was going on?

"KeKe?"

The woman jumped and let out a gasp, but she didn't turn around. Instead, she used both palms to wipe her face. He could see her fighting for control of her breathing.

"Are you all right?"

She whipped around, glaring at him through red eyes.

"Just tell me this, and you'd better be honest. Are you planning on killing your son?"

"What?" Ian jumped to his feet, causing KeKe to back up against JT's bed. "What are you talking about? Why would I kill JT?"

The surprise in his voice and the force with which he delivered his words made her flinch. His mind raced. She had heard something for sure, but what had he said to bring her to make her think he was plotting his son's death?

KeKe wrapped her arms around herself. "You'd better be telling me the truth, because I promise, I will be here to protect him from you. If anything happens to this boy, I'm a witness." She stormed out of the room without giving Ian a chance to deny her accusation or give an explanation.

"KeKe! Wait!" He called after her, but she did not stop.

He waited for her to return later, but he never saw her again. Before he left, he walked the halls looking for her. Ian wanted to assure her he had no intentions of ever harming JT. Giving up, he went back to the room and said good bye to JT. He had some errands to run before he went out prowling. Ian had thought about taking the night off, but now he was flustered and angry and would welcome the distraction.

27

The three vehicles being used for the mission were loaded. The men were waiting for Ahmed to come out of the house and give them the word to begin the operation. After reviewing the plan one more time, Ahmed prayed. He was ready to begin.

He left the house and approached the car he would ride in, not knowing or caring to make note of the make or model. The men were split between the two black SUVs with dark tinted windows. They wore long lightweight coats that covered their silenced fully-automatic weapons. Each vehicle carried three men and a walkie-talkie. Al drove one while the taxi driver was at the wheel of the other. Ahmed drove alone in the car. He would oversee the attacks and lend support if needed.

It was a dark, starless night. At nearly one-thirty in the morning, Ahmed gave the command to move out. They staggered their departure by a few minutes to avoid drawing notice. The three vehicles arrived at the first target, located in a strip mall, within minutes of each other. Ahmed parked at the far end, away from the target, but still in view of it. One SUV went around to the back while the other parked in front. At this time of the morning, it was nearing closing time for most bars. The parking lot was almost empty.

Ahmed watched as the doors opened and the men walked through the front door. Al then drove the SUV around the back so both escape vehicles would be there. Ahmed's breathing accelerated into short, quick puffs. The adrenaline rush was almost more than he could stand, wanting to rush into the kill zone with the men. After all the training and months of planning, the mission had begun. He would not fail.

Inside, the rear and back doors opened together. Ahmed was able to watch the progress in real time on a laptop fed by cameras attached to two of the men. Four men entered and scattered about the room while two more locked and guarded the doors. The business was a small neighborhood bar. Only four men and a woman occupied the bar stools. One bartender worked the bar.

One of the men entering from the back checked both bathrooms.

Finding them empty, he came out and stood guard in front of the back door. His partner went around the bar to check the back room. The bartender moved to block the man, but he moved past her. She grabbed at him, looked as if she said something, then turned and reached for the phone.

The two men in the front stood by the door and waited. The other three men faced the bar. The patrons turned and watched them. Ahmed could imagine the tension growing inside the bar as it also grew within him.

The fourth man came back from checking the office, a security disc in his hand, and nodded to the three at the bar. With the three guns on automatic, it took mere seconds to kill everyone inside. The fourth man ripped a short burst into the bartender, the phone falling from her hand before she completed the call. When everyone had been dispatched, the shooters made for the back door. Ahmed watched with his heart rate increasing as each body went through its death dance from the multitude of bullets tearing into it. Everything went perfectly.

Ahmed stopped watching then. The men knew what to do and where to go next. The last man out would put an adhesive pad on the edge of the door and shut it. The glue would bond within sixty seconds and hopefully keep anyone from entering before they had accomplished the rest of their mission. With the evidence from any security cameras in hand, and hopefully no witnesses, the authorities would be unaware of what had happened on that night for quite a while.

Both SUVs waited outside the rear door to transport the teams to the next location. They had six to do in all before the night ended. The first attack took less than two minutes. As he drove from the lot, Ahmed found himself hoping there would be more victims in the next target.

The second bar was slightly larger and had more rooms to clear. Ahmed had drilled the men on the floor plans for each target. Each man knew their assignments once they entered the bar. Each room, including bathrooms, offices, and kitchens, needed to be checked before the shooting started, if possible. He didn't want the customers to panic or call the police.

At the second location, the men in the rear ran into their first problem. The rear kitchen door was locked. Ahmed cued his microphone. "Knock." One of the gunmen knocked. When he heard someone on the inside start to open it, he looked at his partner and shrugged.

Once the door was pushed open, the shooters stepped in and silenced the three kitchen staff members, then moved quickly into the front room. There were some screams, but like the other victims, they died quickly. Fourteen people died in that assault.

The kill squad continued down the street. One after another, the terrorists marched along with machine-like precision. The kill squad worked through the targets and the death toll climbed. No one was left to identify them. The first five locations had been cleared in forty-five minutes, leaving fifteen minutes before closing time to finish the mission.

At the final location, the men went inside, but before the door could be locked, two patrons entered less than thirty seconds behind the team. Al had already driven around the back for the pickup, and Ahmed instantly recognized this as a flaw in the plan that he would have to correct.

He lowered the passenger side window and drove fast until he was outside the front door. Instantly, the door opened and the two men came sprinting out. Ahmed fired two shots into each man. The next man out was one of his. He grabbed the feet of the bodies and dragged them back inside, leaving a streak of blood on the walkway. The plan, however, did not allow time for cleanup. The streaks would soon be discovered and recognized for what they were. So be it. *Besides,* Ahmed thought. *It's not like we're trying to conceal what we did.* He just wanted to hide discovery until they made their escape.

Thirty minutes later, the men were sitting around the dining room table to debrief the night's events.

Ahmed had no praise to give. These men were trained professionals; he fully expected them to follow orders and succeed. That didn't mean he wasn't elated. He just knew better than to show it. His words were much harsher than any praise.

"You jeopardized the mission by your negligence!" He yelled at the two men who entered the front. "There is always a possibility that someone may enter after the fact. By not locking the door, you endangered the entire mission. It was bad enough that you did not secure the door, but then to let them leave…This is unforgivable." The two men tensed but lowered their eyes as Ahmed raged at them. Their neglect should merit severe punishment, perhaps even death, but Ahmed could not afford to lose the men. They were too highly trained to be replaced. Still, they expected a punishment of some form or another. He would look weak if he did nothing.

He calmed. "The fact that the mission went according to plan and was, for the most part, a complete success allows me to be merciful. We shall learn from this. The mistake will not happen again." He did not need to say *or else.*

He held their eyes and they breathed easier. Ahmed shifted gears. He turned to Al. "The driver in the front cannot leave too early for the pickup. You will watch for anyone trying to enter the building and deal with them—quietly, if possible—before you move for the pickup."

Ahmed looked from face to face. Each man met his gaze.

"You two," Ahmed pointed to the men who entered from the front, "will fast tonight and clean the weapons. You will serve a double watch tonight. That is a fair punishment, considering how well you performed overall."

The men nodded at the judgment as Ahmed left the room. It had been a good beginning. Tomorrow would be better.

28

Unaware of the events that were unfolding in a different part of town, Ian went hunting again. He drove past the storefronts in the neighborhood where he left the body but saw no sign of police presence or yellow crime scene tape marking the space between the buildings. Maybe no one had discovered the rapist yet.

This time, Ian chose the far western part of the North End to search. Even though it was nearly two a.m., this area was much more active than the other side. He hadn't gone half a block before he met a young black couple. As Ian approached, he tried to figure the best way to question them without setting off any alarms.

"Hey, ya'll. You know where I can find Jervis?"

"No man, never heard of him," the man said. The two kept walking. So did Ian.

Next came a lone black man wearing baggy clothes and a Yankees cap sticking out from under his hood. He lifted his chin in acknowledgment.

Ian said, "Hey, you seen Jervis around? Got some business with him and I can't find him nowhere."

"No man; ain't seen him in a while."

"You remember where he was at when you saw him?"

"Nah man. Just around, you know."

"K, thanks."

It went like that for a good hour. No one knew where Jervis was, but, to his surprise, most people knew who he was. That raised Ian's hope that if Jervis had fled town, as the police suspected he did months ago, he was back now. People had seen him as recently as a week ago. Of course, they could all have been lying. Making no headway himself, Ian had to hope word would get back to Jervis and the killer would come looking for him.

He continued his search, but his options seemed to be drying up. He rounded a corner in front of an all-night mom and pop carryout located in the middle of the residential neighborhood and heard a shot come from inside. Ian flattened himself against the wall and started to pull out the .22, but then he thought better of it. Since one shot had already woken up the neighborhood, he decided he wanted more stopping power and fumbled the Glock 9mm out of the left side coat pocket. The Sig Sauer 9 in his belt at his back would have taken too long to get to.

The gun just cleared his belt when the front door slammed open and two hooded figures ran out. They turned in Ian's direction. He could hear one of them laughing. Ian stepped away from the wall, leveled the gun and yelled, "Freeze!"

The two robbers skidded to a stop ten feet away. Small, round white faces peeked out from the cinched hoods. Their dark clothes melding with the night's backdrop gave them an eerie appearance, as if their faces floated above the ground. One raised his hand with a gun attached to it, so Ian pulled the trigger. With adrenaline adding to his rising anxiety, the first shot was rushed and went wide. The blast caused all three of them to jump and burst into motion. The gunman squeezed off his own errant shot while his partner turned and ran.

Ian steadied his hand and fired twice more, blowing the gunman backward and off his feet. The runner stopped for an instant, seeing his partner go down. He shouted a name Ian didn't catch, then started to run again. Ian lowered the barrel and fired twice more, sending the second thief to the ground, screaming and clutching at a wounded leg.

Ian stood there for precious seconds trying to decide what to do next. Remembering the first shot, he chose to go inside to make sure everyone was all right. Lowering his head as he entered in case there were cameras, Ian scanned the small display area and found nothing. A moan from behind the counter drew his attention. He leaned over the glass-front case and saw an older black man lying on his back with a blood-soaked shirt. Glancing up, he could see the cash register drawer was open and the money slots empty. The sight angered him.

Ian pulled out his phone, but before dialing 911, realized it was his own phone and put it back in his pocket. Pulling out the burner phone, he entered the numbers.

"There's a gunshot victim inside the carryout on the corner of Pearl and Elm." He disconnected and hoped he had altered his voice enough.

Ian knew he had only seconds to spare before a police car might arrive, but he didn't want to leave the wounded man without trying to do something.

"Help me, please," the man cried. He was looking at Ian through tear filled eyes. "Can-can you call my wife?"

Ian put his hand on his head. What to do? He scanned the small room and caught sight of a Kotex display. He hurried over, tore open a box of maxi pads, and went back to the man. He opened two pads and covered the wound, then placed the man's hands over them. He propped the man's feet up on the lower rung of the stool behind the counter and put a jacket under his head.

"Please, call…"

He was getting weaker. Ian knew he should leave.

"What's the number?"

The man had to repeat it twice. Ian found the store phone and dialed. On the third ring, a woman answered. "Hold your shorts on, Melvin, I'll have your dinner there in a moment."

"You need to get here fast. It's an emergency." He hung up, knowing there was nothing more he could do. A notepad next to the phone made him pause a few seconds more. Despite the danger of being caught, writing the note was important to him, although he wasn't sure he could explain why.

He wrote, *The scum outside shot him. They will kill no more. A.*

He left the store and heard sirens growing louder. The wounded man had tried to get up and hop away. A burning rage took hold of Ian. The injustice of that good man inside, dying, while this lowlife lived made him see red. He put the 9mm back in his coat pocket and took the silenced .22 out of the right side. Not caring that people had gathered across the street, Ian stalked the man. The thief saw Ian approaching and his eyes went wide when he noticed the gun. He screamed, knowing death was close. Some of the people in the crowd also began screaming and scattered.

Ian stopped over the man and pointed the gun at his head. A battle raged within him. Hadn't he already gone so far that killing this man shouldn't matter to him? Yet as angry as he was, he still couldn't pull the trigger. Instead, he looked up at the small crowd.

"See to it this killer does not escape!" he shouted. Sticking the gun back in his pocket, he turned and walked away.

29

Ian kept checking behind him to see if anyone followed. He was so caught up in the emotions that he lost track of where he parked. He just walked. Twice he had to duck between houses as police cruisers drove by, presumably searching for him. Once a spotlight played across the bush he was hiding behind as the patrol car moved slowly down the street. He was forced to stay there for nearly twenty minutes before the car turned the corner.

He needed to get out of the area before the police closed it off. He couldn't allow himself to be caught yet, not with his mission unfulfilled. He moved cautiously, his eyes scanning all directions and fear building with every step. The car was still four blocks away.

Then, as he passed a house with a large front porch, he jumped when he heard, "Hey man, you looking for something?"

Ian stopped and fingered the .22, keeping his left hand out in the open. He stared hard into the shadows, trying to see where the voice came from. He started to back away, turned toward the direction of the voice.

"You ain't got to fear me, man. I was just wondering if you was the dude axing questions about someone around here." A man materialized from the shadows on the porch of the nearest house.

Ian's heart leaped. His mouth, which had gone dry, tried to reinvent the word. He looked up and down the street. Just as he had hoped, someone made contact. However, with the cops searching for him, it couldn't have happened at a worse time. Still, Ian didn't want to lose the opportunity to find Jervis.

"Might be." He remained suspicious, though, and glanced around him to make sure the man wasn't a distraction. "Whatcha got?" Ian looked back in time to the see the reflections of blue and red lights bounce off the houses on the other side of the street. He dove behind a tree as the police car sped past down the side street, running without sirens. His heart pounded, causing his chest to hurt. His breathing came in short, quick gasps.

He turned to the porch where the voice had come from and pointed his gun. No one was in sight. Ian stood up and moved toward the house.

"Looks like you got someone else looking for you." Ian jumped at the voice, which now came from between the two houses to his right. He snapped the gun in the man's direction, his fear almost causing him to pull the trigger.

The man ducked. "Whoa, man! Stop pointing that thing at me."

Ian looked at the gun and was surprised by how much it shook. He lowered his arm and muttered, "Sorry." Then, after another backward glance, "Tell me what you know."

"Might know where a certain person you been axing about is."

"And who might that be?" Ian stepped closer. He wanted a better look at this gift horse. Despite the situation, he found himself drawn to the possibility of finding his family's killer.

"You don't know who you been looking for all night?" The man's grin showed like the Cheshire Cat.

Ian remained silent.

"Jervis, man. I know where Jervis be staying."

"And where would that be?"

"You sure you ain't the police?"

"No, I wouldn't be down here trying to score if I were. Nope. Ain't no cop."

"Why they looking for you?"

"Someone narced on me."

"What you want with Jervis? He don't sell no more."

"He might have some information I need. It's important to me."

"What information is that?"

"That's between him and me."

"Well, maybe I let you find him on your own then."

"That's fine, your loss."

Ian began walking away. The man hadn't expected that and he stepped forward to cut Ian off. He stammered several times before finally spitting out, "It'll cost you. I ain't doing this shit for free, now."

Ian studied the man now that he was closer. He wore typical dark garb and a baseball hat. He was tall, but Ian couldn't make out his facial features. "All right, how much?"

"How much you got?"

Ian wasn't playing that game.

"I'll give you twenty."

"Twenty? Shit. I want a hundred."

"Well, you outta luck then, cause I ain't got a hundred." He paused, waiting for the man's response or some kind of reaction while considering his own next move.

"I'll tell you what. I'll give you fifty, but after you take me to him."

The man seemed to think it over.

"Yeah, fifty's cool."

He walked past Ian. "This way," he said.

Ian followed a few steps behind and off to the right. The .22 was in the shooting slot in the pocket and aimed at his guide. The man kept a brisk pace and never once looked back, nor did he engage in any conversation. Nervousness became an itch he couldn't satisfy. Ian constantly checked behind him, making sure they were still alone and that no cop cars were coming up behind him.

They sprinted across the street two blocks down from the carryout. In the distance, flashing lights lit the area like a Christmas display. What were the witnesses telling the cops? Had they seen enough to describe him? Had anyone caught him on camera? He pushed the thoughts from his mind. If his guide was telling the truth, Ian could be halfway to his goal.

Two blocks later, the man turned left and kept on for two and a half blocks more before pulling up a driveway. He stopped and flashed another toothy smile. They were at a two-story brick house that had seen better days. The front porch had collapsed. Two front windows were broken; several others were boarded up. The garage in the backyard no longer stood. Only a pile of wood on the cement slab remained. The house was dark and looked as though it had been abandoned for years.

"This the place. Now how about that fifty?"

"I need to make sure Jervis is in there." Ian checked out the backyard and then tried to see in the side windows.

"Oh, he in there. He waiting to see you."

Ian turned to face the man. First he saw the huge toothy smile once more. Then he saw the gun.

"Oh, yeah, he been waiting to meet you. Now get your hands up on top of your head."

Ian had taken his hands out of his pockets when he tried to see through the window. The gun was still in the pocket. *Stupid!* He had no choice but do what the man told him.

The man raised a phone to his ear and said, "We here." He

motioned with the gun. "Now, how 'bout you walk around the back, there?"

A lance of panic pierced his heart. His legs began to go weak. Ian tried to think of a way out or of something he could do to counter the man's obvious advantage, but his mind whirled in fear. One thought kept circling and reminding him that he was not even close to being trained for this. Shooting from a distance was one thing, but hand-to-hand was not something he knew.

As directed, Ian went around the back of the house. A rear door opened and a tall, slender black man stepped out. He held the door.

"After you, meat."

Ian stepped inside. He was standing on a small landing. Stairs ran up to the first floor and down to the basement. The man with the gun pushed it into Ian's back.

"Downstairs to the playroom, man. We gonna have some fun with you."

An icy chill enveloped his heart and for the first time since starting his hunt, Ian knew death was near. He walked with heavy footfalls down the stairs. The basement had been divided into two sections. The side they were on was lit with a very dim bulb and was empty. On the other side of a thin wooden partition, light spilled through cracks over, under, and through the wood paneling that served as a wall. The two men followed him down.

"Through that door."

Ian looked at it but didn't move. He couldn't move. Was this how his life would end? He should have known better, but perhaps this is what he really wanted. At least his mental anguish would end. His only regret was not having finished the job. That and the pain he knew he was about to endure. He swallowed hard.

"Don't be afraid now. You wanted to meet Jervis. He on the other side."

His mind screamed, *'Do something! Go for the one of your other guns. Don't go down without a fight!'* But Ian reached for the latch and pulled the door open. If he'd been any good at all this cloak-and-dagger vigilante stuff, he would have known the time to make his move would have been when the door was swinging toward the gunman. Too slow to realize the advantage and too afraid to make the attempt, Ian stepped through the door.

Two men waited for him. One was a very big, muscular black man standing by a metal folding chair. The chair had been placed over several sheets of plastic. The sight sent a blast of ice through Ian's veins. He froze. A push from behind brought him close to the other man.

The second man was smaller. He had a nasty looking scar running down the left side of his face and a gold tooth that caught the light and cast a dull glint. A sinister smile took his face and he stepped forward. "I hear you been looking for me. You sure ain't no cop." He turned to the larger man. "He look like he about to cry."

The other man replied, "Oh, he gonna cry all right."

Jervis laughed. "For sure."

Despite the situation, the sight of Jervis sparked a fire inside that melted his fear. Ian knew his window of opportunity was slim and his chances next to nil, but he thought if he could get his hand inside his pocket, he still might be able to finish his mission before he was killed. His life would be worth the sacrifice.

His hand had just made the outer edge of the pocket when Jervis lunged forward and buried his fist into Ian's unprepared gut. He doubled over and dropped to his knees, gasping. His cap was torn from his head. From behind, the two men grabbed him and ripped his coat off. When they saw the Sig Sauer in the back of his pants, they threw the coat in the corner without checking it. The gun was yanked free, the barrel scraping a line of the flesh from Ian's back.

"Whooee! Lookie what I found. This dude was ready for war, Jervis."

They searched his pockets and found the Ka-bar knife and the hundred dollars in cash.

"Hey, now. That's mine," said Jervis, no sign of pleasantness in his face or voice at all. The other man hesitated, but gave it up.

"Here," said Jervis graciously. He handed the man back a twenty. "You two can have that." He then passed a twenty to the big man behind him who took it and slipped it into his pocket without looking at it.

"Man, Jervis, that ain't fair. I found the dude and brought him here. We should all get a twenty."

"You not happy with what I gave you?" Jervis said, stepping forward menacingly. "You can always give it back."

He backed up in fear. "No man, we cool."

"Thought so."

Ian found his voice after listening to the exchange. "There's plenty more where that came from. Just let me go."

Jervis looked at the large man behind him. "You hear that, Banger? This boy want us to let him go. He spent all night trying to find me, and now he want to go. That's kinda rude, ain't it?"

Banger grunted.

"No, I think we find out what you want here. Oh, we get the money, sure as anything, but it'd be later, after we get better acquainted. Now, boys, why don't you escort our guest here to his chair?"

The two men lifted Ian to his feet and brought him to the chair. Ian wanted no part of sitting, though. He knew once he was down, he wouldn't be getting back up. He stood up with all four men in front of him.

Jervis said through clenched teeth, "Sit down, boy."

"No, I'm good."

In a flash, Banger parted the others, stepped forward, and showed how he got his name. He slammed Ian in the chest so hard he rocketed backward over the chair, crashing to the floor. He held his chest, thinking the blow had caused a heart attack. The sharpness of the pain made Ian think some ribs were cracked. He lay there, unable to breathe and feeling blood flowing from somewhere.

Banger grabbed the chair and set it back up. Then he dug his huge hands into Ian's shirt, catching a lot of flesh. He lifted him with little effort and pounded him down into the chair. No sooner had his butt touched down than Jervis stepped forward and threw a punch straight into Ian's face, knocking him back over the chair again.

In the distance of his retreating mind he heard, "Oh man, that was a good one."

"Felt good, too. Banger, set his ass back up."

Ian again was lifted and dropped. Again, he was hit; this time with a left. It hadn't been as hard, but he could barely tell anymore. His brain sought the darkness that was closing in. A third time, he was placed back in the chair. This time, however, they let him sit for a moment. He was unable to lift his head. Blood dripped from his mouth, staining his shirt.

"Now, then. It's time for you to tell me what you want with me."

Through his haze, he could barely make out Jervis in front of him. Behind Jervis stood the other two men, looking on with broad grins on their faces. Somewhere behind Ian lurked the monster they called Banger.

Ian shook his head to try and gain some focus.

Jervis grabbed Ian's face and squeezed. "I need an answer, boy. If I don't get one, I'm gonna turn you over to Banger. I promise he hit a lot harder than I do."

Ian spit blood on the floor and made some sounds like he was trying to speak, but couldn't. Jervis slapped his face lightly.

"Focus, fool. I'm talking to you. Why you looking for me?"

A slim plan began to take shape in Ian's head. Ian had little doubt that he would not be ascending from this basement accept in spirit form. He had nothing left to lose, and death would be better than the beating he was taking. He didn't have many options, but if his idea worked, he would have to thank Bonzo. He needed Jervis to react.

"I-I wanted to-to find you..."

His voice was barely a whisper. Jervis had to lean forward to hear him.

"Yeah baby, I know that much. Why?"

"Because...because...I wanted to...to kill you." Ian spit blood into Jervis's face.

"Fuck!" He jumped back, wiping his face. "You fucking bastard. You're a fucking dead man!" he screamed.

At that moment, Banger stepped to the front and pulled his massive arm back. It wasn't exactly what Ian had hoped for. If the big man hit him right, he would be out and most likely never wake up. As the fist fired toward the center of his face, Ian leaned to the side and ducked his head. He tried to roll with the punch, but even the glancing blow he received to the side of his head was enough to stagger him and scramble his thoughts. This time, he flew out of the chair and slammed against the cement wall. He slid down the wall where he stopped, completely dazed.

One of the other men came over and landed a savage kick to Ian's side that dropped him to the floor face-first. Banger had stopped his assault to help Jervis clean the blood from his face.

The man who landed the kick now tried to stomp on Ian. His only defense against the brutal pounding was to curl in a ball. The fourth man came over to lend a foot to his partner's effort. With one hand covering his head, Ian reached the other down to his right ankle. Curled in a ball, it was a simple process to remove the backup gun from the ankle holster without being noticed. The frenzy was upon both men and all they could see was the target that was Ian's head. He pulled the .38 revolver under his chest and waited for his one chance.

"Hold it! Stop! I want him alive!" Jervis screamed.

The two men ceased their assault and stepped away. They were both breathing hard from their efforts.

"Banger, set that fucker back in his chair."

Banger stooped and grabbed Ian under both arms so they were facing each other. Both of his feet were off the floor. Ian's head lolled to the side and he had little strength left to hold it up. With his chest now even with Banger's, the gun was between them. Ian lifted his head and smiled at Banger, angling the gun upward. Banger must have seen something strange in Ian's eyes, because the big man looked at him and knitted his brows in confusion. He looked down as Ian leaned back. The big man's eyes went wide as Ian pulled the trigger twice. Both bullets ripped through Banger's jaw. He fell backwards, clutching his face.

Ian hit the floor, but could not stand upright. He sunk to a squat and fired again. One of the men screamed, but Ian couldn't tell if the shot was fatal. He aimed to the left and fired a fourth round, then to the right for a fifth. He only had one shot left and no idea who was still a threat.

Someone ran through the door into the other room. One of the others fired several shots in Ian's direction. They hit the cement wall behind him. Ian scrambled to the corner where his coat had been tossed. It took a few tries to free the Glock while panicked, wild shots pinged off the walls around him. Ian squeezed into the space between the wall and the furnace, reached the gun around it, and fired blindly twice.

Suddenly, it was quiet, except for moaning. From where he hid, Ian could see Banger's legs. If one of the others was also incapacitated, then he only had two left to deal with. Through a crack in the wooden divider, Ian saw someone on the other side cross in front of the lightbulb and cast a brief shadow. Ian could not see a target, but if the other man drew even with Ian on the opposite side of the thin wall, he could fire through the wood and have a good chance of hitting him. Trapped in that narrow space with no room to duck or hide, Ian had to figure out where that man was, and fast.

A shot was fired on his side of the wall. It hit the furnace above him and exited through the other side, ricocheting off the wall. Now he had an idea where both men were. It had to be Jervis.

Ian peered out, but did not see anyone. Then his eyes stopped at another wooden door underneath the stairs at the opposite end of the room; perhaps a bathroom or laundry room. Jervis had to be in there. They had him trapped if they worked together. But if Jervis tried to escape, Ian would have a good shot at him.

With his left hand, Ian reached the .38 behind the furnace and tapped the wooden wall. Instantly, it drew repeat fire from the other side of the wall. The bullets tore into the furnace. Ian steadied the Glock, and seeing the rounds were coming straight in, he lined up his shot and began firing as fast as he could. The bullets scored a line across the wooden wall from left to right about chest-high. When he heard the grunt and the sound of something falling to the ground, he stopped.

Bullets began tearing through the metal works around him on his right. He slid further into the corner next to the wooden wall. The shots stopped suddenly and Ian wondered if the shooter was out of bullets.

Ian was not sure how many rounds he fired. He also could not be sure of how many of his assailants were still alive and functional. Covering the gun with the coat to deaden the sound, Ian ejected the magazine. Five rounds remained, plus the one in the .38. He shoved it back in place.

Taking a chance, Ian glanced around the furnace. When nothing happened, he stretched his head out farther, taking a longer visual sweep of the room. Besides Banger, he noticed another body lying on the floor near the door to the other room. That might mean Jervis was the only one remaining.

He slid his body in position so that he could run from his hiding place toward the outside door. He would shoot on the way to keep whoever was in the smaller room from shooting back. Maybe he would get lucky and score a hit. He took a deep breath and without a second thought that could change his mind, Ian made his suicidal dash.

Ian shot four times into the paneling and door of the room under the stairs, leaping over the body near the door leading out. He saved one bullet and made it safely to the door in the divider. He stood along the wall, not six feet from where he believed Jervis hid. Ian pushed the door to the outer room open. A fast glance showed the body of the man who had first contacted him sprawled on the floor with at least one bullet hole in his chest.

His raspy breathing was the only sound until he heard the moan.

Ian looked down just in time to see the wounded man lying near his feet try to lift his own Sig Sauer up to shoot him. Ian pointed the Glock down and triggered a round into the man's face. Blood erupted upward, spraying Ian's pants. The very audible sound of the slide locking back brought Jervis bursting into the room. Taking advantage of the situation, Jervis began firing before he was out the door, not knowing exactly where Ian was.

The whites of his eyes were big and dominated the sockets. He began tracking the gun toward Ian, a scream of fear and adrenaline pouring from his throat. Ian lifted the .38 and fired his one remaining shot. The bullet hit Jervis in the shoulder, throwing him backward and dislodging the gun from his grip. Jervis's last round before falling, creased a path over Ian's right bicep. He looked at the welling wound while Jervis tried to get up.

Then, as Ian's eyes came back to Jervis, both men froze. The gun Jervis had dropped lay near his feet. Ian was ten feet away. Jervis had no idea Ian's gun was empty, but he knew his only salvation was to reach that gun. Both men sprung at once.

Jervis gripped the gun, but Ian brought his foot down on his attacker's hand before he could lift it. Ian kicked Jervis in the face with his other foot, but it didn't land very solid and threw him off balance. The gun slipped out from under his foot. Ian dropped on Jervis, bringing the butt of the .38 down across his nose. Ian's left hand found Jervis's wrist and tried to pin it on the ground so he couldn't line up the gun with his target.

Ian hit him three more times before Jervis lost strength. He then pounced on the gun, ripping it from the nearly unconscious man's grip. Ian stood, breathing hard, and stepped back. Now that he had his family's killer in his sights, his hand shook with rage. A small voice deep inside him said, *"No, not yet!"* It sounded so real it chilled him. He looked behind him but no one was there.

Jervis held his hands up in front of his face as defense against the bullet. "Why you doing this, man?" he cried. "I ain't done nothin' to you."

"What? What did you say?"

Jervis looked confused.

"You never did anything to me? You fucking piece of shit. You killed my son and my wife, you prick. You left my other son in a coma."

Ian took a deep breath and fought back the urge to empty the gun into this worthless scum. With great effort, he held the rage in check and changed tactics.

"I-I know it wasn't you who killed them. It was your partner. You give me his name and you'll live."

"Bullshit. I ain't no fool. You'll kill me as soon as the name out my mouth."

"You got nothing to fear from me. I want the person who killed them. You didn't do it, did you?"

"No. Oh, hell no. It wasn't me."

"Then save yourself and give me the name." Ian clicked back the hammer for effect.

"It was Darryle, man. Darryle Lawson. The cops already got him locked up."

Ian lifted the gun and sighted down at Jervis's face.
Panic assaulted Jervis then. He started blubbering uncontrollably. "I told you, man. I told you. It was Darryle."

Ian moved the gun closer and closed one eye.

"You promised, man."

"I know it wasn't Darryle. I want the name of the third person."

Ian kept the gun on him and backed to where his coat was. He picked it up and pocketed the two empty guns. His knife was on the floor. He snatched it and put it in his pocket. Other than the multitude of spent casings, he didn't want to leave anything there that was his.

"See? I'm getting ready to leave. All I need is the name and I'm out of here."

Jervis tried to lift himself to a better sitting position.

"You gotta swear you ain't gonna kill me, man."

"I swear." He used his free hand to make a cross over his heart.

"It was Marcus Davis, man. It was all his idea. He the one who killed your family, man. It was him. I swear."

"Where do I find this Marcus Davis?"

"He gone, man. He left town and never came back."

Ian raged. He stepped forward and kicked the crybaby killer in the ribs. Jervis howled and rolled on his side.

"Liar! This man right here," he pointed with the gun at the body near the door, "told me he was in town." Ian took a chance, hoping Jervis' story would change. "Last chance."

"He around, man.," Jervis whined. He held up a defensive hand. "Please, don't shoot. He not hard to find. The cops stopped looking for us so we came back. He hides during the day and comes out at night. I don't know where he is. I swear. Now, you gonna keep your promise, right?"

"Where would he hang around?"

"Oh, man," Jervis sat up and began crying again.

"Jervis, I'm almost out the door. Where?"

"The pool hall."

"Which one?"

"There's only one in this part of town."

"Okay, you did good. I'm leaving now."

Jervis tensed his palms down on the floor, ready to move if Ian tried to shoot. His eyes had gone wide again.

Ian backed slowly out the door. He stooped to pick up the Sig, then went to the stairs. He ran up and then crept back down. Jervis let out a long sigh and tried to rise.

"Yeah, you were right. I lied."

Jervis's head snapped up in time to catch the first bullet. He didn't feel the next five.

30

Ian spied his ball cap and scooped it up. He brushed at it absently, staring at the mess he made of Jervis's face. He felt neither guilt nor repulsion, but there was also no sense of satisfaction, only a hollowness, as if his soul had fled the carnage. Reaching into the dead man's pocket, he took back his sixty dollars. The others could keep theirs. He pulled out his notepad and wrote, *They will kill no more.-A.* Kneeling down, he placed the note on Jervis's chest and stared at the dripping gore.

He was snapped from his stupor when the first distant sounds of a siren reached his ears. Instantly he was in motion. He raced for the stairs and out the side door. Although every fiber of his being screamed for him to run, he forced a calmness and walked toward the backyard. Glancing left and right, Ian thought he saw someone standing in the next yard. Keeping his head down, he lost control and broke into an all-out run. He hurdled the fence and raced as hard as he could down the alley. He wasn't in the greatest shape, especially after the beating he just took, but his endurance seemed to improve when the fear and adrenaline kicked in.

His mind raced to find an escape route. Ian had now left another witness. Not that he would do anything to the man, he was an innocent. Somethings still separated him from the other killers. Now Ian had another name to hunt. That lone thought pushed his pace faster. He couldn't afford to be caught yet. He made it safely to the end of the alley and turned right on the side street. With some distance between him and the police for the moment, Ian slid into the shadows to catch his breath. He'd escaped so far, yet in his haste, he realized he'd gone the wrong way. His car was parked in the opposite direction.

Ian started to jog. He continued two more blocks north before turning up an alley and heading east, backtracking toward his car. In his panicked escape, he had lost track of how far away he was. He estimated five or six blocks, but in truth, it could have been more. If the police were on the scene, by now the neighbor had given a basic description of him and pointed in the direction he went. The smartest thing for him to do would be to lose the coat and weapons and stay hidden in the shadows.

He found a one-car garage with a flat but slightly sloping roof that backed up to the alley. Using the fence attached to the garage, Ian chinned up on the cross bar, then, with all his remaining strength, pulled upward until he could swing his leg on the roof. He stripped off the coat, slipped the gloves in his pants pocket, and lay down. The roof creaked from the strain of bearing his weight. That's all he'd need—to fall through the roof. He tried to stay still, but the wood underneath him must have been rotted. It continued to groan and then began to sag. He scurried forward to the edge. Checking in both directions, he decided to find a new hiding spot. Ian left the coat and the other two guns, keeping the empty .38. He climbed down and crouched, pausing to listen before moving to the end of the alley.

Both directions on the street were clear. He dashed across the open road to the next alley. His luck was holding; he thought he might actually be able to make it to his car undetected. Ian was midway down the alley when things changed. A light shined his way from behind. Even though he was staying near the garages and keeping low, the light could easily find him.

He ducked behind two large plastic garbage cans and peeked out. A cop car blocked the alley entrance. The spotlight adjusted, moving toward his position. It must have caught his movement as he hid. When he saw the car back up a bit so it could turn up the alley, Ian knew it was time to run. An old rusty gate hung on a wobbly fence behind him. Keeping the garbage cans between him and the light, he pushed the gate open and duck-walked through. Hidden by the garage now, Ian straightened up and ran. Behind him, the sound of the squad car's tires crunching on the stone and debris told Ian the police were getting closer.

Ian went around the front of the garage and started for the driveway where he almost ran directly into the cone of light from another police car spotlight. He leaped for the corner of the house, slamming his shoulder. Fighting back the urge to cry out in pain, Ian saw he was trapped. If he moved to the other end of the house, the cop in the alley could see him. If he went to the front of the garage, the cop in the street would find him. If he stayed where he was, eventually the cop in the alley would still see him. Then, things got worse. The car in the alley stopped and the door opened.

Anxiety gripped him in an iron vise, making it difficult to take a deep breath. Desperately, Ian looked around for a way out. When his eyes lit on a fast food bag crumpled against the garage, Ian made a quick decision and moved to pick it up. He slid the empty .38 inside the bag and moved around the corner of the garage and began whistling. Just inside the gate with his hand resting on his weapon stood a very tall policeman.

Ian feigned surprise and jumped back.

"Jesus Christ, you scared the shit out of me."

The cop put a quieting finger to his mouth, but his posture changed. He crouched slightly, his hand gripping the butt of his weapon, ready to draw and fire.

"Is everything all right?" Ian asked.

"What are you doing back here?"

"Ah, I just finished eating a late-night snack and was throwing the bag in the garbage."

"At this hour?"

"Well, I was kinda hiding the evidence. My wife would be pissed if she knew."

"You live here?" The flashlight beam scanned up and down Ian's body.

"Yes, sir."

"You got some ID on you?"

"It's in the house. You want me to get it."

"What happened to your face?"

The light stopped on his bloodied face, blinding him. Ian raised a hand to block the light and turned his head.

Ian looked down to avoid the light. "I fell down the stairs."

"Come out here into the alley where I can see you better."

Ian went through the gate and lifted the bag. "I'm gonna drop this in the can, all right?"

He didn't wait for an answer. He leaned over the can, lifted the lid and dropped in the bag, bringing the gun out unconcealed. He stepped quickly forward and aimed it at the cop's face. "Don't make me shoot you. Now drop the flashlight."

Ian kept his head down to avoid the cop's eyes.

"You're making a huge mistake. Put the gun down and there's still time to salvage the rest of your life."

"My life doesn't matter, but I'm not through yet. Now turn around and don't make me hurt you." The cop hesitated like he was either going to talk more or be defiant. Ian cocked the gun. "I don't hurt cops if I can help it, but I can't let you take me in yet. Now don't make me add your life to the growing list."

The man turned. A static blast from the cop's shoulder mic made both of them jump.

Ian fumbled in his pocket and said, "Don't. You'll be dead before help can arrive." He unfolded the blade of his Ka-bar and cut through the cord while he kept the gun pressed against the man's spine. He closed the blade and slipped it back in his pocket. Gripping the officer's gun, he pulled it from its holster. With the snap undone it came away easily. The man started to spin, but Ian stepped back and leveled both guns. Anger flushed the man's face.

"Turn back around." When the man hesitated, Ian yelled, "Do it now!"

Ian pulled the cuffs from their holster. He dropped them on the roof of the car and backed up a few steps.

"Clip one around your wrist."

The cop pretended to do so, then spun around so fast that even though Ian expected the move, it still took him by surprise. His lunge fell short and suggested he thought Ian was closer. Startled, Ian pulled the trigger on reflex and whistled a shot past the man's head. The cop stopped then, knowing how close he had come to death. Ian was shaking so bad he couldn't keep the gun on line. It was enough to scare the policeman, though, he attached one bracelet to his wrist.

"Go to the fence now."

The man did so. At the front of the house, a car door opened.

"Clip it on," Ian said sternly. "If your partner shows up, I'm going to have to kill him."

It was a cheap fence and would not hold the man for long. As soon as the cuff closed, Ian ran to the patrol car, jumped in the front seat and shut the door. Putting an elbow on the wheel, he shifted and drove down the alley just as the second policeman came into view.

31

Everything was desperation now. No thoughts, only reactions. His heart pounded an ever-increasing cadence in his chest. Ian slipped on one glove and then grabbed the wheel as shots rang out. Several hit the car as he accelerated down the alley. He watched in the side mirror as the second cop helped free his partner. The car bounced out onto the street, scraping the pavement. Ian turned the wheel hard to the right. He was only a half block from the intersection and there he turned a sharp left. They would be coming soon, as would every other cop in the area.

Ian floored the accelerator, surprised at how quickly the patrol car leaped forward. He tried to get his bearings and decided he was driving away from his own car. He turned another hard left and flew down the narrow residential street, smacking the squad car's side mirror into that of a parked car, before veering left again. Three blocks later, Ian turned another left, so fast that he almost collided with a parked car. He bled off the speed and coasted to the curb where he braked hard.

Wiping the wheel and interior door handle with his shirt, Ian hopped out of the car, leaving the cop's hastily wiped gun on the front seat. If his hurried calculations were correct, his car should be two blocks ahead. Racing the distance, he beeped the key fob to unlock the door as soon as the vehicle came into view. He ripped the door open and jumped in too fast, banging the side of his head against the frame with a loud and painful thud. He doubled over, holding his head with one hand while reaching blindly with his left for the door.

Too much was happening at once. His mind and body were in serious overload: the pain in his head and throughout his body, the door, the ignition, and the pursuit all worked hard to shut Ian down. He fought back the panic and forced himself to take deep breaths. Managing to close the door, he dropped his right hand from his head, but it shook so badly he had trouble lining the key up. A tortured moan released from deep inside him. He didn't want to get caught like in the movies because he couldn't get the key in the ignition.

Pushing back against the seat, he closed his eyes and said, "Come on! You can do this." Two quick breaths later, he opened his eyes and guided the key home. Relief flooded over him. He started the car. It took all his effort not to punch the pedal and race away. Keeping the headlights off, Ian pulled forward to the next street, turned left, and drove away. When he reached the next intersection, Ian saw the reflections of strobing red and blue lights off the houses in the next block down. He flung the wheel to the right and shot down the side street.

Ian continued on in the dark, running stop signs until he reached the first main cross street. There he turned on the headlights and pulled out onto the nearly deserted road. Ian kept a constant vigil in the rearview mirror. He didn't like driving the only car on the road. The police could pull him over just for being in the area. An entrance ramp for the expressway was about a mile away. If he could reach it, he had a chance of escaping. He watched the odometer count down the mile tenth by tenth, like watching the seconds tick away.

At the next main intersection, he turned left. He glanced back down the road and saw flashing lights coming toward him. As soon as he was out of view from the road, he gave the engine a blast of gas and pushed the car as hard as he dared. One block up on the left was a Latino night club. It was closed for the night, but the parking lot was still full and several small groups of people stood around talking. Ian braked as hard as he could without causing a screeching sound. The turn into the lot was too fast and wide. Ian drew a lot of attention. He parked in a spot near the back of the lot and shut off the engine. He ducked down in the front seat, suddenly aware that he was dripping sweat.

He waited, listening for the siren. When he heard it, the volume increased fast telling him the car the siren was attached too was heading his way. Lifting his head, he peered through the side window, preparing for the worst. If they spotted him there, he was as good as caught. He might be able to out run the patrol car, but he'd never outrun the radio.

The cruiser slowed slightly at the club's driveway. The cop gave a quick look, then sped away. Ian waited a minute to be sure it was gone before pulling out of the space. In his peripheral vision, he saw movement. When he looked closer, he saw the club patrons in the lot waving at him. It took a second to understand they were telling him to go back. Ian backed into the parking spot just as another police car flew by with flashing lights but no siren.

When that car passed, the people signaled for him to go. He pulled out and drove out the back exit, waving a thank you to his helpers as he went.

He drove, taking side roads back the same way he came. He stopped for a while on the side of the road and waited. The only sound was that of his ragged breathing. Ian stayed there until it returned to normal.

Driving north two blocks, he reached the long main street in the area that ran east and west. He paused for a moment to decide his best route. He could gamble and take the road west until he hit another expressway ramp, or he could cut across the street and try to get more distance from the area before making a break for it. He opted for the back road's slower path.

He made a dash across the road, relieved he saw no sign of the police anywhere. Once across, he took his time and zigzagged from block to block, stopping often to park in front of a house. It took more than an hour to reach a distance away that he felt was safe to drive on a main road. The one he found took him the long way around, but eventually led to an expressway ramp. Once on the expressway and up to speed, Ian began to relax somewhat. He'd made it this far, but it was only a matter of time before someone IDd him.

As he drove, he forced thoughts of the night's events out of his mind until he pulled into the driveway of his new house. He drove around back, out of sight from the road. Ian sat there for a long while, too exhausted to move. He became aware that he was soaked with sweat and blood. The pain started to arrive in waves with growing and spreading force. Only then did he allow himself to feel a brief sense of satisfaction. Ian had successfully avenged one of his wife's and son's killers and now he had the name of the remaining man. If the police didn't come for him by tomorrow, he had a chance of finishing his mission.

Ian crawled weakly from the car and let himself in the house. He washed and wrapped his wounds and changed his clothes. He took a beer from the small apartment-size refrigerator he'd purchased and closed the door, then reopened it and took out a second one. He deserved two and didn't think he'd have the energy to get up for the second one once he sat down.

Ian tried not to spend time going over what had occurred.

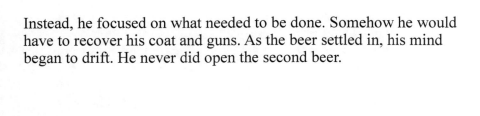

Instead, he focused on what needed to be done. Somehow he would have to recover his coat and guns. As the beer settled in, his mind began to drift. He never did open the second beer.

32

"What a night! Oh, what a fucking night," Stu Marsden, the ME muttered. He had just arrived on the scene outside the North End carryout where two bodies were found moments before all hell broke loose. Before he could even put on gloves he got a priority call about multiple shootings at a local bar. He was redirected to Eddie's Bar on Alexis Road. It wasn't until nearly three hours after the first call came in that they understood the extent of the devastation across the city.

Before he finished at the bar, another call came in about four bodies in a basement back in the north end. He cleaned up, turned the scene over to a detective, and moved on.

One police car was still outside the house, securing the area, but everyone else including the detective in charge had long since gone. Not that Stu was complaining. The fewer people there were at the scene, the easier it was to collect evidence. When he didn't have to constantly stop and answer questions things went faster and after the night he'd had already, faster was what he needed.

He was just finishing up when the cop on patrol walked down the steps.

"I'm supposed to pass you a message. They found another one."

Marsden's mouth dropped open. "You've got to be fucking kidding me. What the hell's going on around here? Did someone declare war?"

"Looks like it, doesn't it? Anyway, it's not far from here and lucky you—you're the closest."

"Thanks," he said, taking the paper with the address, but there was no sincerity in the word.

The next crime scene was in an alley between two buildings. There he met Detective Robinson, who caught all three of the north end crime scenes.

"What the hell's going on, Robinson? We got a gang war brewing?"

"Nah, to tell you the truth, Stu, it's sounding more and more like a terrorist attack. The killings in this area are most likely gang-related." He stuffed his hands in his jacket pockets and shrugged. "But I think this is the work of one man. A vigilante, maybe. Hell, I don't know, but some of the guys chased a lone man. Unfortunately, he seems to have slipped through the net."

"Well, it's madness, that's for sure. I'm just glad I only have to process them. Good luck figuring it all out. You got a vigilante on one end of town and a mad gunman or terrorist on the other. World's gone crazy. How many other scenes were there?"

"They confirmed four, but they were still checking. It's past four a.m. now. Without being able to get into to some of the locations, we can't tell if there's any more bodies. Right now, they're attempting to contact the owners of the other bars on Alexis. The attacks all seem to have been along that street."

"Damn! That's some crazy shit. How come you got left out of it?" He opened his bag, pulled on some gloves, and moved toward the body.

"I'm sure when they have all the details, those attacks will take precedence over these, especially if they determine they had terrorist connections. I got these because they all appear to have been done by the same guy. The two on the street on Monday, this one, the carryout earlier, and four bodies in a basement not far from here."

"Yeah. I was just over there. What a mess."

"I think the shooter fashions himself as some sort of town sheriff, cleaning up the streets."

"What makes you think that?"

"He left notes with each body. I'm sure there has to be some connection between them, but so far I haven't had the time to puzzle them out. What makes it worse is all the work I've done so far will most likely get put on hold until after this mass murder thing is cleared. So, either the guy will get away with it and the trail will turn cold, or he'll be left to kill again with no one running the evidence."

"Yep, it's a crazy world out here."

"And it seems like it's getting crazier."

"Who's in charge of the asylum?"

"Ha, it sure as hell ain't us."

33

Regardless how hard the sun worked to wake him, Ian still could not move. His body ached so much he wasn't sure he'd ever move again without blinding pain shooting through him. It hurt his ribs to draw breath. The touch of his hand moving gently over his swollen face caused him to cry out and gasp for air, which reignited the flame of pain from his chest and caused him to cry out again. It was an endless, torturous circle.

Ian forced himself to lie perfectly still until the nerve endings ceased firing. He breathed softly, not wanting to start the process again. It took a long time before he braved movement. His left side hurt far worse than his right, so he rolled right. Bringing his legs underneath him, he was able to rise to his knees. Ian stayed for several minutes with his head resting on the floor and arms wrapped around his body, allowing the pain to recede. Holding his breath, he lifted his head and elongated his torso. Again, he waited for the flow of pain to subside. If it wasn't for his desire to see his son and tell him the news, Ian would have lay there all day.

Raising one leg, he planted his foot on the floor. Before the pain made him change his mind, he planted the other and was standing...well, almost. He was on his feet, but doubled over. The pain was so sharp he wanted to scream. He didn't doubt he had broken ribs.

Once upright, Ian took long, slow, deep breaths, trying to gauge and control the pain. He would have to pick up some pain pills on the way. It wasn't something he had thought to bring from home. After all, he didn't anticipate surviving a physical confrontation, so really wasn't prepared to deal with pain. He couldn't take the chance of going back to his house. He had no way of knowing if the police would be waiting.

Ian moved gingerly to the bathroom. The low squat to the toilet hurt. The act of twisting with the toilet paper became excruciating. When he felt like he could rise, Ian grabbed the sink to pull himself up and forward. Washing his hands, he bravely splashed cold water on his damaged face. The cold refreshed him, but he dared not attempt to dry his face on a towel. Being dry wasn't worth the extra pain.

The reflection in the mirror bore little resemblance to him. His left eye was halfway swollen shut and the entire left side of his face was a variety of colors. There were two separate bumps on his head that screamed if he tried to touch them. His nose was swollen and dried blood crusted below it. His lip was cut and puffed unevenly. The one good thing about his new look was that few people would recognize him.

The more he studied his face, the more he realized he would need a lot of drugs while he healed.

With much effort, he stripped off his clothes. Using a washcloth, Ian cleaned himself as best he could at the sink. He managed to struggle into a t-shirt and jeans. Getting his shoes on, however, turned out to be quite a challenge. In the end, he slid them on, but tucked the laces inside rather than tie them.

While coffee was brewing, Ian walked out to the backyard with his clothes from the night before and some matches. The land stretched a long way back toward a line of assorted trees. He found an old fire pit, long unused. Gathering dried twigs and some brown weeds, Ian started a small fire. When it was blazing, he dropped the clothes in the middle. He watched as the fire began to eat away at the material. His eyes glazed over. Visions of the previous night danced within the flames.

Ian saw the blood and Jervis's face, before and after. He felt no disgust at what he had done, nor did he take pleasure. The revenge brought a sense of satisfaction, but he knew it had cost him his soul. As the clothes charred to black ash, his lone thought was that he was halfway done.

Ian turned and trudged back to the house. He needed drugs fast but wondered about how smart it would be to be seen in public, let alone go see JT. The police might be there, but even if they weren't, anyone he bumped into would remember his appearance should anyone come checking on him. In the end, the desire to share his victory with his son was overwhelming and Ian decided to go anyway. He knew JT would appreciate what he had done. The thought of relaying the message to his son helped mask some of the pain.

34

Ian arrived at the care facility after stopping for the strongest over-the-counter pain reliever he could find. He purchased a newspaper, a bottle of water, and a tuna sandwich, afraid he couldn't chew anything more solid than that.

Sunglasses and a ball cap pulled low helped cover his face, but nothing could disguise the way he walked. Ian tried to stand erect and move smoothly, but it was like a drunk trying to walk a straight line. No matter how hard he tried, walking normal just wasn't going to happen.

Once inside the building, Ian glanced down the halls in each direction. Seeing they were clear, he forced a quicker pace until he reached JT's room and he peeked inside. Finding the room empty of attending personnel, Ian entered and closed the door. The benefit of paying for a private room was that he could talk to his son without anyone overhearing.

An air of excitement filled the room, and whether from the pills or the adrenaline rush, the pain was under a veil. Only a faint, persistent throbbing remained. Dropping his purchases on a chair, Ian moved to the side of the bed and leaned down close to his son's ear. He watched the boy sleep for a moment and felt the tears rolling down his cheeks. The emotions and raw nerves of the past few days came to a head. Without thinking, he wiped at them and the pain exploded again. He moaned.

He let the sensation subside before he began speaking to his son.

"JT, I found him." It was hard not to let the excitement touch his voice. "I did. I found him. And guess what? He'll never hurt anyone again." He looked for a reaction but found none. His smile faded. He wanted so desperately for his son to share this moment with him. He forced himself to smile again.

"I found this Jervis with three of his friends. Things got a little rough, but in the end, I took them all out. It's true. I never thought I could do it, but I did. I killed all four of them, including one of the bastards who hurt you."

It might have been his imagination, or more likely his intense desire for his son to understand the importance of what he had done, but he thought he saw a small twitch at the corner of JT's mouth. Ian's excitement changed focus. He stared hard at the spot, both watching and praying for the movement to happen again. "Please, God, don't let me have imagined that."

Ian continued with his story, hoping the tale might stimulate more reaction.

"Before I killed Jervis, I made him tell me who the third person was. Marcus Davis is his name. I may not be in any condition to hunt him tonight, but I promise as soon as I'm healed, I'll go after him."

The twitch never returned, but Ian was still bolstered by what he had seen. He refused to think it had been his imagination. The door creaking open made him turn around before he thought about doing it.

"I-I just want to check on…oh my God, what happened? Are you all right?"

"Yes, yes, yes," Ian said, annoyed. He turned his head to avoid her gaze, but KeKe wasn't to be deterred. She moved with him to get a look. Ian kept turning, but eventually she grabbed his arm. She saw the wince and the way he covered his ribs to protect them.

"Stop!" she ordered. "Let me look." She held his arm tight and moved closer to him. "What happened? Tell me the truth."

"I was in an accident. I wasn't wearing my seatbelt."

"Did you go to a hospital?"

"Yes," he said, hoping to back her off a bit.

"Liar. These cuts here would have been stitched if you had. What really happened?"

She touched his side. He jumped, doubled over and groaned. "That hurt?"

"What'd'ya think?" He squeezed out between clenched teeth.

"Good." She turned and stomped out of the room.

Ian fell rather than sat in the chair, sending more jolts of pain through his body. Coming here had been a mistake. He should have stayed home and rested. Gritting his teeth, Ian managed to get to his feet. Gathering his things, he said, "I'll be back later, JT."

Ian was nearly to his car when he heard KeKe yelling for him. He didn't dare look. His pace increased and desperation helped dull some of the pain for the moment. Ian unlocked the door remotely and yanked it open. Her voice was growing louder. The pain exploded inside him as he tried to sit down too fast. "Ahhh!"

Reaching back, he snagged the door. Tears flooded his eyes. "Mr. Kelly, you need help. Don't run--"

The door shut, cutting off the rest. He started the car and could see the nurse closing on him like some beautiful avenging angel. Ian couldn't look at KeKe's face. He felt enough agony already. Accelerating too fast, the car shot forward, tires squealing. He lost the fight not to look in the rearview mirror. KeKe was hunched over in the parking lot, hands on her knees, trying to catch her breath after her sprint toward him. Ian's eyes dropped from the mirror, his heart no longer pumping blood, but guilt.

His drive to the new home was lost in a mental haze. Once there, Ian collapsed on the bedroll. He didn't want to move again. As his breathing slowed and the pain ebbed, he felt his eyes fill with tears once more, but he didn't know why. He had hurt—no, killed— others, and now was running from someone who wanted to help him. What had he become? With that thought primary on his mind, Ian drifted to sleep.

The return of the pain woke him hours later. The piercing agony in his left side was too much to ignore. He fought to sit up. Reaching across his body, he screamed and swore while he grabbed the bag with the water and pills in it. Quickly, he swallowed four pills and slugged them back with half the water. Now he had to wait for them to take effect.

His eyes fell upon the tuna sandwich, trying to remember how long he'd had it without refrigeration, but eventually he just didn't care. He tore the wrapper off and bit hungrily into the now soggy sandwich as if it were the only food left on the planet, thinking of the irony of dying from food poisoning after all he'd been through.

After finishing the sandwich, Ian lay there until the pills kicked in, then levered himself to his feet. The pain was adequately deadened and he was able to move around. Forcing long, slow deep breaths, Ian walked to the bathroom. He would not be hunting tonight. He'd never survive another confrontation. The smartest thing would be to wait until the next night. He winced. Well, maybe the night after that. As Ian tried to sit down, a sharp twinge reminded him about his ribs and he remained standing. Maybe he'd take several days off before resuming his hunt for Davis.

Ian moved to the kitchen where he had set up a card table and folding chair. He spread out the paper to see if his actions had made the news. What Ian read made his jaw fall open.

117 Die in Overnight Attacks
In what Toledo police fear may be a terrorist attack, 117 people were
gunned down in six local bars late last night. It was the worst single-event
death toll in the city's history.
So far, police have little to go on other than that the shooter or shooters
walked in, used an automatic weapon on the patrons, then locked the
doors to prevent discovery of the bodies. "To be able to pull
off something this large in scale," said Police Chief Manuel Sanchez,
"shows planning and purpose; the type of purpose you see with terrorist
actions."

Ian was stunned. The story went on, but he quickly tore through
the paper to see if there was any mention of four dead men in a
basement. Apparently, it hadn't made the news. The police and the
local media were most likely too absorbed in the mass murder to
worry about a few more dead gangbangers, which was good. It kept
Ian out of the spotlight.

Yet on some subconscious level, he felt disappointment not to
be able to see his accomplishment in print. It was as if he had been
cheated his due. The actions of the man known as 'A' were not
important enough to merit mention. A strange thought made him
question whether he was becoming too obsessed with killing. *What
was his focus?* It was vengeance, not notoriety, wasn't it?

What did it matter, though? When he took down Marcus Davis,
his mission would be over and he would no longer care if anyone
knew. But having survived the first battle, now he wondered what
would happen if he made it through the next. Should he run? Should
he go back to Colorado and continue with his original plan? Or
maybe he should just live out his life up on a mountain someplace.

Ian didn't really think staying would be an option. But what if
he did? Eventually they would come for him. They would figure it
all out and arrest him. At that point, he would confess. Why bother
fighting the allegations? Ian hadn't expected to live anyway. Staying
would allow him extra time to be with his son. The investigation
might take a while to put the pieces together and however long it
took would allow him more time to say goodbye to JT.

Of course, the other option was suicide by police. That way, he
could avoid the long trial. His death would end everything and the
story would die. If JT woke up, it would all be over and hopefully
forgotten by then.

Another thought lightened his mood. If he was convicted,

maybe they would place him in the same prison Darryle Lawson was in. He smiled at the idea. He'd be able to get all three of them. What difference would one more murder make? By then, he'd be spending the rest of his life in prison anyway.

The sudden increase in his motivation made him wonder if the excitement was about the revenge or because he had succumbed to the power of taking someone's life? He shook his head, sinking back into a sour mood. In the end, the reasons no longer mattered as long as the job got done.

35

That night, the first that Ian slept through in a while, another attack was taking place. This time, Ahmed's targets were all-night diners on the south side of town. From the list Al had provided, he picked four of them that were about a mile apart from each other, but this time not along the same road. They were chosen because they were the four busiest diners on the route. However, since it was a week night, they wouldn't be so crowded as to be uncontrollable. The body count should still be high enough to spread panic.

The attack would be different tonight. They would not be worrying about trying to keep the killing contained. Ahmed didn't want any witnesses, but once out the door and into the SUVs, they wouldn't be concerned about anyone finding the bodies. Most of the diners had a large number of windows, making it difficult to conceal what was going on inside. Because of that, there would be a strict emphasis on timing.

The two teams assaulted separately this time. One SUV would take the first and third diner; the other, the second and fourth. Splitting the teams allowed for two assaults to be going on at the same time, thus shortening the actual time the fire teams were exposed.

Ahmed followed the first team. He would catch up to the other team on their final attack. Once more, Ahmed warned them to stay alert. The police would be mobile and ready. He insisted the missions be completed in fifteen minutes: five minutes at each site and five to make the drive between them. Each team had an escape route that would take them away from the safe house. If there was any trouble, they would drive until the others could catch up and help. Whatever happened, no team member was to be taken alive. The only way to survive the week-long mission was not to get caught.

The parking lot was almost full at the first diner. The crowd was bigger than expected. Ahmed held the three-man fire team for a minute to check the flow of patrons. It seemed steady with some diners coming as others were leaving; not the best situation. There were too many possibilities for interference, cell phone calls or videos, and witnesses, but it was too late to alter plans now.

Ahmed called the driver. "Patrol the parking lot. Shoot anyone you see as a threat or witness. I will signal you when it is time to go around back." His final instructions given, he gave the signal and the driver pulled up to the front door.

The masked men ran inside and immediately opened fire. Screams could be heard in the parking lot. Ahmed observed through the large windows as the chaos and death toll mounted. Two men made it through the door, running for cover, but the driver swung around and shot both before they reached their cars.

Ahmed nodded to himself. His team was working well. He gave the signal over the radio for the pickup and the driver sped around the building toward the rear. As Ahmed continued to watch, a car pulled in and parked on the far side of the lot. Ahmed pulled in front of the diner and waited. A man and a woman holding hands and laughing approached.

The woman stopped and threw her hands to her face as she discovered the bodies between the two rows of cars. He had to stop them or the alarm would be given too soon. Ahmed couldn't take the chance on a long shot. If he missed, he would have to expend a lot of time and energy tracking the couple down without being seen. He got out and walked toward them. The man bent down to check for vital signs.

"Alice, call the police. They've been shot."

Alice pulled her cell phone from her purse, then noticed with a start that Ahmed was approaching her.

"What is it?" Ahmed said in perfect English. "Is someone hurt?"

Alice relaxed for a moment and turned back to the body. "Yes, it looks--"

Then the bullet tore through her throat. The man was just coming to his feet to see who Alice was talking to when two shots ripped open his chest and threw him back on the hood of the car behind him. He slid to the ground and Ahmed returned to his car. Another car turned into the lot as Ahmed was exiting. There was nothing he could do. The bodies were bound to be discovered. He averted his face and drove to the next destination.

Ahmed called Al for a report on team two and was told their first target went as smoothly as planned. There were not as many customers as hoped, but they all went down in a hurry. The team was out and heading for their second target in less than three minutes.

By the time Ahmed arrived at the second location the team was already inside. Muzzle flashes pulsed through the windows like strobe lighting. He picked up the radio to give the driver his instructions only to find he was already in position. A surge of annoyance struck Ahmed. He no longer felt in control. Pushing the feeling aside, he replaced it with a sense of pride. His team was performing exactly as instructed. He allowed himself a smile realizing his plan was working.

The driver called less than a minute later, advising him they were on their escape route with no problems. The tension began to melt.

While Ahmed drove on his own escape route, he received word from Al that the second team was being pursued by a lone cop car.

"Can you escape?"

"No, but we will deal with him."

Ahmed diverted to catch the second team. He would lend assistance if he was able. It was far too early in their mission to lose three men.

"Give me your route. I will catch you if I can. But you must deal with your pursuit quickly before they can get out information on you and bring in backup."

Al said, "We can lose them."

"No, you fool! You cannot outrun a radio. They will have cars converging on your location as we speak. You must eliminate your pursuer. I am on my way to help." Ahmed checked his GPS. "Where are you?"

There was a brief pause, then the voice said, "We are on Barton Road."

Ahmed found the road on his display. "Turn right on Middleton."

"Middleton." There was some shouting and then the man returned. "We are on Middleton now."

"Keep going."

Ahmed came to a red light at a busy intersection. As he stopped, he saw the black SUV fly past with the pursuing police car close behind, lights flashing and siren blaring. He made the turn and followed.

The man behind Al in the SUV leaned out the window and fired a long burst at the cop car. Ahmed moved to the curb lane to avoid taking an errant bullet. The shooter was not trying to hit the car since his rounds would not penetrate the windshield. He was trying to keep the policeman's attention on him.

Ahmed tried to gain on the squad car. He intended to nudge the car and hopefully cause a wreck, but at these speeds, catching the pursuit car was difficult. He picked up the radio. "Slow your speed."

A voice responded, "No, back off now. Do not make your presence known. We've got this."

The boldness of the man and the sharp tone with which the words were delivered sent a flash of anger through Ahmed, yet he respected the command and backed off. As he watched, the rear passenger side door opened a crack. A hand reached out and dropped something onto the street. Ahmed knew instantly what the man had done. He hit the brakes hard and veered to the right. A few seconds later, an explosion rocked the night, lifting the rear end of the squad car into the air and dropping it on its roof. The car skidded about twenty feet, hit a parked car, and spun around like a turtle on its shell.

The SUV faded in the distance. Ahmed slowed and gripped his handgun. If the policeman got out, he would shoot him. But as he waited, traffic began to gather and stop. People were getting out of their cars and running to aid the officer. Ahmed had no choice but to leave. He turned down a residential side street and worked his way back toward a main street. Almost an hour later, Ahmed was the last to arrive at the safe house. The men were cleaning their weapons while they laughed and talked. Their excitement filled the room.

As soon as Ahmed appeared, the silence was as sudden as if someone flipped a switch. He looked around at the men as they avoided his eyes and continued with the maintenance of the guns.

"It was a wonderful victory tonight. You did very well. Continue with your celebration, but keep in mind that each night our missions will get bigger and more dangerous. Do not allow our victory tonight to make you overconfident. That is when someone will make a mistake that not only will affect the mission, but may get some or all of you killed."

Ahmed walked past them and up the stairs to his room. Shutting the door behind him to muffle some of the laughing that had resumed, Ahmed sat on his bed and stared blindly at the wall. Two days down, five to go. The search for them would be intense. He wondered how much information the cop was able to relay before he'd been stopped. They would have to be very careful from here on. The authorities would be prepared now and would have descriptions of the vehicles and maybe of the men. His team would be very lucky if any of them survived the next attack.

36

The morning news was ablaze with stories of the horror of the prior evening. When the local news ended, the national news took over and confirmed that similar attacks had happened in six other mid-size cities around the country.

Local governments had initiated curfews and wherever possible, called in the National Guard for added security. The terrorist alert level was increased to the max. President Andrew Morales issued a statement that threatened severe retribution to any and all terrorists involved. He called out the army and offered assistance to the governors and mayors of the affected states and cities.

Behind closed doors, President Morales tore into the directors who had falsely advised him the country still had another month to prepare. He would have asked for all their resignations, but if word ever got out that they had been given a heads-up on the attacks and did not move on that information, another Democrat would never hold office again anywhere.

"How did this happen on our watch? I need answers now!" He yelled the words as he paced furiously around his office.

"Sir," Arthur Penn, Director of Homeland Security said. "With the compiled information from all the agencies, we were able to stop three leaders of what we believe to be terrorist cells from entering the country. They are in custody now. That's three other cities saved."

The president interrupted him. "I don't want to hear that. It's as if we're saying 'yeah, some people died, but look how many were saved?' We fucked up here, people, and we need to be accountable for it, at least within this office. If the truth ever got out, we'd all fry. We need to find the other cells and wipe them out before they do any more damage. And I do mean wipe them out. The people will accept nothing less. They will want to answer blood with blood."

"Besides," CIA Director Foster chimed in, "if they are dead, there will be no one to interrogate. No interrogation means no information to leak out about how long the operation has been in the works."

The President stopped his pacing. "So, what do we have?"

FBI Director Knight took over. "From the CIA's agent, we knew there were twelve cells. He had no idea where the targets were. The time frame we were told was two months. They must have stepped it up when they learned they had a spy in their midst. Along with the three captured terrorist leaders, information was sent to all city leaders to be prepared for some sort of attack. That information led to the arrest of another cell in Tulsa before any attack could be initiated. The report I received was that they had enough weapons and explosives to start a war.

"In Fort Worth, there was a shootout with suspected terrorists by local law enforcement. A very observant state trooper followed a carful of men. When they got out, they were brandishing assault weapons. The trooper called it in and attempted to stop the men. When they started firing, it became an all-out gun battle that lasted nearly an hour before the last terrorist was killed."

"All right," said the president. "We stopped three before they got started. We arrested one cell and killed another. With the six already in operation, that still leaves one. Where is the twelfth cell?"

No one had an answer.

Penn spoke. "To be able to pull off what they done already, they are obviously well-funded and have competent leadership. But there is no way they could have accomplished this without inside help. They must be getting aid from people already living in this country."

"I have sent out more than a hundred teams to the local offices to start surveillance and interviews on various known sympathizers," Knight stated. "We are concentrating on the six cities where the attacks have occurred, but are also hitting other cities of the same size in case more attacks are still to come there."

Penn added, "They have avoided the large cities as obvious targets since there is more security. By striking the smaller cities, they have hit hard at the very heart of the country. The panic and fear they have caused already will go a long way and create a debilitating paranoia. No one will know where or when the next attack will take place. People will put their lives on hold in lieu of safety."

"Gentlemen," the president said. "That is why this must end now. We have to find who sent these assassins into our midst to retaliate in such a way that no one will dare attack us again. These aren't American soldiers that are dying. They are men, women, and children." He wiped an angry tear from his face. He whispered,

"They look to us for protection. Go. Find these killers and protect our people."

The meeting dismissed, the men rose and left without a word.

***

Ian sat listening to the radio in complete shock. His country and his city were under attack. The death toll made all his troubles seem small by comparison. With all the added security and patrols scheduled around the city and the citywide curfew, hunting Marcus Davis would be all the more difficult. On the other hand, with the attention focused on finding terrorists, it might be easier to get to him. He would have to give the idea some thought.

His body still hurt, but other than the periodic stabbing pain in his ribs, the rest was manageable. The bruises covering his face were turning wondrous shades of yellow, purple, blue, and black. His lip and forehead were not nearly as swollen. The eye had opened a few centimeters. Ian held a baggie filled with ice against his face. He would not look normal again for a few days, if ever, but he still wanted to see JT.

Ian was fairly certain today was one of KeKe's days off. This would be his best chance to avoid seeing her. He wished he knew what kind of car she drove so he could cruise the lot to make sure she wasn't there. He decided to call the care facility and ask for her. When told she was not scheduled to work, he moved.

With his stomach growling like a hungry lion, Ian stopped at a diner. He bought a paper from a machine outside the door, then ordered a large breakfast. Ian took his time reading the horrid details of the most recent attacks. He wasn't looking for anything in particular; he was just following where the story told him to continue. But as he finished the article and folded the paper to set it aside, he found himself staring at a drawing of his likeness.

The first page of the second news section held an artist's rendering of the man accused of killing four men in a basement and assaulting a policeman as he fled the scene. The story said the killer was suspected of multiple murders and considered to be extremely dangerous. Ian studied his face. It had to have been from the policeman's perspective because the neighbor never saw his face. The beaten and bloodied face and the swollen eye gave a distorted impression. He wasn't sure if he would be easily recognizable to others, but when Ian looked at the drawing, he knew it was him. With nervous eyes, he scanned the dining room over the top of the paper then lifted it higher to cover his face.

He skimmed through the article and stopped at the description. The hair, build, and height were about right, but this article said the man walked with a limp and spoke with a lisp. Ian hadn't been aware of it, but with his lip split open he could see how it might sound that way. And he had been kicked enough that he could have been limping without noticing it.

If anyone pieced together that one of the deceased was wanted for murder and the description of his killer suspiciously matched the man whose family had been killed, he would be caught immediately. Eventually, someone would put it together, especially if Robinson was involved in this new case. Ian had to make his move to catch Davis while he was still able to do so. He would have to work around all the security on the streets. If he delayed and another attack happened, the city would be locked down tight. He had to hunt tonight.

Ian kept his head down while he finished his food. He had to be very careful. In fact, visiting JT might no longer be safe. Ian tried to think the process through. Even if someone thought he might be the killer, would they be able to find him this soon? Maybe. But this might also be the last time he could visit his son. If they hadn't figured out today, they certainly would by tomorrow.

A quick drive-by would be the first step. If no obvious police presence was in sight, Ian would pull into the parking lot and decide then whether to go in or not. With KeKe off, the other nurses might not be aware of how often Ian visited his son.

Just this one last time, Ian prayed. Things would be coming to an end soon, but he wanted to say goodbye to JT.

His arrival was later than normal, which was on purpose. From now on he needed to avoid routines. Nothing seemed out of the ordinary, so Ian drove into the parking lot and parked near the rear. He left the engine running while he scanned the lot. Would he know if there were any cars that didn't belong? Of course not. He had never paid any attention before. Besides, if the cops were inside and expected him, they wouldn't have any vehicles in sight. They would wait until he entered to spring the trap. That would have to happen as soon as he walked in, though, because the police wouldn't risk the safety of the patients.

The risk was too great and too much was at stake. If he was caught, his mission would never be completed. Ian shifted into drive but didn't lift his foot from the brake. The thought of not saying goodbye to JT was too strong a pull. He turned the car off and got out.

Putting the ball cap on and sunglasses in place, he walked toward the entrance as fast as his aching body allowed. He stopped with his hand on the outer door and looked through the glass. The lobby was empty. If the police were waiting inside, that would be by design.

Fighting to stay calm, Ian pulled the door open and stepped inside. The anticipation of being surrounded and cuffed weighed on his mind, making it difficult to move. He was surprised when he made it to his son's hallway unchallenged. They wouldn't be waiting in JT's room, would they?

Inching the door to his son's room open, he peered inside. The anxiety was so intense that Ian felt lightheaded. When he realized the room was empty except for his son, he gripped the knob tightly to keep from collapsing. Sucking in a quick breath of relief, he entered and closed the door.

Ian leaned against the door, waiting for his legs to find the strength to support his weight. He stood watching his son, saddened but no longer capable of tears. The events of the week had hardened Ian beyond feeling much emotion anymore.

He spent more time than intended reliving past happy memories with the boy. After a long silence, he explained his plan to his son, if only for his own benefit. The details unfolded as he went. Hearing them aloud made it easier to visualize and make changes. When Ian had his final hunt worked out, he was ready to say goodbye.

"I have one more target to complete my mission. I may succeed. I may not. Regardless, this will be the last time I'll be able to see you. I'm sorry. I wish it didn't have to be this way, but if, by some miracle, I'm successful, the police will be looking for me. It won't take long before they figure out I did it. I don't want to draw them here. I'll be leaving and won't see you again. I just want you to know that what I am doing, I'm doing for all of us. I love you. I pray for your recovery. I hope someday you will have a happy life. Who knows; maybe you'll get married and have a great kid like yourself." The sorrow hung like a weight from his heart.

"But do me a favor. Just tell him good things about his grandpa, okay?"

Ian leaned forward and kissed his son goodbye.

With his head hung low and his heart breaking anew, Ian turned and walked out the door.

37

Ian made it back to the house and began packing up whatever he would no longer need. He fully expected that if he was lucky enough to find Davis and end his mission tonight, he would not be coming back. Ian felt bad for old Mr. Jackson, but at least he made some money off the house and now the plumbing worked.

With his arms full, Ian was almost to the back door when he heard the knock. Startled, he froze. He hadn't heard anyone approach. Afraid any movement on the old creaky old floor would give up his presence, Ian stood still, allowing only his eyes to move. *What if it's the police?* After a long silence, Ian stepped back behind the kitchen counter and ducked out of sight from the door. The knock came again, harder this time.

Ian struggled, trying to think of an escape plan. He needed to sneak a look out a window to see what he was dealing with. He set his belongings down. The knock changed to pounding and a voice shouted out, "Mr. Kelly, I know you're in there. I saw you drive up and go in." It was a woman's voice. *Who could it be?* He didn't know any women, or at least none that would know his location.

"Open this door now or I'm going to get someone who can open it."

He recognized the voice now as KeKe's. She must have followed him from the nursing home. She was a threat, but why didn't she call the police? He put both hands on his head and tried to think. If she went away to get help, he could load up and be gone by the time she returned. He decided to wait her out.

The pounding stopped, as did her demands for him to open up. He was starting to think she was gone when he heard a noise at the kitchen window. To his surprise and dismay, KeKe had grabbed on to the window ledge and pulled herself up so she could look through the window. She was now looking directly at him.

"Mr. Kelly, you open the door right now or I swear I will break this window and crawl in."

Ian could see she was straining to hold on. Even so, her gaze did not waver. It was the tone of her final plea that made him move.

"Mr. Kelly, please."

Ian unlocked the door and stepped out. When he went around the corner, KeKe was hanging from the window ledge, dangling above the ground. *She must have jumped to catch the ledge,* he thought. She was definitely determined. Ian reached up and grabbed her waist with both hands and guided her to a soft landing. Upon lighting, KeKe spun. They stood facing each other, eyes locked, before Ian realized he still had his hands on her waist. He felt his face heat and pulled his hands away. He backed up, then turned and went inside. KeKe followed.

She didn't bother closing the door. When Ian stopped in the living room, he turned to face her. From a back pocket of her blue jeans, she pulled out the day's newspaper. It was folded so the sketch was the only thing showing. She looked from the paper to him and held it up for him to see.

"When I overheard you the other day with your son, you weren't talking about killing your son, were you? You were talking about doing this." She touched the sketch. "This is you, isn't it?"

Ian made no comment to either deny or confirm.

"You didn't think you were going to survive this, did you? From the looks of it, you barely did."

Again, Ian said nothing.

"Damn you, talk to me!"

He turned his head. He couldn't look at her.

In frustration, she let out a little scream and shoved him in the chest with both hands. It wasn't hard, but one hand landed on the right spot and he let out a cry, grabbed his injured ribs, and doubled over. He staggered back until he touched the wall, using it to stabilize himself so he didn't fall as he waited for the pain to cease.

"Oh, I'm so sorry. I didn't mean to hurt you." She followed him to the wall. He wanted to say he was fine and to leave him alone, but it hurt to draw a breath, let alone speak.

"Here, let me look."

He raised a hand to ward her off.

"Stop being so damned stubborn. If you fight me, you're going to get hurt again." She kept at him until he couldn't fend her off anymore. She got past his defenses and snagged the bottom of his t-shirt. She stopped then and forced her face in front of his. "Stop! Now! I'm going to take a look and I would prefer not to hurt you. Not that you don't deserve it, but I'm going to try not to."

He gave up and raised his hands to his sides. KeKe lifted the shirt gently.

"Oh, shit."

She glanced up at him and then back to the bruise, which took up nearly his entire side. The assorted colors could only be described as angry. Ian jumped at her touch.

"Did that hurt?"

"Not really. I was anticipating pain."

"Tell me when it hurts."

Her fingertips glided over the discoloration, starting from the top down. Every few inches, she probed slightly. The first two were just sore, the third caused a wince, and the fourth made him jump even though he was prepared. She sighed like a mother checking a child for an injury. He waited for her to tell him to stop being a baby, but she examined him in silence.

She pressed her fingers against his bruises twice more, and both were painful.

"I think you have two cracked ribs. You really should get them x-rayed. If there's any bone splinters on the inside, you could puncture an organ. I can tape them for you but if it's more severe, you need a hospital. I have no way of telling."

She backed away, letting his shirt fall back in place. Her arms crossed under her breasts as she studied him, her lip curled under her top teeth. Then she shook her head and threw her arms in the air.

"Why are you here?" Ian asked.

"I-I, I'm not sure really. I was curious, I guess. I thought you were going to hurt your son and I wanted to protect him. Then when I saw you yesterday, I knew something else was going on. I guess I was being nosy, but I wanted to help. Don't ask me why."

She bit her lower lip then turned away from him.

He wanted to ask her just that. He chose an alternate, if not more important question instead.

"What are you going to do now?"

"I don't know that, either. I suppose I should call the police, shouldn't I?"

But the question sounded more like she was looking for confirmation, not an answer.

"If that's what you need to do, go. I won't try to stop you. I won't be here, of course, but do what you feel you have to."

"And you wouldn't care? And if the police caught you, would

you make them kill you? Is that what this is all about—your pain? Or do you feel guilty about what happened to your family?"

His eyes avoided hers when she said 'guilty.'

Ian ignored the question and walked past her to the kitchen. He pulled a bottle of water from the small refrigerator.

"Would you like something to drink?" He held the bottle out to her.

She looked completely dumbfounded.

"What?" KeKe slapped the bottle out of his hand. It hit the wall, dropped to the card table and rolled. Ian caught it. "We're talking about your life, or the end of it, and you calmly ask me if I want something to drink? What is wrong with you? No, I don't want something to drink. I want you to explain to me how I'm going to tell your son when he wakes up that his father is dead—shot down by the police—because he had a vendetta to kill the people responsible for hurting his family."

She stepped forward as if trying to corner an opponent in a boxing match. "If you throw your life away, you give up on your son. Don't you understand that? Hope is the only thing he has. There is always hope that he will wake up one day and look for a familiar face. He will need that face to get through the trauma of remembering how he got there. That's your obligation—your duty— to your son: to help him recover and try to fit back into the world, a world where random violence has taken his mother and brother. Do you really want him to have to face that alone?"

"No, but he will have one good friend to help him through."

Her jaw moved up and down, but no sound came out.

"Oh, no you don't, you selfish bastard. You're not dumping this burden on me. You take the chicken shit way out and expect everyone else to pick up your pieces. No. Uh-uh. No way."

She glared at him, daring him to make another stupid comment. The hands on her hips had curled into fists.

"Why are you here?" Ian asked again.

"No. Don't change the subject."

"Tell me."

"No. It's none of your damn business."

"KeKe, why are you here?"

"Why should you care? You're gonna be dead soon anyway. And don't call me KeKe." She pointed one finger at him. "You don't have the right. I'm Ms. Brogan to you."

"Ms. Brogan? Not Nurse Brogan?"

"What?"

"Never mind. I'm sorry."

"You're sorry? Don't tell *me* you're sorry. Go tell your son."

"I'm sorry I'm making you so mad. I just don't understand *why* I'm making you so mad."

"You don't…you don't understand why I'm mad? Of course you don't, you pin-headed, self-centered moron. You're a man. You're only capable of thinking of yourself. You don't care what you do, or how it affects others, or who you hurt, for that matter. You just do what you want, when you want, regardless of the consequences."

She stomped her foot and turned away. "Ahhh!" she screamed in frustration. "I don't even know why I came here. It's been a complete waste of time. You want to kill yourself? Go ahead. Why should I care?"

"Why do you care?"

"'Cause you just totally piss me off."

"I can see that. I'm sorry."

KeKe stood with her back to Ian, shaking her head and letting the steam escape. After a minute, she faced him, her voice softer.

"It's just that, well, I've seen you with JT. I've heard you talk to him. I-I kinda listen sometimes from the hall as you talk about the memories you've shared. The good times you had with your family, and-and, those amazing memories, and I…"

Tears began cascading down her face. She attempted to wipe them away as fast as they fell.

"I think it would be a shame that after he wakes up, he'll be haunted by the fact that you won't be there to talk with him about them anymore. How do you think he'll react, finding out his father is in prison? It would be such a waste. Don't you see that?"

Without warning, KeKe flung herself against his chest and cried. It took all of Ian's effort to keep the scream from escaping. Gently he put his arms around her and held her while she cried. He was confused by her actions and the raw emotion with which she made her plea. They didn't even know each other. Why was she getting involved?

Feeling KeKe in his arms brought back a flood of memories when he'd held his wife in this same way. The time she had hit the mailbox with the car. The time she turned his Notre Dame t-shirt pink. When she told him she was pregnant with Jonathon Thomas.

Before he realized it, his eyes had begun leaking, too.

38

They stood that way for the better part of five minutes. When KeKe stepped back, they both wiped their eyes, attempting to be inconspicuous.

Ian opened the refrigerator and took out a second bottle of water.

"Here," he said. "Let's sit down and talk."

KeKe sat and accepted the water. They took long drinks; not just for thirst, but to help compose themselves.

"I don't understand why you're crying."

She waved his comment off. "Tell me what's happened. How did you get those bruises?"

"I'll tell you if you tell me why you're here."

"Okay. Deal. But you first."

So Ian told her. He left nothing out, starting from his drive to Colorado right up to the gunfight in the basement.

"What you're saying is that they captured you, beat you, and you feared for your life. That makes it self-defense."

Ian shook his head. "Except that I went there with the idea I was going to kill this Jervis. I'm not trying to sugarcoat what I've done. I killed those men out of necessity, sure, but I would have tried to kill Jervis, no matter what."

"I'm sorry, but I see it differently. I want to spin it my way, if you don't mind. I don't want to think of you as a bad man."

"That's kind of you, but you took a very dangerous gamble coming here alone. What if I wasn't the person you think I am? You could've gotten yourself killed."

"I had a good feeling about you. I sensed that you were in trouble and needed help. No matter what, I think you're a good father and that counts for something in my book."

"I'd like to think I was at a good father, at least. I know what I am and what my intentions were. It's too late for me to undo what I've done. If I survive, I will have to live with that for the rest of my life."

"But you don't have to do this anymore. You've already proven yourself. Just let the police deal with this last guy. Call and tell them this Davis is back in town."

Ian watched her as she spoke. There was an anguish in her expression that was born from some deeper emotion. She was a very attractive woman and he could see that her passion ran through her soul. If their meeting were under different circumstances, he would enjoy getting to know her. But it wasn't, he reminded himself. And he would never stop loving or thinking about his wife. He could never hope to find another love like that. It wouldn't be fair to anyone who came afterward.

"Why are you here? Are you some self-appointed guardian angel who tries to save lost souls?"

KeKe bristled at the slight mocking tone. Her words came out harsh. "No. It's because I'm a fool. It's because I allowed myself this fantasy that you might be a decent person. My reason is the most basic there could be: I liked you. And even knowing it might never be anything more than friendship, I still feel it would be a waste if you throw your life away.

"I know you're thinking that you don't even know me, but sometimes things just click inside. There's no rhyme or reason, but they do. Don't get me wrong; I never would have been so bold if I didn't think your situation was desperate. But there it is. I liked the way you were with your son. You were hurting and my heart went out to you. I wanted to get to know you better. I'm sorry. It was nothing more than a fantasy; more like a schoolgirl crush. There are so few really decent men out there and I just felt you were one."

"Until now that you found out the truth, right? That in fact I'm not so decent? I've killed people and may try to do it again?"

She hung her head, accepting the facts. "I wish you hadn't, but I do understand why you would want to."

"A decent man would have let the law handle it. Instead, I became the law. I'm sorry, Ms. Brogan. I can't be what you want. My soul is tarnished; my heart is numb. I have nothing left to give anyone, even if I wanted to."

"I think you're wrong. I think it might take time, but decent men always have a lot left to give. No matter what you say, that's how I choose to see you. And for God's sake, I cried on your chest. Call me KeKe."

He smiled. She was certainly funny, if somewhat unpredictable. "Okay KeKe." He paused a beat, then said, "Where's KeKe come from, anyways?"

"It's a nickname I picked up decades ago. I'll tell you about it someday, if you live that long."

"KeKe, I'm not sure what my future will be, but if I have one, I promise to give your words some thought."

She was suddenly angry again. "You do have a future, mister, and it's with your son. Don't think of my words. Think of him."

She stood up abruptly.

"I think I've said more than enough. I hope common sense takes hold of you. Your son needs you and I would certainly miss seeing you with him. I'd better go. I'm sorry for the intrusion. Oh, hell! No, I'm not. See a doctor. Bye."

Before Ian could say another word, she was out the door. He stood and watched her leave, confused by the visit, what she might do and by his own feelings. She was certainly a fireball. He liked that. As she drove away, Ian pictured his wife's face and sadness took him again.

39

After KeKe left, Ian unpacked what he needed for the night and then put the rest in the trunk of the car. Suddenly, his urgency to leave was gone. He decided to stay one more night.

Before Ian lay down on his bedroll, he turned on the small twelve-inch TV he brought from home to watch the news. He wasn't expecting to see anything about his activities but he was hoping not to hear there had been new attacks on the city. The story was a replay of a report earlier in the day. The reporter was in mid-sentence when she stopped. She was live on scene, covering some story, when her emotions had gotten the better of her. She tried to compose herself.

"I'm sorry. I'm sorry," she repeated as she tried to wipe the tears away with the hand that held the microphone. "I've never seen such atrocity. Who would do this to innocent people? There were children in there. Lots of children…" And she lost it again.

The camera scene cut back to the studio and a solemn pair of nighttime news anchors seemed at a loss for what to say next. The slender man was first to recover. The woman lowered her head to avoid the camera.

"There is no doubt now that Toledo is under siege by some yet unknown terrorist organization. The FBI has descended on the city and has taken over the investigation. They have yet to make a statement, but we expect Special Agent in Charge, Madison Atwater, to make one any minute. We have a crew standing by at One Government Center."

He took a deep breath and the camera moved in closer to cover that the emotional female anchor had gotten up and left the desk.

"To recap: today, just before closing, bombs exploded in six different public library branches around the area." He listed the bomb sites. "There is no word yet on how many casualties there are, but estimates put the number of patrons in the downtown branch alone at several hundred, not counting staff. The bombs detonated at approximately the same time, leading investigators to believe they were synchronized with timers. Speculation is that one or more persons entered each branch, stayed for a while and left, leaving behind a book bag with the explosive devices inside."

His voice grew weaker with each sentence.

"Three of the buildings caught fire and crews rushed to the scenes and quickly gained control of the blazes. The most destructive blast occurred at the downtown branch, where a section of the roof on the newly remodeled four-story building, collapsed.

"Police, fire rescue, and EMT crews are working feverishly to clear the debris and searching for survivors.

"Violence around the city has escalated over the past three days."

The man stopped talking and put a finger to his ear.

"I've just been told the Mayor will address the city in five minutes. We send you now to Rob Wiercinzski at City Hall.

The screen changed to a view of City Hall. The camera drew in closer on a tall man with serious eyes and a nervous manner about him. A row of sweat beads lined his forehead. He nodded at the camera and started speaking.

Ian turned off the set and lay back on the bedroll. He stared at the ceiling for a while. One of libraries destroyed was the local suburban branch Margo went to once a week. She loved to read. He wondered if she would have gotten caught in the blast if she were still alive. Would Ian have taken up arms against terrorists to avenge her death then, too? What had this world become? He couldn't believe people could kill so indiscriminately. For what purpose? They obviously felt that whatever the reason, it was justified.

A new thought made him cringe. They had killed for a purpose, but hadn't he done the same thing? He was no different than the terrorists. He killed because he felt he had been wronged and wanted to take his revenge, but wasn't that their claim as well? No. He shook the thought off. No matter what the comparisons, Ian would never be like one of them. His hatred was against three individuals, none of them innocent. The terrorists' hatred ran deeper and they didn't care who they hurt. No, he was not a terrorist. He was a killer, yes, but there was a difference.

40

The morning news was full of facts about the explosions. Day three of the siege had claimed more than two hundred confirmed dead so far, with the potential to add to that number from the many severely wounded. Crews were still sifting through the rubble, searching for survivors.

The mayor announced the city was now under a strict curfew. Those who had to work past the curfew needed to apply for a pass at City Hall. Employers, like newspapers and medical facilities, or any company with a third shift, were being asked to submit lists of key personnel who had to be at work after curfew. Other companies were being encouraged to shut down by ten. The biggest losers in the curfew fight would be bars and all-night diners that made the bulk of their money during the late hours.

Gripping fear had the entire city ready to explode. The National Guard was called in to help patrol the streets. The mayor threatened Martial Law if there were problems with people disregarding the curfew. He wanted the city shut down tight.

Finding Davis would be impossible for Ian now, let alone killing him. Ian doubted the pool hall would be open. Regardless, he was going out tonight. He didn't care about his pain and wasn't going to worry about the patrols. His opportunities would be extremely limited from here on. At least he wanted to get a look at the pool hall.

He showered, dressed, and packed everything back up. Taking one last look about the house, Ian closed the door for what he thought would be the last time.

In the car, Ian called the care facility and asked for Nurse Brogan. When she came on line, he said, "Hi, it's Ian, ah, Kelly. I was wondering if the police are there."

"No."

"Would you tell me if they were?"

Silence descended over the line. For a moment, Ian thought she had hung up. Then he heard her breathe. Thinking the silence was her answer, he was about to hang up when she spoke. "Yes, I would.

Come see your son. He needs you." Then she did hang up.

No longer feeling KeKe was a threat, Ian drove straight to see JT.

Except for JT, the room was empty when he arrived. The only change was a small bouquet of flowers on the table near the bed. Ian stared at them for a few seconds before moving toward them. There was no card.

"I thought they would help brighten the room," the voice behind him said.

Ian spun to see KeKe standing in the doorway. Her brown hair was swept up and pinned to the top of her head, revealing the long, slender lines of her face that ended at the point of her chin. Her face didn't display the usual KeKe-like smile or the sparkle in her eyes, but there did seem to be peace in her manner. She brushed past him without a glance, lifted the small vase, and held it in front of JT.

"When he wakes up, I want him to see beauty. Maybe it will help him to overcome all the ugliness in his life. And the fact he no longer has a father."

The verbal blow struck hard.

"Breathe in the scent, sweet boy. Let the fragrance awaken a nice memory that will bring you home before your father does something stupid."

She held the flowers in front of JT for another moment before placing them back on the table. "Well, if anything, maybe the horror that has hit this city will prevent you from adding to it."

"Ms. Brogan, er, KeKe… I'm sorry…"

"You're sorry for what? For throwing your life away? Don't tell me, tell him. I don't have any vested interest in your life. In fact, I take back all the nice, happy thoughts I had about you. I was wrong. You're not a decent man at all. I'm the one who's sorry. I'm sorry I ever thought you might be different; someone I could have fantasized about being with. Of course, I knew it was just a fantasy at the time and that nothing would ever come of it, but it was my fantasy, and now you've killed that, too. Evidently, killing is all you're good for."

Her words struck like a barrage of automatic weapon fire. Each word slammed into him, sapping life energy. She was right about one thing: he had killed that bright, friendly person who used to look after his son. She would never again flash that wondrous smile in his direction. A week ago, he wouldn't have cared; now he felt the loss wholeheartedly. There was no going back and no longer any need to. Ian drew himself up, and in a voice harsher and colder than he would have thought possible, he said, "If you'll excuse me, Nurse Brogan, I'd like to spend some time alone with my son."

Her face reddened and her eyes narrowed. She rushed past him, hurt showing on her face. The door closed hard in a symbol of finality. Ian stood there, staring at the door for several minutes before he moved to JT's side.

"Well, JT, it's almost over. Just one to go. I think I'm gonna do some recon tonight. If I see him, I'll take him out. Just so you know, if that happens, I may not be back again. I wanted you to know it wouldn't be because I forgot you. I will never forget you. How could I? But with all the extra patrols out and the curfew, finishing the mission unscathed is no longer a realistic possibility. But then, I never expected it to be."

Ian ran his hand through JT's hair.

"I just want you to know I love you. I should have been there for you. This is my way of making it up to you. To all of you. After what I've done, I don't imagine I'll be seeing your brother and mother in heaven. Do me a favor. Someday when you get there, tell them I love them, too."

Not knowing what else to say, Ian sat down and forced old happy memories past his mind's eye like he was watching home movies. He might not have a chance to relive them again.

41

Ian exited the facility just before eight. A different nurse looked in on JT after Nurse Brogan left. She stayed out of sight the rest of the time Ian was there. In a way, her absence saddened him, but he knew it was for the best.

Stopping at a pharmacy, Ian bought tape and gauze. He drove home, and following directions he found on the internet using his smart phone, he attempted to wrap his ribs. He ran his hands up and down the wrap when he finished. The bandage would help some, but he couldn't afford any more physical encounters. If he couldn't get a clean shot at Davis, he would abort. Swallowing extra pain meds, he left the house.

Taking the expressway, Ian was soon across town. He took a pass by the pool hall to make sure it was open. It was in an older one-story brick building with small windows located near the top of the wall. There was no way to see in except for the double glass doors at the front corner of the building.

It was still too early for anything clandestine, so Ian drove down the alley where he left his coat and guns the night before. He slowed as he passed the garage and checked the yards. He couldn't see anyone watching, so he stopped behind a garage two down from the one he needed. Driving the car into the alley was a risk, but out of necessity, one he was willing to take. Someone might see him climbing up on the roof, get his license plate number and call the cops. Of course, that would only lead the police back to the woman he bought the car from.

He walked past the garage. Seeing no one, Ian turned in a slow circle and checked out each yard and house that had an angle where someone could see him. It looked clear, but he couldn't be sure. Deciding to go for it, Ian stepped up on the crossbar of the fence and with great and painful effort, pulled himself up to the roof. With his head above the edge, he saw the coat was still there. He scrambled up and crawled toward the bundle, trying to stay low. Sliding the coat on, he checked to make sure nothing was left behind before he retraced his path.

Lowering himself to the fence, he missed the bar but was unable to hold his weight, falling on his hands and knees on the gravel. The fall seemed to reawaken his other sore spots. He hobbled to the car and drove off. Two blocks away, he pulled over and rested until the pain diminished.

When he was able, Ian got out of the car and pulled boxes of 9mm and .22 bullets from the trunk. He drove to a nearby park and loaded both weapons. When finished, he covered everything with the coat and dined on granola bars and an apple and washed it down with bottled water.

The sun was setting. Curfew was less than an hour away. He donned the coat and pocketed the guns and ammo, then strolled to a garbage can to stretch his body. He dumped his trash and looked around. The park was peaceful, reminding him that soon he would have his lasting peace. With one deep exhalation, Ian returned to the car and drove back to the pool hall.

The pool hall appeared to be open, judging from the cars in the lot and the lights on inside. Ian swung around and drove past again. This time, he pulled over to the curb and stopped. Through the window he could see two black men playing at a table near the door. In the next row, a tall, skinny white kid with long dreads played alone. No one else was in sight, but five cars were in the lot. If one belonged to the owner or an employee, there might be others inside, too. The only way to make sure was to venture in, but he wasn't ready for that yet.

He turned down a residential side street. Pulling into an alley, Ian reversed and parked on the street with a view of the front door of the pool hall. There he sat and watched until past curfew. During that time, a few other cars arrived and others left. The exchange left only two cars in the lot. Two hours after curfew began, a car pulled up and dropped off two men, then left. Ian found that to be very curious. Could one of them be Davis? How many others were inside? Ian began to picture what his odds would be if he confronted Davis with the others in the pool hall. Even if they didn't intervene, they would be witnesses. One way or another, Ian knew he was going down tonight.

After the men entered the hall, someone came to the front door, pulled shades down over the glass, turned the *Open* sign around to *Closed*, and locked the door. Seconds later, the outside lights went dark. Ian's mind began reeling. Now what was he going to do? There had to be a way to get inside without making a full-frontal assault.

While he tried to think of a way to get to Davis, a military jeep with four National Guardsmen inside, rolled down the main street. The city was taking the curfew seriously. Ian slid down in his seat and watched. They stopped for an instant and one of the Guardsmen hopped out and tried the pool hall door. When it didn't budge, he climbed back in the jeep and they moved on. Ian would have to be careful.

After the jeep drove off, Ian got out of the car and, leaving his weapons behind for now, crept to the street corner. He crouched and peered down the main street in both directions. To the left, the receding taillights of the jeep were red pinholes against the black backdrop of night. To the right, headlights appeared in the distance, but he judged them to be a long way off.

He bolted across the street, ran past the pool hall and a cement alley behind it, stopping behind a bush on the side of the corner house. His breathing came in short, painful gasps, his ribs not approving of the exertion. From the bush, Ian could see the entire length of the rear of the pool hall. A metal door was at the far end of the building. A light attached to the building hung over the door, but it wasn't on. Ian hunched down and waited, his legs keeping track of time for him. Several position changes later, the rear door opened.

Two white men exited and stood under the darkened light fixture. Their loud voices carried a long way in the eerily quiet night. One man fired up a lighter and lit a cigarette. When he passed it to the next man, Ian knew it was more than a regular cigarette. A black man joined them for the second round of passes. Now Ian wished he had brought his gun, even though he had no idea if one of the men was Davis, or, if in fact, he was inside. All he knew for sure about Davis was he was white. The scene did give him an idea, though.

He waited for the men to finish their joint and move back inside before breaking cover and retracing his steps to the car. This time when he crossed the street, headlights approached in the distance, perhaps less than a quarter mile away. He sprinted past his car and sought cover between two houses. From there, he saw the police car turn down the street and flick on the spotlight.

Ian backed away until he came to the fence at the rear of the house. Climbing it into the backyard, he walked around the house and waited. The spotlight probed the spaces between each house and moved slowly on. Minutes later, Ian scaled the fence and moved cautiously to the front porch. The police car was two-thirds of the way down the block. Ian became anxious, having to wait for the car to turn the corner. He had to be more careful. He was too close to finishing what he started to get caught now. If the cop saw him cross the street, he would stay in the area for a while.

A short jog brought him back to the car. Ian opened the door and slid across the seat, lying down. He was thankful for having the forethought to take out the dome light bulb. While he waited, Ian tried to picture how he wanted the events to unfold.

His plan was to find a closer undercover vantage point to watch the rear door. Hopefully, the men would come back out again. When the men were about to go back in, Ian would dash for the door before anyone could respond. Holding the grenade that he purchased from Bonzo in one hand and the gun in the other, he could control the situation and determine if Davis was one of the men inside. Of course, the pin would have to be pulled for the grenade to be a real threat. Hopefully, he didn't blow himself up before he got inside.

The grenade should give him their instant cooperation. He had no desire to hurt anyone other than Marcus Davis, but then, that would be up to them. The problem was that Ian had no idea what Davis looked like. His only hope was that those inside would give him up and one shot would end it. He would put the pin back in the grenade and walk out into the street, not caring any longer if he were discovered.

Ian toyed with the idea of suicide bombing Davis. That way, both of their lives would be over. He could avoid being captured and going to trial and any publicity that would follow, at least while he was alive. However, that plan would mean taking out others who might be innocents and didn't deserve to die by his hand. There was also the possibility of something going wrong and missing Davis. Suicide bombing didn't offer second chances.

Lifting his head enough to see if the street was clear, Ian crawled out of the car. Staying low, he made his way to the trunk and popped it. Instantly, the light came on and to his panicked mind, it seemed as though the entire area was lit up. He lowered the lid so fast that it locked. He had forgotten to remove the trunk light.

He froze, hoping the quick flash of light and the slamming of the trunk were both much brighter and louder in his mind than in reality. The crunch of a tire on gravel drew his attention to the alleyway in front of him. Ian dropped to the ground behind the trunk.

The sneaky cop had turned off his lights and circled the block for a second look.

Ian was in a panic. Had he been seen? His mind raced for a solution. Glancing out from the underside of the car, he could see the cruiser had stopped at the end of the alley only one house-length away from where he hid.

His fear exploded when the car door opened. The heavy, accelerated thumping of his heart made his bruised chest hurt. The officer stepped from his vehicle and peered over the roof of his car. The cop moved toward the houses and started walking down the sidewalk. A bright cone of light shone as the cop swept his Maglite from the house to the street. It encircled Ian's car for an instant, then moved back toward the house. If the light was moving, it meant he had not yet been seen.

In his mind, Ian believed the policeman could hear him breathe. He was afraid to move. This close, any tiny noise could send an alert. Ian had no weapon, and in a few more steps, no cover. He would have to risk moving to the side of the car.

As slowly as possible, Ian stretched out one leg and placed the toe of his shoe around the tire. His foot landed without a sound. The policeman moved closer. Ian lifted the other leg. He rushed this one. The cone of light was moving back in his direction. He was going to run out of time if he didn't hurry.

Just then, a crackle of sound broke the quiet and made Ian jump.

"All units…officer—make that officers, in need of assistance. All units respond."

"126. What's the situation?"

"Multiple gunshots. Two locations. Officers under fire."

The dispatcher gave the locations.

"Roger. Moving to the Central Avenue site. 126 out."

The man swept his light around once more, then jogged back to the squad car. Ian collapsed to the ground in relief as the car sped away.

His heart pounded a furious cadence against his chest. *I'm really not cut out for this shit.*

42

Ian fought the urge to drive off. He might not find Davis again. If he was in the pool hall, Ian would have to kill him tonight. His luck would run out eventually and he had been lucky so far. Besides, driving at this time of night would draw too much attention. He was safer staying put, even if he did nothing.

However, he knew he couldn't stay there. The cop could come back at any time. Ian might be making his escape from shooting Davis and run right into the policeman. As much of a gamble as it was, Ian opted to move the car to the other side of the main street.

With the headlights off, Ian pulled up to the corner. A glance in both directions showed the way to be clear, so he turned left, drove a half block and went right, parking in front of a boarded-up house on the street behind the pool hall.

Ian studied the surrounding homes to see if anyone was watching. When he was as sure as he could be that he wasn't being observed, he climbed out. Unlocking the trunk, he held the lid down this time to prevent the light from coming on. Snaking his arm inside until he could grasp the light bulb, he twisted it out. Again, he felt relief, but also a little absurd. You had to be smart to pull off crimes without getting caught. Wasn't it always the little things that tripped up most criminals? One simple mistake had almost cost him.

Is that what he was? A criminal? Yeah, he thought, that's exactly what he'd become. So be it. He slid into his coat and loaded his pockets, hoping it would be for the last time. He started to close the lid, but had a thought and lifted it again. He reached in and fumbled through one of the duffel bags and withdrew the grenade. Staring at the unstable explosive, a chill played a concerto along his vertebrae. If he couldn't get inside one way... He slid the grenade into his pocket and hoped it didn't go off until he was ready. He shut the trunk lid.

Ian moved to a point behind the pool hall where he could see if anyone came out the back door and possibly catch a glimpse inside. Now it had become a waiting game. He sneaked a look at his cell phone and saw it was almost two. Sunrise was a good four hours away. He did not want to have to come back tomorrow. No, if he had to, he would use the grenade to blow the door. This was going to end tonight.

After an hour with no movement from the building, Ian had taken to sitting on the ground. He could no longer find a comfortable position his legs would agree with. From this position, his reactions might be slower, but it would keep his legs from cramping so he could respond when needed.

Staying awake was the next problem. His head kept bobbing and he felt so sleepy he had to fight off the desire to go back to the car and nap.

His head had just snapped up, his eyes fluttering open, when he heard voices. Ian jumped up and almost ran toward the building. His brain was foggy. He rubbed his eyes to wipe away the sleep. The men were back. He settled back to the ground just as one man glanced his way. Ian must have dozed for a minute because he never heard or saw the door open.

Outside the back door, the same two men as before stood passing a joint between them. They were talking in low tones and Ian couldn't make out their words. He felt his muscles tense as he grew anxious for the right moment to make his move. He was on edge with anticipation, ready to spring, yet unable to move. The joint had to be six inches long for it to be taking that long to finish.

As soon as the first man reached for the door, Ian pushed forward. He pulled the pin from the grenade. The door opened and Ian walked faster. By the time the second man was through the door, Ian forced his legs into a full sprint. The door began to swing shut.

Ian began to fear he wouldn't make it in time. The door moved in slow motion, yet he seemed to be moving even slower. The light seeping from inside was slightly more than a sliver. Ian stretched as far as he could and stuck the gun barrel inside the door before it shut, but the metal-on-metal contact rang loud. As Ian pried the door open and stepped inside, all eyes turned in his direction. Seeing the gun, everyone scattered and ducked.

Ian stepped inside, letting the door close.

"Freeze!" he screamed. "Don't anybody move. I'm holding a hand grenade."

A hand holding a gun emerged above one of the pool tables. Pointing it in Ian's general direction, the shooter fired repeatedly. Others added their own bullets to the barrage. Obviously, they didn't believe him about the grenade.

With wild shots smacking into the walls around him, Ian was forced to dive for cover. With his heart pounding, he landed on his knee, which sent a shard of pain through his body. The collision with the floor was enough to jar the grenade from his grasp and it rolled a few feet away.

His breath caught in his throat. Looking across the room, he realized he was now at eye level with everyone else. While they adjusted their shots to fire under the pool tables, Ian crawled desperately toward the grenade. Bullets pinged off the floor around him as he reached the explosive. Bonzo had warned him the grenade might either be a dud or unstable and could go off at any time. Now was not a good time to find out which he had.

A bullet ricocheted off the floor in front of his face, causing him to flinch back. *How much time had elapsed?*

"Shit! He really does have a grenade!" one gunman shouted.

With a cry of alarm and feeling like his bladder was about to release, Ian swatted the grenade along the floor toward the shooters.

Leaping to his feet, he grabbed the side of a pool table and lifted with all his strength, flipping on its side. A bullet tore a path across his calf before the table shut down the shooter's line of sight. Another grooved the top of his shoulder when he stood.

Ian dropped to the floor just as an explosion ripped apart the room. Someone screamed. Ian thought it might have been himself. The shock waves moved the pool table. While there was still smoke filling the room, Ian crawled to his left to change his location. He kept going until he was across the room from where he had been. One of the men had been shooting from there before the explosion, but there was no sign of him now. Ian kept going.

The ringing in his ears began to subside, replaced by screaming. The survivors were shouting and swearing. Then the gunfire started again, directed toward his previous location. Ian crawled further along the wall where the tables were either blown apart or tipped on their sides.

Ian reached a line of tables near the front door that offered cover. He lay down and inched toward the end of one of them. When he could see past it, he saw three men shooting blindly over the tables. Another battered body lay lifeless against the wall.

Ian reached his gun around the table. The barrel struck a wooden leg as it cleared, alerting one of the men to Ian's presence. He yelled and spun on Ian, giving him little choice but to fire. He released two shots that hit the man in the chest, pitching him back into the next man. He stood to shoot over his friend, but Ian shot faster and dropped him as well.

A voice from the far end of the tables cried out. "Don't shoot! I give up! Don't shoot!"

"Toss your gun out."

"You gonna shoot me if I do?"

Ian thought of a better approach. He also knew he didn't have much time left. Someone was bound to have heard the explosion and called the police.

"What's your name?"

"Desmond. Desmond Jenkins."

"I'll let you live if you tell me where Marcus Davis is."

"Marcus? He gone."

"Gone? What'd ya mean, gone?"

"He run out the front door after the explosion."

"Shit," Ian said softly. "Where can I find him? Where's he stay?"

"Man, I don't know."

Ian started backing away. Something in the man's voice raised the hairs on the back of Ian's neck. He had slid backward to the end of the pool table when the man made his move. He had been buying time to get a shooting position on Ian and he jumped up and screamed as he fired. He shot several rounds before realizing his target was gone.

He turned, searching, and when he found Ian, it was too late.

"Nice try." Ian fired twice. The body lurched back against the table and hung there. The man tried to raise his gun, but Ian stood and shot him once more.

Ian stared at the carnage for a moment. Had Jenkins been telling the truth? He walked to the front door and pushed. It opened. Someone had gone out that way. Looking around the room he tried to form a mental picture of who was missing. He tried to remember, but his mind was too aware of time passing. Then, it came to him, the guy with the dreads was missing. He felt mentally and physically depleted. *All for nothing,* he thought.

Using a towel he found on the floor near his feet, he rubbed it in the man's blood and wrote on the bottom of the table. As he worked he thought about the absurdity of taking the time to leave his message. Who would care? It would serve him right to get caught, yet, still he continued, knowing someone had to have called in the explosion. Standing, he tossed the towel and read his script. *They won't kill again. -A.*

They won't, but Davis is still alive.

He was out the rear door and heading down the street as the sirens wailed nearby, filling the night. A small crowd of people milled around on the street, curious about the destruction. Ian slipped the gun into his pocket and kept his head down.

"What happened?" asked one man.

"Damn druggies blew themselves up."

With adrenaline still coursing through him and his ears still ringing, he walked at a fast pace down the side street toward the car. He slid into the front seat, trying not to throw up. The combination of the loud, violent attack and the near-death experience had rattled his nerves.

Keeping the headlights off, he drove away. Someone was apt to have noticed his license plate number. If he had succeeded in killing Davis, he wouldn't have cared if he had seen him, but his job was still unfinished. Ian needed to survive another day. The thought of continuing the hunt added to his exhaustion. How much longer would this go on? How much longer could this go on before he was caught or killed?

Needing to find a place to park until morning, Ian kept to the side streets until he reached the next main road. Across that street, he found his hiding place: a small two-story apartment building. Ian checked for clearance and then darted to the other side of the street. He drove to the back of the lot and parked.

As he let his weight sink into the seat, the pain released. He peeled off his coat and fingered his new wounds. In the dimly lit parking lot, Ian could barely see them, but they burned. He stepped out of the car and dug through the trunk for the first aid kit and then lay down in the back seat. He cleansed and bandaged his injuries by feel. Though both bullet wounds probably required stitches, the tight wrap Ian bound them with would have to do. He dry-swallowed some pain pills. Placing his hands behind his head, he stared at the roof of the car.

He lay there, exhausted yet not ready for sleep. Had Jenkins told him the truth? Did Davis really make his escape, or was he one of the men Ian had killed? He might never know for sure now. Why hadn't he taken the time to check for IDs? He should have done that instead of wasting his time writing that stupid message in blood. What was he thinking? But he hadn't been thinking, that was the problem. With the adrenaline rush and bloodlust upon him, no rational thought could have penetrated. That was dumb. Now he had to continue hunting and no longer had a lead to follow.

He let out a long breath, his body suddenly feeling very heavy. "I'm sorry, JT. I almost had him."

Minutes afterward he drifted to sleep and dreamed about KeKe.

43

He was awakened by the sound of a car door shutting. He blinked away the sleep and momentary confusion and peeked through the car window. A red compact car was backing out two parking spots away. When it was gone, Ian opened the door and stepped out into the unseasonably cool air, stretching. Moving both hurt and felt good at the same time.

With the apartment building coming to life, Ian got back in his car and drove off. Curiosity kept trying to talk him into cruising past the pool hall, but common sense won out. Ian took a roundabout route back to his safe house. He hadn't planned on returning, but now that his mission would continue, he needed a safe haven again.

Taking only the first aid kit and the duffel bag containing his clothes and toiletries, Ian went inside and showered. Checking the wounds again, he put on more triple antibiotic cream and wrapped them tight. He stared into the steamed mirror, trying to recognize the face that looked back. He gave up, too exhausted to care who it was. Part of him wanted to lie down and sleep forever, but he wanted to see JT again first. Sleep would have to wait.

He repacked the car and drove to the diner. Ian bought a paper and ordered up a large breakfast. While he waited for his food, Ian read about the most recent terrorist attacks.

The paper highlighted what it called 'The Fourth Day Under Siege'. The report chronicled the events in order, listing the number of casualties from each attack. The article went on to say three other cities had gunned down terrorist cells as they attempted similar attacks there. The death toll throughout the country had risen to well over nine hundred, with almost half of that total being local.

Evidently, whoever was planning the assaults here had decided to target policemen this time. Eight city policeman, four deputy sheriffs, and three state troopers had been shot last night; perhaps that was the call the officer who pursued him last night had responded to. Five of the officers had died. Three were in various conditions in local hospitals. The others had been treated and released, their injuries minor. Another seven officers had been shot at, but did not sustain injuries.

Witnesses described the shooters' vehicles as black SUVs. Two different people stated there were at least two men inside each one.

Ian was angered by the attacks. He hoped the assassins were caught and killed and not brought to trial. The police probably wanted it that way, too. But in his outrage at the events that had taken so many innocent lives, Ian tried to discern what made his attacks any different. Wasn't he just an assassin, too?

He flipped the pages until he hit the second news section. His fingers froze and his eyes went wide. With everything going on in the city, he hadn't expected there to be a story about him.

Vigilante Serial Killer Strikes Again

Vigilante? Well, at least he wasn't being considered a terrorist. This time, there was a more accurate description of him. Someone had noted his dark blue Chevy Impala and remembered the first two letters of the license plate. It wouldn't be long now. Of course, since he never registered the car, it might take a while to find him. The car would be traced back to the previous owner, but although she could describe him, she had no other true information. He'd paid her cash for the car.

Ian wondered now if it was a good idea to visit JT. Each day it was getting more difficult to make that decision. Could the police have made the connection? He doubted they would have gotten that far yet, but he needed to be cautious. This may be the last chance to visit, as he had come to believe each time would be, but he kept gambling. Sharing his late-night escapades with JT was important, like they were accomplices in the revenge.

Was he trying to get caught, or was the adrenaline rush and the power he felt from killing and surviving starting to make him feel invincible? Wasn't that the kind of thinking that got most villains caught? Their over-confidence? When his food arrived, he shoveled it in, left money on the table, and rushed off.

44

"So, we're it? We're the task force to stop this vigilante?" Officer Ben Thornton asked. With all the detectives running the terrorist cases, no others were available. The rookie, Thornton, was assigned to Robinson to do his grunt work.

"Yep, that's it. You, me, and a computer geek. You should be happy though, Thornton. Any other time, there'd be a slew of detectives on this. You'd still be out trying to bust car thieves. You've been given a golden opportunity to work homicide with the big boys. But now, you're quite literally under the gun. We have to stop this guy before he kills again and before the media tears us apart enough that we become an embarrassment to the department. That's a good way to get our asses chewed out and me transferred back to the lowly job of chasing car thieves."

"Hey, busting car thieves ain't so bad."

"Yeah, well that's what would happen to me. Your career would go straight in the shitter. No more promotions. You get handed shit assignments. You'd start drinking and become an alcoholic and eventually get shit-canned from the force for being a boozer. You'd end up on the streets alone, broke, and friendless, where you eventually eat a bullet."

"Thanks for the pep talk, sir. Can't wait to get started."

"That's the spirit. Welcome to homicide."

Robinson opened several files and spread them on the conference room table.

"There's a connection here somewhere. We need to find it. Start charting everything we have. There's a reason he's targeting this area. I'm gonna go check the medical examiner's report."

Robinson had just exited the building when his phone chimed.

"Robinson."

"Detective, this is Jolson."

Robinson didn't recognize the voice or the name.

"Yeah, ah, Jolson, what can I do for you?"

"I think I found a connection in the Vigilante Case."

Then it came to him. Jolson was his computer geek.

"Okay, what's that?"

Robinson jogged down the steps and turned right at the sidewalk. There was a lot of foot traffic out today, he noticed. Probably a lot of lawyers either picking up new clients or talking about last minute details for court appearances.

"Did you know that we were looking for one of those guys in the basement?"

"Ah, no, which one?"

"Cummings. Jervis Cummings."

It wasn't ringing a bell. "Ah ..."

"He's wanted for murder in the Kelly shooting about a year back."

At the mention of the name Kelly, something clicked. Robinson stopped abruptly, causing a lawyer to run into him. Robinson didn't notice or hear the comments that followed him.

"Kelly?"

"Yeah."

His mind reeled, remembering back to the courtroom scene and the wild look in Kelly's eyes. In a blur of mental imaging, all the pieces came together. "Ah, no. Don't tell me."

"What was that, sir?

But Robinson was no longer listening. He spun around and ran back to the station.

Back at his desk he said, "Hey, Jergens, you still there? Time to earn your keep. Call up the case and send it to my computer. Use your skills and find me Ian Kelly."

"Yes sir. And it's Jolson." But he was speaking to dead air.

Things were starting to fall into place now. He recalled when he had to tell Kelly about what happened to his family. That was the worst part of his job: telling someone, especially parents, that their loved one was dead.

For a while, Kelly had called him almost every day. He seemed desperate for news. When was the last time he had called? Robinson fired up his computer and clicked on the file. As he scanned it, his excitement grew. He thought about the man and remembered thinking there was no way Kelly had the balls for revenge. Well, maybe he'd grown a pair since then. Having his family killed could have been all the fertilizer he needed. Robinson checked the address and ran straight to the conference room he left Thornton in.

"That was fast. What's up?" Thornton said.

Robinson slid photos around the table until he found one of Jervis Cummings. He nodded. *Yeah. It felt right.* Then he studied the different witnesses' composite drawings of the suspect. They varied, and in truth, didn't look much like Kelly, but they were close enough. He pressed both index fingers on the two pictures and said, "I think we found our connection."

45

Ahmed knelt silently on his prayer rug but he wasn't praying. Instead, his mind reviewed the previous missions. So far, they had been very successful. Each attack had increased the death toll and the chaos within the community. It was so easy to send the Mighty American Machine into panic. Considering what had happened with the other cells, his group had accomplished far more than expected. If you could believe the American media, it appeared only one other cell was still in operation. His cell had yet to lose a man. Yes, they had done well.

They had been lucky so far. The local and federal law enforcement organizations had very little to go on, although they now knew about the black SUVs. Ahmed had tried hard to ensure that no witnesses were left. Of course, he wasn't naïve enough to believe the authorities were reporting all they had found, either. Ahmed would have to be very careful in order to complete the entire mission. The men were beginning to feel confident about their chance of survival. Overconfidence could lead to failure and Ahmed was determined not to fail.

Today's mission would be the most ambitious and offer the greatest threat to the men. They had a good chance of being seen and of perhaps even losing a man. The attack would occur in early evening while there would still be some daylight. They would be drawing the enemy's forces toward them into a deadly ambush. There had to be exact timing and attention to detail to pull it off. The men's discipline and training would win out. After today's attack, the city would live in fear for a long time. If successful, the men would get one day off to prepare for the final assault.

Two of his men were out securing a new vehicle. Ahmed sent his Al to scout out the site of the last and most destructive assault. Everything else was in place. It was just a matter of the clock winding down.

Ahmed bowed his head again. This time, though, he prayed.

***

Ian stayed all day by his son's side. He took a lot more frequent short walks to the front door of the facility, telling himself he was checking for any signs of surveillance, but his ulterior motive was to catch a glimpse of KeKe. He'd seen her twice in the hall, but she either hadn't noticed him, or was ignoring him. Twice so far, she had entered the room, but neither time did she speak to him nor answer when he said hi.

Ian was disappointed, but not only because she was the only person he had talked to in quite a while. As much as he fought against the pull, Ian couldn't deny his interest—his attraction, even—to the woman. Her visit to the house had sealed it. He wasn't sure how KeKe would respond if anyone came around asking about him, but so far, no police arrived to arrest him. Of course, the other fear was that she now knew where he lived.

Ian shared his fears with JT, including every bit of information, every tiny detail of his exploits.

"I had him, JT. He was mine. I had him but the bastard—oops, sorry for the language—but he got away. Now I have no idea where to find him. I'm not even sure what he looks like. But don't worry, son. I won't let you down. I'm going to find that bas—find him, and finish what I promised.

"The problem is that some people saw me yesterday. There's a description of me in the paper. It won't be long before they put two and two together. It looks like I'm safe today, but it might be harder for me to get here tomorrow. If they show up here, I won't be able to come back to see you. I'm sorry."

He stared out the window. He could feel it was all coming to an end. If they put Jervis together with Ian's description, they would swarm around his house. When they couldn't find him there, they would come here. Ian wasn't certain how he felt about that, but it was too late to change things now.

He leaned down and kissed his son's forehead.

"Bye again, JT. I love you. My gut tells me this will be the last time I can see you. I know I've said that before, but this time..." he shrugged. Ian's heart was breaking, but there were no more tears to shed. Only the reality of the situation remained a load on his mind, but no longer a burden to his hardened and scarred emotions.

He left the facility without looking down the halls. It was getting late and he had to find a new car.

***

Robinson and Thornton walked around the nice suburban home. There was no sign anyone had lived there for a while. The grass was long, junk mail was piled in the mailbox, and the house looked deserted. A '*For Sale*' sign stood in the yard.

They peered in the windows. Nothing moved inside. Robinson would have to get a warrant to search the house, but he felt fairly certain they would find nothing. If Kelly was still in town, he was staying somewhere else.

"Check with the neighbors. Find out when the last time was they remember seeing him."

While Thornton went off to canvass, Robinson called Jolson.

"Start a request for a search warrant on Kelly's house."

"I'm on it."

Robinson went to the garage door. It was locked and the tiny windows were too high to see through. Thornton returned shortly.

"Neighbors haven't seen him in quite a while. One said he thought Kelly had left town."

"Lock your hands together."

"Huh?"

"You heard me. Give me a boost so I can see inside."

Thornton wasn't happy, but he did it.

Inside the dark space, Robinson could make out a car. If Kelly wasn't there now, he had been at some point. *What he was driving now? Was it a dark blue Chevy Impala?*

"You think this guy could kill?" Thornton asked.

"Anyone can kill, given the right circumstances. And this guy lost his whole family."

"Or he could have hired it done."

"Yeah, there is that. Nothing surprises me anymore. Let's go get that search warrant."

Could Kelly kill? Robinson asked himself again. What would he do if he were in Kelly's shoes? How could anyone know until they were put in that situation? He paused before getting in the car and glanced back at the house. "I hope it's not you," he said to himself.

46

After spending an hour trying to pay cash for a car without having to sign for it, Ian gave up. He was going to have to find another old lady to buy a car from. The lost hour's one saving grace was being able to steal a dealer plate from the back of a car when the salesman went inside to answer the phone. With the extra plate, Ian thought perhaps the best and least expensive way to get a new car was to have it painted.

Barely an hour of sunlight existed. He toyed with the idea of sitting home tonight, fearing patrols would be on the lookout for his car, but he wanted to at least walk the streets a bit and see if he could dig up some information, though he wasn't optimistic about his chances.

Ian made a right turn and started for the expressway ramp fifty yards ahead. In the distance, the sound of multiple sirens approached from the opposite direction. Jolted, Ian felt a tightness across his chest. They had found him. With a start, Ian jumped and slammed on the brakes as the sky lit up in a streak of fire. The bright flash ended at a firetruck that was now in view. The explosion lifted the truck, engulfing it in a ball of flames.

"Oh God," Ian said. "Someone just blew up that firetruck."

As he watched, a second bolt shot out and another vehicle, Ian could not see through the smoke and fire, exploded. He jumped the curb and parked in the grass along the side of a grocery store. Racing around the car to the trunk, he pawed through the equipment until he found the binoculars. Ian then jogged to the corner of the bridge that crossed the expressway and trained the glasses on the spot where he'd seen the rockets launch from.

His gaze stopped on a produce market that was closed. A large overhang served as a cover for people entering the market against rainy or snowy weather. The top of the overhang was a four-sided glass structure that resembled a small square lighthouse. The glass had been broken out of the two sides Ian could see. A masked figure moved inside from window to window, searching out the next target.

Rifle fire erupted, drawing Ian's attention across the street to a two-story office building where two men with rifles were shooting at the police who were arriving on the scene. From his vantage point Ian saw both officers go down. "My God! It's an ambush." It had to be the terrorists. Ian grew angry. He had to do something to help.

Before he could move, another police car screeched to a stop. The first two cops were gunned down before they could fire a shot. This policeman jumped out of the car and was dealt a similar fate.

Ian raced around to the trunk of his car. His hand shook violently as he took out the key fob and pressed the trunk button. When the trunk popped, he let the lid rise without concern for covering the weapons cache inside. He pulled the rifle from its case and grabbed the box of bullets. Then he jammed the handgun in his belt. Slamming the trunk shut, Ian raced for the corner of the bridge. Other than at the firing range with Tex, Ian had never shot the rifle. As Ian readied the weapon, he tried to recall everything he'd been taught.

Tex had taken him out on the porch so he could shoot at a greater distance than was possible inside the underground range. The man's raspy voice filtered through his mind now. "Use something to stabilize the barrel. Don't trust your arms to keep it steady. Check for wind. If it's strong from any direction, compensate slightly the other way. For distance, aim low to start with since the rifle will kick up, at least until you get used to it. For longer distances, you have to allow for drop, so aim above your target. This is a crash course. I can't get you into the finer adjustments, so just use some common sense. If the target is moving, try to lead them, like throwing a pass to a wide receiver. Squeeze the trigger. Don't jerk or pull. Most important thing is to relax. Breathe in, breathe out, and shoot."

The voice faded as he lined up his shot. The distance he'd shot with Tex was only about fifty yards. This shot was nearly a hundred yards long with a slight breeze moving from left to right, fading light, and small moving targets that were half-concealed. Perhaps not a difficult shot for someone with training or maybe even a deer hunter, but he had never attempted anything like it before. He just knew he had to try, if only to force the snipers to keep their heads down and prevent them from killing anyone else.

Ian watched through the scope and noticed a pattern. The two shooters would first move to a location and scan the area in front of them, wait about thirty seconds, and then move again. He positioned the rifle, running through Tex's check list. Ian rested the barrel on top of the cement guard rail, sighted through the scope, and made some adjustments. Then he set the crosshairs on one of the shooters' heads, but the rifle would not stay still. His short, quick breaths and racing heart made it difficult for him to stay on target. Pulling his head back from the scope, Ian forced slow, deep breaths in through his mouth until he was calm enough to try again.

This time, his hands were more steady and the sight stayed on target. He thought he should try a body shot to have the best chance of hitting his target, but the snipers weren't showing much of anything. The roof was about three feet below the surrounding brick wall, like a short castle rampart. When the shooters knelt behind the wall, the only visible target was from the shoulders up.

Ian took several more of the slower breaths, steadied his body as he exhaled and squeezed the trigger. Nothing happened. He dry-fired, but there was no round in the chamber. Swearing to himself, he jacked a round and started over.

This time as he found his target, the snipers moved. Rather than rush the shot and perhaps waste a round on a moving target, Ian waited for them to settle again. He tried to relax. More sirens were fast approaching. He knew this shot was important; it might be the only chance he got. If he missed, they might direct their attention toward him, and he had no doubt they were better shots than he was. He had to make the first shot count.

As he let out his breath, a siren blared behind him. Ian's target turned toward the sound. The sniper's face was now fully in Ian's scope as he fired. An instant later, the man disappeared behind a red cloud. The other shooter turned and noticed his companion was down. In a fraction of a second, he acquired his target, aimed, and fired. Ian, seeing it all through his scope, knew he was the intended target and panicked. He fired as he ducked, knowing his shot didn't have a chance. The sniper's bullet, however, nicked a corner of the cement bridge a mere inch from where his face had just been.

Ian's body began to shake. The man had fired that quickly and still been on target. Ian had to move positions or the next time he raised his head, the man would bury one through his scope and into his eye.

He stepped a few feet down the embankment toward the expressway. On a steep slope now, he dug his left foot into the grass and placed his right on the base of a small tree's trunk for balance. Testing it to make sure he had solid footing, he tried to find a shooting angle. The bridge had thick, decorative cement spindles that lined the first ten feet of each side, and Ian slid the rifle barrel through the second and third spindles. It gave him a very narrow angle at the target, but it was enough. He tried to sight on the second man, but amazingly, cars were still crossing the bridge, unaware of the danger in front of them.

More shooting and another explosion occurred on the opposite side of the expressway, but, Ian couldn't see what blew up. When the traffic cleared, Ian readied himself. He had a good line on his next shot and was squeezing the trigger when he heard, "Put the gun down and step out of there. Do it now, or by God, I'll shoot you."

The voice was loud and angry. Ian turned his head to see a policeman with his weapon aimed at him.

"Sir, the terror--"

"Last chance. Step away from the gun or die."

The look on the man's face left no doubt he was serious. Ian released the gun and grabbed the small tree to pull himself up the slope. The police cruiser had parked behind his car and another one was driving over the curb at that moment. Cars were backed up as people gawked at what was happening. A few motorists had left their cars and fled the overpass.

"The terrorists are shooting people over there," Ian said, pointing behind him.

"Yeah, and you're one of them."

Then it dawned on Ian how the situation must have appeared to the cop.

"No. I shot one of them. Up on that roof." He turned to point this time.

"Get on the ground now. I want to take you alive, but if you give me an excuse, I won't hesitate to shoot."

A second cop ran up behind the first to lend support. Ian started for the ground, trying to think of a way to make the cop understand he wasn't involved. A shot echoed in the distance, and Ian felt the heat as it passed over his head and plowed into the cop. The force blew the cop off his feet, knocking him backwards.

Ian showed his empty hands and screamed. "It's not me! It's not me!"

The second cop dropped to one knee and pointed his gun at Ian.

"It's coming from the rooftop over there. They're targeting all first-responders. Stay down. You're a target." Ian pointed to the injured man. "I'll grab him and drag him to you."

He waited to give the cop a chance to assess the situation and agree. The cop looked over the front of Ian's car in the direction of the shooter. Another bullet hit the hood inches from his face, causing him to rock back and fall on his butt. The shot seemed to convince him. He nodded toward Ian.

Staying low, Ian ran to the fallen officer, grabbed under his arms and dragged him backward until they were past the cover of the car.

"I saw them shoot rockets at a firetruck and an ambulance, I think. They've been shooting everyone else who's tried to help. I shot one of them. You need to get officers here to stop the traffic."

They both looked around. The street was now clogged with cars, many now abandoned as the drivers ran for shelter.

"If you bring in an ambulance, you should keep it behind the building there so the EMTs don't get shot. Your partner's still alive. Drag him out of sight. I'm gonna go back down and see if I can get another shot at that last terrorist."

"Are you law enforcement?"

Ian hesitated, then nodded. "Yes." Not wanting to say any more, Ian hurried back to his rifle.

Sighting in a hurry, he saw the sniper stand and move for the back of the building. He appeared to be dragging the other man. Ian fired, but the shot was too hasty. The terrorist vanished from view. Next, Ian saw a body flying over the edge of the building. The second shooter jumped onto the ledge and grabbed a rope. Ian fired again and the bullet chipped brick mere inches from the man. As he disappeared from view, Ian ripped the rifle from between the spindles, snatched the binoculars and bullets, and climbed up the hill. The sniper was bugging out and he wanted to catch him.

Just then, the ground rocked as an explosion lifted the rooftop of the shooter's building into the air. Ian stood, gaping at the destruction. A large cloud of dust and debris obscured the building. The explosion must have been set to cover their retreat. Moments later, the produce market exploded and a wall of smoke filled the air.

47

Ian gasped. Reflexively, he flinched and ducked. When the debris had finished falling, he lifted his binoculars and tried to locate the shooter. Through the haze, he spied a man wearing a ski mask crossing from where the produce market had once stood toward the blown building the shooters were on. Ian surmised it to be the man who fired the rockets. He tried to raise the rifle but he was way too slow. The runner disappeared behind what was left of the office building.

Ian ran hard up the slope back to the car. All around him, people were screaming and running from the scene. He jumped in, tossing everything on the seat. He had little room to maneuver the car. The street was blocked with vehicles and backed up for a long distance. A cement walkway lined the road across the bridge, but it wasn't wide enough for the car. Despite the narrow passage, the sidewalk offered the best chance of getting through the jam. Angling toward the curb, the car bounced hard and the right side lifted, tipping upward. The left wheels stayed on the road while the right ones rode the walkway. Driving sideways like an exhibition driver, Ian went across the bridge while other drivers hiding in their cars watched him with amazement.

When the car cleared the bridge, Ian stopped and looked around, searching for signs of the gunmen. Too many buildings offered cover and the smoke from the blasts and the burning vehicles made it difficult to see beyond them. The office building was on a corner. The terrorist had to have gone down that street. But where did it lead? Wasn't that street a dead end?

Ian got out and stood on the door frame to see above the other cars. Using the glasses, he scanned the area. Movement to the left drew his attention. Down the entrance ramp on the opposite side of the overpass, Ian saw a brown service van parked along the shoulder of the expressway. Gawkers. They must have pulled over to see what was happening above them. He was about to move on when several men broke from the cover of the tall weeds and brush at the top of the slope. One of them carried a body slung over his shoulders. They slid down the embankment and piled into the van. Before the sliding door was closed, the vehicle took off, bouncing onto the roadway heading north.

Ian jumped back in his car and pushed the pedal down. The car leaped forward, sideswiping a Lexus. The car bounced down from the walkway, jarring Ian. He drove onto the grass until he came to the entrance ramp. The ground began to slope and the car tipped dangerously sideways. If he didn't make it to the ramp fast, he feared the car would flip over. Jerking his wheel to the left, he floored the pedal and banged hard into the back side of the curb. The car bounded over and bounced hard on the other side. He went diagonally across the ramp, hit the median, and swung right. The bumpy ride seemed to waken all his injuries as wave of pain washed over him. He gasped.

Ian lost control, driving over the cement divider and down the up ramp before regaining command of the car. He swung the wheel hard again and the car bumped over the median to enter the proper lane, then sped down the ramp. Taking the curve too fast, Ian almost drove off the road. At the bottom, traffic still moved along the expressway, unaware of the deadly rampage that had happened above them. Ian shot out in front of a semi and accelerated. The van was nowhere in sight.

At high speed, Ian guided and angled the car around and between other vehicles, trying desperately to catch a glimpse of the van. His speed hit one hundred, and the car shook so hard he feared the body would disintegrate beneath him. Ripping past another semi, his heart pounded and a harder, less emotional type of anger than he felt for his family's killers burned inside him.

As he raced down the road, Ian swept his gaze quickly in all directions, desperate to catch a glimpse of the fleeing vehicle. In the distance, Ian caught sight of the van climbing the next exit ramp. Ian became more reckless as he tried to close the distance. With his target in sight, he kept his focus on the van and was no longer aware of the other cars around him or how close he came to causing accidents. Only one thought occupied his mind: catching that van.

Maybe what drove him was that he considered himself a patriot. Perhaps Ian wanted to make amends for the things he had done, or maybe he just needed to know in his heart some good was still left within him. But what Ian didn't think about was what he would do if he caught the terrorists.

Ian reached the top of the ramp, braked slightly, and squealed around the turn. No other vehicles were in front of him. *No!* His chest tightened as did his grip on the wheel. He panted as if he been running instead of driving.

Ahead, the road curved and he could not see what was in the distance. Ian pushed the car, screeching the tires around the bend until he reached a section of road that stretched on straight for a long way. Nothing moved in any direction. He braked and sat staring.

"Shit!" He slammed the wheel with his hand. Somehow he'd lost them.

48

With no idea where to look for the van, Ian could do nothing but turn around and try to avoid any cops on the way home. He debated calling 911 on one of his burner phones, but decided against it. Making a one-eighty turn, Ian pulled into the westbound lane. The sun was but a fine line above the horizon; daylight was fading fast. Suddenly very tired, Ian sagged in the seat, so much so that he almost missed the van hidden behind an abandoned warehouse.

The driveway and surrounding area was overgrown with weeds and brush. A deep drainage ditch ran along the road and right side of the property. The old cement block building had six loading bays that slanted downward to a cement a platform. At the back of the building, the tail end of the van was barely visible. It couldn't be seen by drivers coming from the other direction.

Ian turned up the driveway, veered right, and inched toward the building. His hand sought and found the handgun on the seat. He gripped it for reassurance. The van was out of sight from the driveway. Angling further toward the right to get a view of it, Ian lifted the gun, ready to shoot. As he passed the rear corner, the van was in sight. He braked and studied the vehicle. No one moved inside. He inched closer, his eyes darting from the van to the building.

Creeping forward he noticed the rear doors were open. The van appeared empty. No one was outside, either, or at least they weren't being obvious about it. The hairs on the back of his neck stood up, sending a chill through his veins. He stopped thirty feet from the van next to the side drainage ditch in a position that allowed a view of both the front and back of the structure. There, he watched with his heart pounding. Ian didn't want to get too close in case of an ambush.

The haziness of the setting sun made it more difficult to see if anyone was stalking him through the brush surrounding the property. He reached for the phone. He had to call in his discovery. Before he could punch in the numbers, an engine accelerated from somewhere close. From the far side of the building, a black SUV shot out, racing through the weeds. It turned down the drive to the street. A second black SUV followed seconds later. Both vehicles turned west on the road.

Throwing the car into reverse, Ian was about to give chase when a dark four-door sedan pulled out from the far side of the building and stopped, blocking the driveway. Ian braked hard. His mouth went dry. *What was this?* His neck hairs stood up again, but this time the chill he felt seemed to stop his heart.

The driver, a tall man with black hair and a short beard, got out of the car and opened the back door. He leaned inside. Ian watched him, not sure what to do. Then he reacted. He had one of the killers right there in front of him.

Ian shifted into park and put his hand on the door, about to open it, when the driver pulled a long tube from the back seat. When Ian realized what it was, he hit the gas in panic. The car revved, but it didn't move. Panicked, he realized he wasn't in gear. He yanked the shift and the car jumped backward, plunging into the ditch. The rear end hit the far bank, leaving the car suspended about four feet above the bottom of the ditch with the front end angled upward. The car was stuck.

Ian dove for the passenger door. He pushed it open and glanced behind him. The man lifted the rocket launcher to his shoulder and sighted on him. Ian swallowed his panic and crawled out the door, dragging the equipment on the front seat with him. He dropped into the ditch with a thud as the rocket hit the car and lifted it off the ground.

Closing his eyes, Ian rolled sideways as fast as he could. Pieces of the car showered down around him. The flaming remains of the chassis dropped not three feet from him. A fiery ember flew off, landing on his shirt and setting it on fire. Ian rolled, furiously trying to beat out the flames before they could spread.

Ian swatted out the last of the glowing embers on his chest. Then, seeing that the car was on fire, he jumped up and ran to the trunk before the car became engulfed, or the gas tank exploded. The trunk lid had blown open and the contents were smoldering. He looked to the road and saw the shooter turning his car in the same direction the SUVs went. He lifted the rifle too late to get off a shot. Turning his attention back to the trunk, he saw the duffel bag had just caught fire. He couldn't afford to lose his weapons and equipment. Sliding the barrel through the handles, Ian yanked the duffel bag out of the rapidly spreading fire and ran from the car. He dropped the bag and threw dirt on it until the flames died. The rest of his belongings and equipment were gone.

He dragged the bag further away from the car. Gathering the binoculars, he jammed them inside the duffel bag. Hoisting the bag over his shoulder, Ian walked around the building, keeping close to the brush. The fire would draw someone's attention and he wanted to be long gone when it did.

Ian reached the road and was crossing the bridge over the expressway when another explosion occurred. He dropped to the ground, felt for his gun, and looked back. The van exploded. The terrorists must have set a timed charge to destroy it. A vision of the man with the rocket launcher came to him. Ian wouldn't soon forget his face. Ian got up and ran toward the other side of the expressway. He didn't want to look suspicious, but he needed to get clear of the area.

Darkness had fallen and it helped obscure his escape. Headlights came toward him. Stepping off the road, he ducked into some tall weeds before the vehicle reached him.

Ian had a long way to go and probably not much time before the area was overrun with law enforcement. He couldn't afford to be found anywhere near there, especially with what he carried in the long black bag.

In the distance, the bullets he couldn't reach cooked off, sounding like a fireworks display without the visuals. Hopefully, no one would get injured. He continued on without looking back.

Ian thought about stopping at the diner down the road but he smelled of smoke and charred flesh. He moved on, his fast pace making it hard for him to catch a breath. The burned flesh was right above his broken ribs, creating pain on top of pain.

More than a mile from the bomb site, Ian stopped at an isolated gas station that was closed for the night. Two pop machines lined the side of the building. Ian dug in his pocket for two dollars and purchased a bottle of water, which he guzzled so fast he had to buy another.

Pulling back the tatters of his shirt, he poured the remaining water over his scorched chest. He cried out, stomping his feet. It might have been his imagination but he thought the water sizzled when it touched his burned flesh.

Ian sat down against the wall next to the machines to give him some cover and to rest. He rummaged through the bag until he found one of his burner phones. He rifled through his wallet until he found the card with the number he wanted and placed the call.

"Detective Robinson, please."

"He's in a meeting. Can I take a message?"

"No, he's gonna want to talk to me."

"And why's that?"

"'Cause I've got information he needs for his Vigilante Case."

"Just give it to me. I'll make sure he gets it."

"Guess he loses, then."

"Wait. I'll see if I can get him."

A minute later, Robinson took the phone.

"This is Robinson. What've ya got for me?" He sounded annoyed. There were probably a lot of calls coming in saying they had information on the Vigilante Case.

Ian altered his voice. "The men who blew up the fire truck today escaped west in two black SUVs."

"What? What's this got to do with the Vigilante Case?"

"I'm trying to help you. They appeared to be Middle Eastern. There were maybe five men and a body. They escaped the scene in a brown van. I followed them to an abandoned loading dock on Sterns Road where they blew up the brown van."

"Okay, that's helpful. Anything else? Anything about the Vigilante?"

"There was another man in a separate car. He's tall with short black hair and a beard. He fired a rocket at me."

"Why tell only me? You could have called 911."

"Because I trust you. Because I'm the person you've been searching for. I wanted you to know that it was me who shot the terrorist on the roof."

"Yeah? Well up until that part, I was believing you. How do I know you're really him?"

"Because I know what the A stands for."

Ian hung up. He could imagine the look on Robinson's face. For some strange reason, he began laughing. Not in a humorous way, but a nervous, somewhat crazed laugh. It continued for over a minute as though the harsh sound emanating from his throat had a life of its own. It wasn't until Ian felt the tears rolling down his face that he stopped laughing. *What had he become?* He hadn't given one thought to the dangers of chasing down a group of terrorists, but a month ago, he had seldom touched or thought about guns. Now, here he was, carrying a bagful of weapons and thinking he was some sort of special agent.

Ian let the tears flow. He had lost whoever he had once been to the bitter hatred that now festered deep inside. This quest was driving him insane. Perhaps his bravado was a mask for his cowardice. Not strong enough to take his own life, he thrust himself in the middle of a gun battle and chased down trained killers, hoping they would do the job for him.

Ian wiped his tears and stood. He stared at the bag for a moment, trying to make a choice. Finally, he bent and picked it up. Regardless of who he had become, he still had a job to finish.

He walked into the darkness.

49

The news broadcasts were full of the ambush. In all, six firefighters, six EMTs, five policemen, and eleven civilians died in the attacks. Seven more were wounded. Many others sustained injuries in the explosions.

In national news, during a similar attack, a SWAT team in Fort Wayne, Indiana, took out the cell operating there with only one local casualty. The six-man cell had been gunned down to a man. After all the deaths the cell had caused, the thought of taking someone alive was slim. The only cell still in operation appeared to be the one in Toledo.Federal agents descended upon the city by the dozens. Until they found the terrorists, the city was shut down. The residents were told if they weren't going to or coming from work, they should not be on the streets. Schools were closed, children encouraged to stay in the house. The entire city was in shock and at a standstill.

Since he had gotten in so late, Ian slept past noon. He turned on his regular cell phone for a few minutes to check for messages, which he did several times a day in case someone called about JT. Ian was surprised when the phone beeped several times telling him there were multiple messages. He scrolled down the phone log, but didn't recognize any of the numbers. Punching in his code, he listened to each one.

"Mr. Kelly, this is Detective Robinson. We have some news about your family's killers. Please contact me asap."

There were two more similar messages, but in each one, the voice held more force. The next message came from his attorney telling him someone had put a bid in on the house, and he needed Ian to call so he would know how to respond to the offer.

The last call surprised him the most. It had come in earlier in the morning.

"Mr. Kelly, it's Nurse Brogan. I thought you might want to know the police were here this morning, asking about you. I told them I hadn't seen you in a few days. Look, I know you're in trouble and that you're still hurting, but I think you need some help. If I can do anything, please let me know. I still think you're a good man who made some bad choices. You should talk to someone before it goes too far. Ah, I don't know what else to say. But don't worry about your son. He's in good hands. Be careful…and call. Bye."

Ian didn't know what to think. He had been prepared for the police to figure things out, but he wondered whether KeKe's call was real, or if the police had asked her to make it. He needed to call her but he couldn't do it from the house. And since Ian no longer had a car, leaving would be difficult. How was he going to handle this?

Pacing the house, Ian tried to come up with options. He couldn't risk getting his car from the garage at the old house. By now the police must have it under surveillance. He could take a train or bus to Chicago, but he had to get downtown to do either. Then it came to him. When the police were done with Margo's minivan, Ian had it towed to a detail shop to have it thoroughly scoured. He wasn't sure why he had done that, since he knew he would never drive it. Months later, it was still there…at least he hoped it was.

Another problem was that he didn't have any more clothes. Everything he brought from home had been burned in the car. He would have to walk the three miles to his old home, make sure it wasn't under surveillance, and sneak inside. Leaving his weapons behind in the safe house, Ian started the long hike to his house.

His chest burned and itched as the sweat began to trickle over the blistered wound. The ache in his ribs seemed secondary now. He had become so accustomed to the pain that it had been relegated to mental background noise. Ian wrapped the remnants of his shirt around the burn to protect and conceal it. He took his time and tried not to overexert his already strained body. More than an hour later, he arrived on the street that ran behind his house.

Various small businesses lined the street and behind them a condo community backed up to Ian's property. He walked through the neighborhood until he came to the split-rail fence that bordered his property. He glanced around, trying not to look too conspicuous. Then he hopped the fence and jogged up the deck to the patio doors. He used his key to unlock the door, then ran inside to turn off the alarm. He stood for a moment, waiting for someone to jump out and scream, "Freeze!"

When that didn't happen, Ian could breathe again. Locking the patio door behind him, he went into the living room and peered through the windows that bordered the front door. There were cars parked on the street, but none were in front of the house. He could get to the stairs without anyone outside seeing him.

Once upstairs, Ian went to the front bedroom windows and parted the curtains enough to see down the street. Half a block up there was a dark blue sedan parked with a man sitting inside. He had his arm out the window and his fingers tapped the roof. The police were definitely onto him.

In his own room, Ian packed underwear, socks, blue jeans, t-shirts, and toiletries in a small duffel bag until it was stuffed. Grabbing a pillow case, he threw lotion and first aid supplies inside. Ian applied a burn medication and placed several small pads over the area and wrapped gauze around his body. He swallowed four aspirin to try to ease some of the pain. Back downstairs, he used a burner phone to call a cab to meet him outside one of the businesses behind the house. He was told a car would arrive in about thirty minutes.

Checking once more to make sure the watcher was still down the street, Ian made himself a peanut butter sandwich. He washed it down with water. The sandwich went down so easy that he made a second and packed the remaining three bottles of water in the pillowcase.

He took one more look around the house then left, locking the door. Carrying his goodie bag, Ian retraced his steps. Several people from the condos saw him, but none challenged him. Ian stopped in front of an old-fashioned ice cream parlor and waited. Ten minutes later the cab pulled up and Ian gave him the address. The driver stared at the pillowcase like he was trying to use x-ray vision to see what was inside. The cabbie looked at Ian and raised a querying eyebrow, but when Ian made no remark, he drove off.

Ian paid the driver with his remaining money. He would need to go to the bank to replenish, but wondered if the police were watching his accounts. He could use an ATM to see if his accounts were frozen. He wondered about the legalities of that and if the police had enough hard evidence to cause his access to the accounts to be denied.

The minivan detailing had been prepaid, so he picked up the keys and was off. Ian drove to a state liquor store where he knew there was an ATM. Relieved his account was still active, he pulled out the maximum daily allowance and then went to fill up the gas tank. From there, he planned on hopping on the expressway and heading toward Chicago. It seemed silly to drive that far if they were indeed monitoring his accounts. All they had to do was check his activity and they would know he was still in town. If they hadn't progressed that far yet, he still had some time. He would know soon.

Just before turning down the exit ramp, Ian changed his mind. Feeling like it was a good sign that the ATM spit out his money, he decided to try a suburban branch of his bank. He entered the drive-thru. He wasn't afraid the police would be staking the bank out, but was wary about how the teller would react when she punched in his account number. If she hesitated or moved away from her window for any reason, he would bolt. With a deep relief, he accepted the thousand dollars from the smiling woman. Money meant freedom and Ian was now free to hunt a little longer. He took the ramp and began his trip.

Ian called Stern on his way out of town using one of the burner phones. He countered the offer made on the house, which surprised the attorney. "I thought you just wanted to be rid of it at any cost?"

"Changed my mind. The more I can make on the sale, the longer I can keep JT in a first-rate facility."

That made sense to the lawyer.

Three hours out, just short of Chicago, Ian used his personal phone to call Detective Robinson.

50

"Kelly, where are you?"

"Why, Detective? Has something happened in my case? Have you finally caught those animals?" Ian tried to keep his tone even, but he couldn't hide his emotion. His response seemed to cause the detective to pause in thought.

"Yes, there have been some new developments. I'd like you to come down to the station so I can explain what we have."

"Is it something that can wait? I'm not in town at the moment."

"Oh? And where are you?"

"I'm in Iowa."

"Iowa, huh? How long have you been there?"

"I think three days, now. Yeah, three."

"You realize it would be easy to check your story."

"I don't understand, Detective. Why would you need to check my story? I'm not the one who killed my family. I'm not sure I like your tone. You said you had news. What is it?"

Robinson sighed into the phone. "I have a feeling you know exactly what this is about. Mr. Kelly, you need to be in my office by tomorrow noon or I'm issuing a warrant for your arrest for murder."

"Murder? Now you're just pissing me off. Here's my attorney's number." He quoted it off. "I'm not giving up my much-needed vacation because you think I killed someone. That's absurd. You can work out the details with him. I'll be back when I'm back. End of story." A sudden rage swept through him.

"I wonder, Detective, how you would react if your family had been murdered, your life destroyed, and some inept policeman not only couldn't find the killers, but decided to accuse you of their murders. Doesn't bode well for cooperation, now, does it?

You need to increase your efforts at finding those punks. I'll be back when I'm ready." Ian pushed 'end' and turned his phone off. That was that. They had their suspicions about him now and would soon know he lied to them about when he left town and where he was going. The time that he would remain free was limited. He couldn't afford any more mistakes. Somehow, he had to find Davis

---

and end it, but if the police caught him, it would no longer matter.

Ian turned around and headed home. He had no time to waste. The sun was setting as he returned. He had to start taking chances.

***

Ahmed watched his men celebrate. He didn't mind. It was to be their one day off before the big assault. After that, he knew there would be few survivors. They had all gathered in the garage to honor their fallen brother and send him to his glory. They placed him in a shallow grave behind the garage, covered him, and like the true professionals they were, pushed his memory aside.

The mission was almost finished. From what the news was reporting, he had been the only team leader to make it through to the end. At least he would not have to travel to the other cities to eliminate the surviving cell members. His cell was a true killing machine. They might not live through the final stage, but they would at least get to it.

Ahmed wondered if his sponsors were proud of what he had accomplished. Would they reward him and give him a bigger, more involved role in the planning of operations should he walk away on the final day?

A loud burst of laughter shook him from his thoughts. He missed whatever the joke was, but could see the men glance nervously at him, afraid he would object to their good moods. To ease their minds, he smiled broadly and lifted his cup of tea in salute. He needed to leave so the men could relax. It would give him a chance to go over his escape route and review the possible targets.

Casually, Ahmed stood and walked to the kitchen, where his second in command was cooking something special for the group.

"Save some for me, my friend," he said. "I'll be back in a few hours."

Al knew better than to ask where Ahmed was off to. He kept stirring the contents of the pot and nodded.

Ahmed nodded toward the front room where the men sat laughing. "Let them have whatever they want, but do not let them leave or stay up too late." He left, not needing a response.

Ahmed had plotted three possible ending scenarios. The first was the minor league baseball game being played at a downtown stadium. The game started at one. The pros were that there would be a lot of people in a confined area for maximum damage and the escape route would be close to the expressway. The cons were the heavy concentration of police because of the close proximity of the downtown police station and security at the park. They would have to shoot their way into and out of the park.

The second was a local mall. They would enter, form a shooting square, and move from one end to the other, cutting down everyone in their path. The plus there was it was not as well protected by armed security and would be fairly easy to escape from. The downside was that by the time they made it to the opposite side, the entire place could be surrounded. Also, there was no guarantee how many people would be there and they would be dispersed throughout mall, giving too many a chance to escape and call in the police.

The third option was his favorite: a local professional women's golf tournament. There had been much talk about canceling the event because of the terrorist threat, but the politicians had succumbed to pressure of the financial supporters of the tournament, citing that if canceled, the LPGA would move the money-making event to another city and may not return the next year. With the thought of losing so much revenue, the mayor had grudgingly agreed to allow the tournament to proceed, although, he insisted security be beefed up considerably. The mayor had also made a brave statement that they would not allow terrorists to alter the way the residents of his city lived their lives. This statement pleased Ahmed.

The police presence would be substantial, yet he still liked their chances. Four men would enter the golf course and stow timed explosives about the grounds under the many bleacher structures that had been erected for the event. The fifth man would lend support should any of the bombers be discovered. The sites were chosen as to where their impact would cause the most death and chaos. There could be hundreds to thousands of people in the grandstands.

With confusion and fear turning the crowd into a panicked mob, the men could open fire at will. The property was so large that police would not know where all the shooters were. The golf course had many open areas for Ahmed's men to escape from after they had emptied their weapons.

Three men would buy tickets and enter the grounds. Another man would remain hidden in the SUV across from the gate. After the explosions, using an automatic weapon, he would eliminate as many police as possible, then turn his attention to the hordes of people that would be attempting to exit through the narrow gate.

The second SUV, driven by the taxi driver, would hold Al and the final soldier. They would drive down the street and spray the grounds along the length of the fence.

Ahmed had an unusual chill of anticipation course through him. Perhaps it was a sign from Allah. Yes, the chosen target would be the golf course. With his decision made, he drove back to the house. He still much to do before the onslaught began.

51

Ian was almost home when his personal phone rang. It was Stern.

"Mr. Kelly, I had a very unusual phone call a little while ago from a Detective Robinson. He encouraged me to convince you it would be in your best interest to turn yourself in at the downtown police station by noon tomorrow. I take it you know what this is in regards to, since evidently you told him to contact me?"

"Not necessarily. His accusatory tone angered me. Instead of looking for my family's killers, he has turned his attention towards me as a possible suspect. I don't understand it, but I'm not going to stand for it either. I'm out of town, as I told you, taking a stress-relieving vacation. I spent a lot of time with my son last week, and quite frankly, the thought of him confined to that bed, perhaps for the rest of his life, depressed me to the point where I had to get away for a while."

"Well, I can tell you he was quite serious about your being there tomorrow. It may be in your best interest to show up. I will accompany you, of course. The alternative will be to have your life turned upside down and made public. I'm sure a warrant and subsequent manhunt will ensue."

"In case you haven't been paying attention, my life has already been turned upside down and couldn't be made more public than it is now." Ian's tone took on a hard edge.

"My apologies, sir. I meant no disrespect. I know full well the burden your heart carries and the turmoil it has caused in your life. I merely wish to prevent any more stress by nipping this entire situation in the bud."

Ian cooled. It wasn't the attorney's fault. As he pulled into the driveway of his house, he said, "I'll give it some thought and call you in the morning with my decision."

"Very well, Mr. Kelly. Do give it serious consideration and let me know as early as possible so I might plan my day and inform the detective."

***

Stern replaced the handset in the cradle and turned to his burly investigator, sitting across the desk from him. "If what you suspect is true, make sure Mr. Kelly never sees you. I don't need his actions being connected to us."

The big man stood and stretched. "Who'd a thunk? I never thought he'd actually do it, let alone succeed. I was only trying to give him a reason to live."

"Well, I think you've created a monster. Take a few days off and go for a long ride. I don't want you anywhere near here when he arrives."

***

Ian unfolded his weary body from the minivan and stretched. He ached and his chest itched. Time to change the bandages and apply more ointment. What he really needed was a good night's sleep, but that wouldn't happen. Remembering the old movie saying, 'you can sleep when you're dead,' Ian went inside, thinking he could be sleeping well very soon.

He took care of his needs and dressed for the hunt. Without his long coat, he had to settle for a dark windbreaker. A sense of relief came over him as he made his way back to the minivan. It would all be over soon, one way or the other.

Ian parked down the side street from where the pool hall stood. The building was taped off, but someone was scrounging through the debris. Now that he was driving the minivan, he no longer worried about having his vehicle recognized. He stopped in the shadows between two street lights. Ian got out and looked around, zipped up his jacket, and went on foot patrol. Four hours later, frustrated, exhausted, and hurting from his multitude of different injuries, Ian called it a night. People were too afraid to be on the streets. On his long walk, Ian had only seen one other person and he had gone to great pains to keep his distance.

Back inside the van, he attempted to sleep. Sprawling on the floor between the two rows of seats, he tossed and turned. He hadn't thought to bring any medication, bandages, or lotions for his now peeling and raw chest. Weariness was starting to have an effect. He was forgetting things and making mistakes. With no comfortable position for him to curl into, he climbed onto the into a rear seat, and not caring if he could be seen, reclined it as far as it would go, eventually falling into a fitful sleep.

Ian dreamed of JT. His son was standing outside and tapping on the minivan window. "Dad, what are you doing?" To which Ian replied, "I thought I was trying to make things better. Now, I just don't know."

***

Ahmed gathered the men together in the small room he used for planning. After the next day, there would no longer be a need to keep the door locked and his plans secret. This was the final stage.

He went over each person's assignment with them from entry points into the golf course to escape routes. A map showed the grounds and the approximate location of the grandstands. Each man had an explosive device and location to place it. Ahmed decided to have the bombs set for remote detonation, instead of on timers as originally planned. He would do it himself from the clubhouse terrace where he would place his own device.

There would never be able to pass through security carrying the bombs and weapons, so they would go in tonight to place everything. Ahmed was sure security would be patrolling the course tonight as well, but on acres of land in the dark, there would be plenty of shadows to hide them.

When each man could repeat his job without hesitation to Ahmed, they were ready to move. They took the two SUVs into the neighborhood of high-priced houses that bordered the rear of the golf course. Two vacant houses that backed up to different sides of the course had been selected from previous reconnaissance. Each SUV pulled up a driveway and the men climbed out quickly. They gained access to the course through the backyards. From there, they dispersed.

Ahmed waited on the outskirts of the course with a silenced pistol. He was in contact with his men via earbuds. If any of them were discovered, he would move to rescue them.

With great stealth to avoid detection by the security patrols and dogs, the men were able to get all their equipment hidden. They were instructed to bury the devices behind trees and mark the location. The men would sneak into the woods during the tournament to collect the devices and place them without being noticed.

Ahmed had fretted about the best way to have the men retrieve their weapons, which was the only flaw in an otherwise perfect plan, so the weapons were buried as well. After the bombs went off, the men would use the ensuing chaos and panic as a distraction to open fire and make their escapes.

If the plan fell apart and one of the men were discovered, the others were ordered to shoot at random targets and run toward their assigned placements with the explosives. Ahmed would then remote detonate the bombs when his men were close to large groups of people. The men would be sacrificed, but then, they would be anyway. Ahmed had not told them he could detonate the bombs, however. They were professionals. He was certain they would know.

Thirty-five minutes later, back at the safe house, the job was done and the men were quiet. Four bombs had been buried, including the one he would set in the clubhouse. The patrols had been thick and one of the dogs had picked up a scent, barking the alarm, but the group had escaped without notice.

An anxious tension filled the air. Ahmed paced. He wondered what had happened after they left the golf course. Had the bombs been discovered? Were the dogs bomb sniffers? There would be no way to tell until the morning. He stopped and turned to his men.

"You know what is at stake and of the promised rewards. You have done well so far. You have gained much glory from your successes, but this last mission will lift us to such heights that our people will shout out your names in praise. One more day to survive and make good our escape, and a lifetime of wealth and honor will be yours. You know what to do and what is expected of you should something go wrong. Pray and sleep, my brothers. Tomorrow, glory will be yours."

The cell members went to their beds, knowing the next day would be their last, either in this city, or in this world. Only Allah would decide which would be their fate.

52

The rising sun through the van window and his itching skin woke him around six-thirty a.m. He glanced out the window, hoping he would see JT. A yawn split his face as he stretched, causing him to wince in pain. Climbing into the driver's seat, Ian drove toward home on autopilot. He was groggy and thought of nothing but lying back down. His stomach growled, causing him to laugh out loud as his body registered yet another complaint. Food would have to wait. He needed more sleep first.

Before he could give in to his body's demands, Ian called Stern and left a message that he would meet him at his office at eleven-thirty. He set the alarm on his phone and flopped on a blanket he spread out on the living room floor. Despite his exhaustion, sleep eluded him. His thoughts turned to his son. He missed being there with him. He closed his eyes for what seemed like seconds, opening them when the alarm beeped.

Though it felt like he hadn't slept at all, he roused himself and stood under the shower for a long time. He saw to his wounds and dressed in clean clothes. Ian had a feeling the state might soon be providing his wardrobe.

In the kitchen, he made coffee and sat staring at the cup, lost in a thoughtless trance. The phone rang snapping him back to reality. He had a brief flare of excitement, thinking it might be KeKe, but it was Stern.

"I called Detective Robinson and told him we would be there by noon. If there is anything you wish to share with me, now would be the time."

Ian didn't like misleading the man, but he wasn't about to give anything up to anyone, at least not yet. He wanted to see what Robinson had first.

"No. There's nothing. I have no idea what this is about."

The hesitation on the other end told Ian the attorney wasn't buying it. "All right. I will see you here at eleven-thirty." He disconnected without any goodbye.

Ian decided to leave all the weapons and equipment. No one

knew about the house, so the guns were safer here. Plus, there was a good chance they might want to search his car. He imagined their surprise when they saw he was driving a minivan. He tried to make sure it held no obvious evidence, knowing as thorough as he was the police could still find enough trace to put him away. Ian finally decided there was nothing more he could do. He drove away, wondering who might find the guns if he wasn't allowed to return.

Turning on the radio, Ian discovered there had been no new terrorist attacks yesterday. Maybe they moved on, having done enough damage and leaving the city in a state of paranoia. A mile from the suburban city of Sylvania, traffic was suddenly thick. His first thought was that the police had set up road blocks. The next one was if the snare was for him or the terrorists.

When he came to a red light, he rolled his window down and called to the driver of the car next to him. The man lowered his window a few inches and eyed him warily.

"Do you know what's going on ahead?"

"Yeah, it's the LPGA Golf Tournament. It starts today." The man buttoned his window up as Ian waved a thank you.

The golf tournament. Ian had forgotten about it. In the wake of the recent attacks, the news had been full of debate as to whether the event should be canceled or not. Ian tried to think of an alternate route, but in his lane, there were no good options. He drove another few blocks before getting caught at another red light. From the southbound lane, a black SUV turned on the street in front of him. A second followed a few seconds and several cars later, but neither of them set off an alarm until he saw the car directly behind the SUV and the silhouette of its driver. With a heart-pounding start Ian recognized the man who blew up his car. Though the distance and short time Ian had seen the man before the rocket was launched did not offer a great look, something about the man in the car triggered the memory, leaving no doubt in his mind. That it was traveling so close to black SUVs sealed the deal.

His thoughts swirled. Could he be mistaken? He was tired. His eyes and brain might not be in sync. Ian had to check, to get closer to make sure. In his excitement, Ian jumped the light by a fraction, but cars still turning in front of him from the northbound lane caused him to fall farther behind the convoy.

The traffic inched forward. Ian craned his neck to keep track of the SUVs but lost sight of them when a courteous driver allowed a delivery van to turn in front of him. Ian's vision was blocked with no way of getting around the backed-up cars to follow them. He thought for an instant of calling the police, but decided he wanted to know where they were going first.

Up ahead, a policeman directed traffic and stopped him with a big authoritative hand held in the air, but the truck in front of him made it through. Space began to open up, giving Ian a better line of sight. He sat taller in his seat, then stuck his head out the window, but to no avail. The SUVs were gone. More importantly, so was the car.

The policeman finally motioned him forward after what seemed like five minutes. Ian's head swiveled side to side as he tried to locate any sign of the vehicles. The golf course was located in the middle of a residential neighborhood. High-priced homes surrounded the venue. Ian drew up even with the clubhouse on the right and would soon be past the entry gate. Had the terrorist's convoy driven through or had it turned down one of the side streets? Could the tournament be their next target? Again, he was tempted to call the police. There were certainly enough of them around. The golf course's fence that ran along the street was lined with cops.

With mounting tension, Ian drove past the gate. The terrorist and his vehicles were nowhere in sight. Ian kept looking, deciding they must have driven straight through when he caught a glimpse in his rearview mirror of a man walking across the street. He hit the brakes and spun his head around to get a better look. The cars behind him were forced to stop short, and several slammed a hand on their horns.

Ian ignored the blares and concentrated on the tall man with the black hair as he neared the front gate. It was him. Ian was sure of it. He drove into the turn lane and pulled up in a driveway where two teenage girls were motioning for spectators to park on their lawn. Ian lined the car up with the one in front of him and shut the engine down. Hopping out of the car, he fished out his wallet and handed the bleach blonde suburban woman he assumed was the girls' mother a ten-dollar bill. Not waiting for the change he was due, Ian sprinted for the street. He started to cross, but a policeman yelled at him to go down to the crosswalk. Ian waved and jogged the half-block distance. There, two officers were crossing a steady flow of excited fans.

When Ian was close, the policeman held up a hand to stop the pedestrians so traffic could take a turn. Frustration boiling up, Ian wanted to scream. A knot began forming in his stomach. Ian rose up on tiptoes to search over the crowd. He thought he saw the man stop at one of the vendor's booths just inside the gate. In his impatience to cross, he glanced around to see if anyone had taken an interest in him. That was when he saw one of the black SUVs parked a few houses down from where he stood, almost directly across from the entry gate with its tail facing it. Though the vehicle appeared to be empty, the sight of it sent a chill up his spine.

If he what he was thinking was right, he had to tell someone or this could turn into a massacre. He feared, though, that if he told one of the numerous policemen patrolling the grounds they would hold him in custody. Eventually, they would discover he was wanted, although Ian didn't think Robinson had put out anything official on him yet. Ian felt he needed to be free to find the black-haired man who had tried to blow him up with a rocket. He might be the only person who could identify the terrorist. But how was Ian going to stop him without a weapon.

The officer motioned for the people to cross and Ian went with them. Though the morning was already warm, the sweat rolling down Ian's face was not caused by the heat. He scanned the crowd, amazed at the number of people attending the event. No one seemed to care that their city was under siege. Many could die if he didn't find the killer or at least inform the authorities. As soon as he located Rocket Man, Ian decided he would call Robinson. He would let the detective handle things while he roamed free to search out the others.

Without a ticket, Ian had to wait in line to purchase one. The wasted time worked to increase his building tension level. At the gate, officers on both sides of the flow checked bags for anything that could be considered a weapon.

He forced himself to breathe while one officer swept a wand over him as another stern-faced cop watched with his hand resting on the butt of his gun. His stomach fluttered and it was all he could do to keep from running away as fast as his feet would take him.

Once through the gate, Ian realized how enormous the task of finding one man was going to be. The tournament drew thousands of people. According to the TV news reports, the tournament officials had been afraid the terrorist attacks would keep attendance down, but if this was low attendance, Ian couldn't imagine a normal crowd. Obviously, the mayor's message had been persuasive: this city's residents were not going to allow terrorists to change their lives.

Ian walked, pivoting around in all directions to the annoyance of fans who wanted to get inside. He stopped in front of Vendor's Row, where tents were set up on both sides of the walkway into the course. A multitude of companies were trying to sell and promote their products or solicit e-mail addresses, a sign that no matter what, business must go on. Most were giving away free gifts, which caused the tents to be packed. The compressed walls of humanity made it difficult to see anything.

Ian turned in slow circles as he walked toward the end of the line of tents. A small hill lay before him. As he crested the slope, his jaw slackened. In front of him, the wide-open space stretched on for a great distance. The grounds were filled with countless people unaware of the potential danger that surrounded them. A long row of constantly changing people lined the first tee like a gauntlet. Fans moved to find a spot where they could watch each golfer drive their first tee shot.

A burst of applause erupted from the gallery as each golfer was introduced. Almost instantly, the noise ceased as if someone had flipped off a switch. The silence was somehow disconcerting to Ian, like the calm before a storm. Applause sounded again as the drive soared down the fairway in a long, high arc. It was hard not to be drawn to the woman golfer as she waved to the crowd and stepped aside for the next pro to tee off. Ian forced his eyes back to the gallery, but his efforts seemed futile. His heart sank as the band across his chest tightened

As he moved, Ian tried to take in the setup. It would help to know where he was on the course. After about twenty more paces, he realized how impossible the task was. He needed help. He could never live with himself if he had the opportunity to stop whatever was about to happen because he was afraid to call the cops. He would gladly sacrifice his freedom if it meant saving so many innocent lives.

He grabbed his phone from his pocket and found the number, but before he pushed send, he had another thought. He needed help, but maybe there was an alternative to the police. Locating the other number, he pushed send.

When it was answered, he said, "It's Kelly. I need help."

Silence greeted him.

"I'm on a burner."

The voice in his ear said, "I thought I made it clear you should never contact us again."

"You're the only one I can turn to."

"Not my problem. Besides, if I'm reading the paper right, it sounds like you've been doing all right. We can't help you."

"Please, I'm desperate."

"Sorry. You knew the risks. Don't drag us into your problems and don't call here again."

"I found the terrorists," Ian blurted.

The phone didn't disconnect, so he continued. "They're going to kill lots of people if I don't stop them and I can't do it alone. For obvious reasons, I can't go to the cops. I'm pretty sure they know who I am by now and are looking for me."

The silence was unbearable. Ian was about to say 'forget it', when he heard, "Where are you?" He couldn't stop the sigh of relief that escaped him.

"They're going to hit the golf tournament."

"We're fifteen minutes away. I'll call you when we get there."

"Ok. But there's cops everywhere and they're checking for weapons."

The phone disconnected.

Ian didn't know what that meant, but he couldn't wait for them. The terrorists were here somewhere. Ian walked on, searching.

53

Ahmed found the solution to one of his problems almost as soon as he passed through the gate. The various businesses were all giving things away. One of them, a co-sponsor of the event, was giving away large green plastic bag with handles to carry all the other free goodies in. Ahmed waited in line to receive one.

Another of the free gifts was a visor with the company's logo on it. He had no idea who the company was, but he slid it on to help cover his Middle Eastern appearance. As he climbed to the top of a small hill, the other three men were waiting at a distance, spread out. They had been instructed to watch each other enter in case of a problem.

They made no acknowledgment, but looked for a signal from Ahmed. Walking past the others, Ahmed tapped the bag with his hand and motioned over his shoulder with his head. The three men understood and went back to get bags for themselves. They would make retrieving and transporting the bombs and weapons easier.

Ahmed didn't wait for the others. Too many in the woods at one time might draw attention. He took a leisurely route around the first tee, walking on the outer fringes of the gallery. He stopped and leaned against a large tree, setting the bag down next to him. Ahmed stood there watching the women tee off and applauded along with the rest of the crowd. He waited until after the next woman teed off, then scooped up the bag and walked casually into the woods, angling deeper every few trees.

Periodically, Ahmed would stop and pick up a pine cone or twig, examine it, then pitch it. It took several minutes to find the marked tree where his buried weapon and bomb were. He leaned against the tree. Lowering his head as if looking for something, he glanced up to see if anyone was watching. Judging the coast clear, Ahmed knelt and pretended to tie his shoe as he scooped up the loose dirt and leaves spread over the bomb.

Several inches down his fingers scraped the device. He couldn't help the excited catch in his throat. A quick glance to make sure he was still alone and he lifted the bomb out of the hole and placed it in the bag. Covering it with papers he picked up from the various vendor tents, he slid the gun in his belt, camouflaging it with his baggy shirt, then stuffed the extra magazines in his pockets. Brushing the dirt from his hands and pants, Ahmed made his way back to the gallery. He looked at his watch and hoped the others were as successful. If they stayed on schedule, less than an hour remained before detonation.

***

With each passing second, Ian felt time running out. To the right and twenty yards behind the first tee stood the clubhouse, a long one-story structure with seating on an outdoor patio. Further down the fairway on the left, a large white tent housed VIPs. Behind the tent, a large grandstand that wrapped around the eighteenth green had been erected. Right now, those stands were empty since none of the golfers had reached that point yet. Ian followed the first fairway past the tent, scanning the crowds as he went. To his knowledge, he had not passed any of the terrorists, but he wasn't sure he would know if he had. The only one he'd gotten a clean look at was the man who tried to blow him up. He was getting desperate to locate him, but in this mass of humanity it seemed hopeless.

He stopped and slapped both palms on his cheeks. What should he do? He was at a loss. *Think, stupid. Think.* He let out a breath and tried to regroup his thoughts. *If I were a terrorist trying to get the most bang for my buck, where would I be?* They would want an area that grouped the most people together.

Ian spun around to the tent. Many VIPs were already taking advantage of the extra price they paid to lounge and sip drinks under the cooler covered space. The grandstand would also be a good target once the field had reached the eighteenth green. Would the terrorists wait that long for them to fill up? His eyes continued to the clubhouse, where even at this early hour, some patrons had already staked out seats.

Ian looked down the course. In the distance were several smaller bleachers built around the greens. They would all be good targets. Ian decided to walk toward the back of the course. He wanted to get a look underneath one of the bleachers.

The first green had more than a hundred fans gathered around it watching one of the golfer's putt. The applause announced she had made the shot. Ian skirted around the crowd and followed the flow to the second and third holes. He crossed to the opposite side of the fairway, walking directly to the bleachers near the fourth green. He stopped behind them and bent to tie his shoe. The underside of the bleachers appeared free from any unnatural attachments.

Standing up, he looked across the green. Nothing struck him as odd. Ian turned around and looked behind him into the woods that separated two of the holes, and there he saw movement. Amidst the trees, too far away to see any of the golf shots could be seen, was a man carrying a green bag. He was walking away from the course. It could be nothing, maybe just someone looking to take a leak. But it was also the best lead Ian had to go on so far. He took off in that direction, stalking the man.

Ian made it to the trees and reacquired his target. The man ducked behind a tree and knelt. Ian tried to hurry without making too much noise. With all the brush and leaves, stealth wasn't an easy task. At one point, after kicking up a branch, Ian darted for the cover of a tree. It wasn't a large tree, so he couldn't be sure he hadn't been spotted. He waited a few very long seconds before peeking around the opposite side of the trunk. The man was no longer in sight.

Breaking cover and moving far faster than caution dictated, Ian arrived at the tree where he had seen the man. A small hole at the base of the trunk had been hastily covered. He kicked away the leaves exposing the dimensions of the hole. A picture of what might have been hidden there came to mind. *Oh, boy. This isn't a good thing.* His pulse quickened and his mouth was suddenly very dry. A rustling of leaves behind him was the only warning that someone was on to him. Instinctively, he ducked and moved right as the man lunged past him, sticking a knife blade into the tree.

Ian reacted with wide eyes and a pounding heart. While the assailant pulled at the knife to free it, Ian drove his foot into the side of the man's knee, buckling it and sending him to the ground with a stifled scream. As the assailant fell, the knife dislodged and was now in his hand. Without thinking, Ian dove on him, pinning the knife between them. Both men grunted as Ian's weight drove the air out of his opponent's lungs.

They grappled for the knife and Ian felt he was winning the battle until his hands became slick from sweat and slipped free from the handle. A vicious blow to Ian's head dazed him. An elbow to the other side of his head darkened his vision for a second. This man was more than Ian could handle, but he could not allow him to get free.

The terrorist rolled away. Ian followed, jumping on his back as the man tried to stand. His weight drove the knife wielder to the ground again. Using both hands, Ian grabbed the man's head and slammed it down on the ground where it struck a small protruding root. The first thud made it easier to repeat the action and Ian drove the man's head down again and again until he ceased to resist.

Ian straddled the body and tried to catch his adrenaline-driven breath. The man evidently had no energy left for a fight, either, because he didn't move. After a moment, Ian thought it strange that he'd been able to best a trained killer with such ease. He lifted a leg and rolled the man over carefully to ensure he wasn't playing possum. He had nothing to fear. The man was dead. His eyes stared blankly at the trees above him, the knife buried to the hilt, just below his heart.

He examined the man's face. He couldn't be sure if he was the same man who had fired the rocket at him. That man had a beard, this man didn't. Of course, he could've shaved. Ian decided he couldn't be sure. He would have to continue his search.

Looking down, he saw his own hands were covered in blood. Ian wiped them on the dead man's shirt as best he could. His dark jacket had taken some of the blood splatter from the man's wound. He stripped it off and checked the rest of him. He was clean. Maybe not under a close examination, but to the passing crowd he shouldn't cause concern. Pulling the knife from the body, he wiped it on the man's shirt, then stuck it in his pocket. At least now he had a weapon.

Before he did anything else, he looked around to make sure he was still alone. Seeing that he was, Ian propped the body up against the tree to hide it. He wiped the nylon jacket on the dead man's pants. Much of it came clean. Then he checked the man's pockets and found some money, which he took, and two magazines for a handgun. There was no gun, however. Maybe the gun had been in the hole. *Wasn't the man carrying a green bag?* Pocketing the magazines, Ian went in search of the gun.

He found it in the bag, two trees back, along with something that scared him breathless. In the bottom, covered by some papers, was a small rectangular block that looked like an explosive device. A circular metal rod stuck out of putty-like substance attached to two wires. He was afraid to touch it, but he couldn't leave it lying about. Someone could stumble across it and get blown up.

Picking it up as carefully as he could, Ian carried it back to the hole. Using the knife, he dug the ground out deeper, then placed the bomb inside. He covered it with the dirt and then with leaves. Last, he took the knife and marked the tree before noting a small, white chalk X was already there.

Checking the gun, he found it loaded and jacked. He tucked it behind him in his belt, slid the knife into an inside jacket pocket, and went hunting terrorists. Ian felt better, knowing if he found one, he could now do something to stop them.

Not wanting to exit the trees from where he entered, Ian walked farther toward the rear of the course coming out along the fifth hole fairway. How many others besides the black-haired man he had recognized were there? He thought back to the SUVs, but they had tinted windows, leaving no way of knowing how many men had been inside each. All he could do was walk and keep looking. He kept the tree line in view in case anyone else emerged.

Going back to his original idea, Ian looked for large groups of fans knotted together. Now knowing explosives were on the grounds, Ian hunted for places where they could be hidden from view. He walked the fifth green and crossed behind the semicircle of people watching a putt. Once again he found himself turning in circles. Small bleacher sections were all around, too many to check by himself before something happened. He couldn't afford to wait any longer. He needed more help now. He yanked out the cell phone and dialed the number that perhaps he should've called first.

"Yeah?" Robinson clearly was not happy.

"This is the person you've been looking for."

"Yeah. And?"

"You need to listen. This is--"

"No, you need to listen. You get your ass in here--"

"Shut the fuck up!" Ian screamed. People around him moved away, perhaps thinking he was dangerous. This was not going as he wanted it to. He walked away from everyone and stood near the trees, turning his back to the crowd.

"Just shut up and listen."

Robinson tried to respond, but Ian yelled over him.

"I found the terrorists. Now listen before they start killing people."

Ian didn't wait for a reply.

"They're at the golf tournament. I saw the black SUVs and a separate car. The driver of the car is the same guy I followed after that last attack. They're going to hit the tournament. And you know how many people are here. Call someone. I'm searching, but I can't find them all. There's just too damn many people here. I found--"

"Go to a cop and tell him what you told me."

"I don't think so. I need to be free to find these guys. I'm the only one who knows what they look like. Somehow I think if I go to a cop, you'll fix it so I won't be free to do that."

"This had better not be bullshit, or I swear--"

"You'll swear what? You'll kill me when you see me? Do you really think my death matters to me, especially when so many others' lives are at stake? Look, Detective, you may not like me or what I've done, but I'm not a bad man. I can help save these people, but you have to trust me and act now. When it's all over, you can have me, but this has to be dealt with now."

"All right, I'll make a call. I'll tell them to be searching for you. As far as I'm concerned, you're the only terrorist out there."

"Listen, you stupid son of a bitch. I found one of them. He had a bomb, asshole. Does that get your attention? A bomb. I'm not the enemy here. I managed to stop him and bury it, but there are others here. What if they all have bombs? Are you willing to risk these peoples' lives? I'm not. I'm going to do what I need to do to stop these animals before they kill any more Americans. Now act like the policeman I think you are and make some calls."

A more subdued Robinson replied. "Is the bomb still live?"

"Yeah, I think. I don't know anything about them."

"Describe it."

"A clay-like brick with wires and a metal tube that I guess is a detonator. I buried it behind a tree in the southwest corner of the course."

"Fuck. It sounds like C4. All right, do what you can. I'll make some calls. Keep me informed if you find anything else."

Ian was about to hang up when he thought of something else.

"Oh shit, I almost forgot. You have to be careful not to create panic. One of the SUVs is positioned directly across from the gate. It may be nothing, but if a stampede of people burst out of those gates, it would be a perfect place for a bomb—or an ambush. The shooter could hardly miss."

With that, Ian disconnected. As he was putting the phone back in his pocket, Ian noticed that in his haste he had used his own phone instead of the burner. He gave a mental shrug and said, "Oh well, he knows for sure now."

A few steps farther, the burner rang. Ian pulled it out and answered.

"We're here," Bonzo said.

"Things have gotten worse. I took one of them out."

"How's that worse?"

"He had a bomb."

"Ah, yeah. Worse."

"I need you guys to search under all the grandstands and around any buildings you come to. I think it's C4. You know what that looks like?"

"Fuck yeah."

"You know how to defuse it?"

"Probably. Where are you?"

"Back between the fifth green and the sixth tee."

"Stay there. I'll come to you. We'll take care of the search up here."

54

Ahmed took a seat on the patio of the clubhouse. He ordered an iced tea from an overly excited waiter and sat back to watch the crowd roll by. Retrieving his package had been easier than anticipated. After his tea arrived, Ahmed went to the bathroom and placed one brick above the ceiling tiles in the men's bathroom. He returned to the table, keeping the other explosive in the bag at his feet along with the gun. The spare magazines were in his pocket.

The others should have set their bombs by then. Otherwise, he would have heard some sort of commotion. His men would not go down without a fight. Gunshots would be his signal to detonate the explosives and make for his escape route.

Ahmed picked up the tea and sat back to enjoy the minutes remaining before the show. Glancing at his watch, he saw he had a half hour before he started the slaughter. The crowds continued to pour through the gate. That elated him. The more to add to the carnage.

Look at them all, with their expensive clothes and their money to burn on unimportant things like a sporting event. The money spent to purchase one ticket would be enough to feed a person for a month in many parts of the world. These ignorant Americans deserved to die here, if only for their wastefulness.

He sipped the tea and wondered if his bombs would kill more than a thousand. The steady stream of people still entering the grounds made him smile. He toyed with the idea of delaying the explosions to allow more people to enter. Maybe it would be ten thousand then.

***

Ian recognized Bonzo's large frame from a full green away. He waited until bulky man got closer and then moved to intercept. He nodded at Ian but kept walking. Ian fell into stride next to him.

"Show me where. No, don't point."

Ian dropped his hand.

"To the right, about fifty yards in. I marked the back side of the tree and covered the…er, it with some dirt and leaves. It's not deep."

"All right. I'll go in and take care of it. You keep searching out here. Since you know they're here, I take it that means you know what they look like."

"Well, one of them, anyway."

"Go get 'em."

Bonzo veered to the right. Ian went left.

Ian made his way toward the ninth green where the second largest grandstand had been erected. As he neared, he noticed a large man duck under the stands and disappear. Ian began jogging. As he did he reached around his back to get a quick grasp of the gun if needed and to prevent it from falling. Closer to the bleachers now, Ian slowed, approaching with caution. People were looking at him, but he ignored them. If he caught another terrorist, they would understand his behavior.

He tensed, ready to pull the gun as he caught sight of the man. However, the body that emerged from the bleachers was Big Jim's. Seeing Ian, he nodded and gave him a thumbs-up, the detonator pressed between his large fingers. He was all smiles. Ian stopped.

"You found one?"

"Yep. No more boom."

He seemed very pleased with himself.

"I hope there aren't many more," Ian said. "I'm going to where that big tent is. I went past without checking it."

"Roger that," Big Jim replied.

Big Jim strolled off, seemingly unfazed by the fact he had just diffused a bomb.

Ian walked with haste toward the VIP tent. He was feeling better about his chances of stopping the assault now. He only wished he had an idea of how many bombs there were. With his mind so focused, he never heard Bonzo come up next to him. Ian jumped sideways, fearing he was under attack.

"Have you noticed the increased police presence?"

Ian looked around as if for the first time. Cops were walking through the crowds trying to appear casual in their intent. Robinson must have made the call. Blue shirts dotted the scene in all directions.

Bonzo lifted his phone to his ear.

"Yeah?" He listened. "Do nothing. There are too many cops."

They're liable to think you planted it. Find a cop and tell him what you saw and let him deal with it. Then drift into the background and get out of there."

He clicked off. They kept walking until they were next to the tent.

"Tex said he saw a guy duck under one of the bleachers. He was under there when he called. You heard what I told him. How many of these bastards you figure there are?"

"I don't know for sure, but from what I saw the other day, there might be five or six left. Unless they have more I didn't see, of course."

"Huh."

"You see how this tent backs up to the large grandstand? It would be a perfect place to hide a bomb. No one could see, 'cause it's blocked by the tent wall."

"Okay, let's look," Bonzo said.

"Let's double our efforts. I think the two most likely places are here and the clubhouse. I'll check up there."

Bonzo nodded and ducked under the tent's support ropes. Ian headed for the clubhouse a hundred yards away. As the distance closed, he began scanning the patrons sitting on the awning-covered patio. The shaded interior made it difficult to make out details, but his eyes locked on one target. In the very middle, sitting by himself at a small round table, was a man wearing a visor. Black hair stuck out the open top. From that distance, the man looked very tan.

The closer Ian got, the more convinced he became that this was the same man that shot the missile at him. For his part, the man looked relaxed. He held a glass in his hand and his legs were stretched out under the table. A green bag sat near his chair. He glanced at his watch and then went back to watching the crowds. Ian continued on, his eyes locked on the man as if he were a missile. Ten feet closer, the man stiffened, suddenly aware of Ian's gaze. He focused on Ian. Ian couldn't look away. He was positive now this was his man.

Very slowly, the man put down his glass and slid his legs underneath him. His hand reached into the bag sitting on the ground next to him. Ian wasn't sure what to do if the hand came out of the bag holding a weapon, but he surely wouldn't shoot into the crowded area. As soon as the thought entered his mind he knew how absurd it was. This man was a terrorist; a stone-cold killer. He would have no hesitation shooting anyone in sight. Ian had to get to him before the hand came out. But even as he thought it, he knew there was no way that would happen.

Ian increased his pace and the man stood, pulling the bag up with one hand while the other stayed inside it. Just then, from some distance behind Ian, the sound of gunshots echoed over the grounds and froze the action in the gallery. Without thinking, Ian reacted to the shots and ducked. He glanced behind him. Cops from all over were bolting toward the sound, guns drawn. By the time Ian brought his eyes back to the patio, the man was gone.

Desperation gripped at Ian's chest. He scanned the nervous patrons from center to right then back left. Somewhere behind him more shots were fired and answered. From the corner of his eye, Ian saw blurred motion and turned in time to see the man hurdle the small decorative fence that surrounded the patio. As soon as his feet touched down, he was off running around the far side of the clubhouse. Ian gave pursuit as though he had done that type of thing all his life.

The terrorist's hands were full, but of what, Ian couldn't be sure. The time for pretense was over. He reached behind him as he ran and pulled out the gun. The terrorist ran toward the fenced corner of the course. His only options were to climb the fence and escape or turn and fire. Ian couldn't give him the chance to do either. Then, as if slamming into an invisible wall, Ian came to a panicked stop. The terrorist was not holding the bag. Ian spun and scanned the patio. The bag had been pushed under the table.

With a hateful look at the man escaping, Ian realized he had to make a choice: the terrorist or the bomb. Ian turned and raced for the patio. With his gun now prominently out in the open for all to see, the customers who were left in the clubhouse ran screaming in all directions. Ian added to the chaos by shouting, "Bomb! Get out of the way! There's a bomb! Everyone get out of here!"

He ran past the stampede and snatched up the bag. One glance inside confirmed his fears. "Oh, dear God!" He slid the gun back in his belt, reached inside the bag, then thought better of it. He scrunched the bag shut as if that would prevent the blast from escaping. He should have asked Bonzo how to defuse the explosive. Could it be as simple as pulling out the metal stick thing?

To further complicate the moment Ian heard, "Freeze! Don't you move. Drop the gun."

"It's a bomb. I've got a bomb." Which of course was the entire wrong thing to say. Now they thought it was *his* bomb. "Get these people out of here."

Ian slid his hand inside and fumbled for the protrusions as he made for the open spaces. Ice shards stabbed his heart. Even though he fully expected to die, he realized he didn't want to be blown up.

The cop, not knowing what to think, repeated, "Freeze." When Ian didn't obey, the cop turned toward the crowd and shouted for them to run. The officer reported into his shoulder mic, asking for backup.

Pushing all pain aside, Ian ran as fast as he had ever run before, trying to put distance between him and everyone else. He heard the cop yell something behind him. Ian didn't look, but he was sure the cop was in pursuit. He had no idea if what he was about to do would work or if it would be the last thing he ever did in this life, but he grabbed the tube, yanked it free, and flung the bag. However, it wasn't three feet from his hands when the explosion occurred.

The concussion blew Ian off his feet. He had a momentary feeling of flight before he crashed to the ground, rolling over numerous times before a tree brought him to an abrupt stop. He wasn't sure how long he lay there, but eventually, the world began to come back into focus. Echoes came from everywhere and he thought he must be in hell, because heaven couldn't be this loud.

When at last Ian looked around, his first clear image was of the explosive brick he'd tossed, now only a foot from his head. Ian was confused until he looked around and noticed the clubhouse was no longer there.

55

"I have the interior in sight," the SWAT sniper reported to his commanding officer.

The number two sniper said, "I have no line of sight from here. I'm repositioning."

The commander said, "Anything?"

"No sir. Looks like the back is covered in blankets. By the shape there could be something concealed beneath them."

"All right, keep an eye on it. Someone thinks it's important and with everything that's happened in this city lately, we can't afford to be lax."

"Roger."

The commander turned to Robinson. "You're sure about this?"

"No, but I think my informant is reliable."

The easily recognizable sound of gunshots reverberated across the golf course. The commander tensed and looked in that direction. His earbud came to life.

"I have movement within the SUV, sir. One male. He's got what looks like a .50 cal. He just popped the rear window and is rising, setting the weapon. He's ready to fire."

The first sounds of panic came from the course, spreading fast and growing louder. The fans would stampede the small entryway. In moments, it would be jam-packed with easy targets for the shooter in the SUV. He had seconds to make his decision and give the order to fire before the slaughter would commence.

"Two, what's your status?"

"Setting up, sir."

"One, do you have a shot?"

"Roger."

An explosion rocked the ground. The commander saw the smoke rise above the clubhouse and knew they were now in a combat situation.

"Take it, one. Take it now."

The crack of the shot was lost in the aftermath of the explosion and the resulting screams from the patrons fleeing the area.

"Ground Team, advance and secure."

Four heavily armed and armored men moved with practiced efficiency to control the SUV.

The commander swung his binoculars toward the golf course. Police inside the gate were trying to stem the stampede before it reached the street by having everyone hit the ground. A line of uniformed and suited enforcement agents from many different departments lined the outer fence with guns readied.

A crackle in the commander's ear gave him the report. "One dead, sir. The scene is secure."

Then, "Two, sir. I have eyes on another black SUV coming around the corner at high speed."

The commander turned and saw the SUV barreling toward them. It appeared the terrorists had a backup plan. Both passenger side windows were down and machine pistols extended out toward the row of officers that were set up along the front of the fence. Many of them had already pulled their weapons, but were looking at the golf course rather than toward the street. In an instant, they would be mowed down.

"Two, take the shot!" the commander shouted. "Take the shot!"

A second later the bullet hit the windshield a fraction after the vehicle veered toward the police line. The driver jumped in his seat as the guns opened fire. As one unit, the police sent a deadly barrage at the SUV, drilling holes all through its body. The vehicle swerved back to the left, the driver hanging half out of the window. Full automatic fire still raged from the rear window, but with little accuracy. The vehicle jumped the curb and crashed into the rear of the other SUV, scattering the SWAT members.

***

Robinson, weapon raised, ran toward the grounds as soon as he'd heard the first shots. Kelly had been right, but that didn't change the fact that he was wanted for murder, and Robinson was determined to capture him.

Too many people were trying to escape through the gate at the same time, creating a wall of panicked humanity. Robinson had no choice but alter his course toward the smoldering ruins of the clubhouse. Kelly was on the grounds somewhere. He hoped the man hadn't been part of the bombing, but it didn't matter. He had to be caught. Finding him amidst the chaos would be difficult.

56

When Ian regained his senses, he looked for the bomber, but he was gone. He scrambled to his feet, wincing at the pain that seemed to cover his entire body. His phone rang. He looked at the screen, thinking it was Bonzo. Instead, he recognized the number of JT's care facility. He feared it was bad news about his son, but he couldn't take the time to talk now. Sliding the phone back in his pocket, he was about to give chase when he saw the policeman lying on the ground. He ran to the man and dropped beside him.

"Are you all right?" The man's eyes were unfocused, as if he had a concussion. The cop's gun was a few feet away. Ian picked it up. The man groaned, his eyes coming to rest on Ian.

"Just relax, you're all right. I'll call an ambulance."

The man tried to speak, then tried to rise. Ian saw fear on his face.

"It wasn't me," Ian told him. "I saw the man who left the bomb. I was just trying to remove it so it didn't hurt anyone."

The man studied Ian's eyes and seemed to relax.

"I saw where he went. I have to go after him before I lose him. You stay here. I'll call for help."

Ian stood but felt a hand grab his leg. He looked down.

"Get the bastard."

Ian nodded and the man let go. He hadn't taken two steps when he heard, "Kelly, freeze."

Ian swung around toward the voice and saw Robinson fixed in a shooter's stance, the gun leveled at him.

"It's over. Don't make me shoot you."

Ian dropped the gun and lifted his hands half way up. He still had the gun at his back, but to pull it would be to invite death and as ready as he was for that to happen, it couldn't be now.

"Detective, the bomber just climbed that fence. I would have had him, except the explosion knocked me down."

"Get on your knees and clasp your hands behind your head."

Desperation crept into Ian's voice. "Look, I pulled that bomb from inside the clubhouse so more people would not be hurt. Ask your man here." Ian pointed toward the fence, but before he could say anything else, Robinson yelled.

"Get your ass on the ground now!"

"Which would you rather have, Robinson? The terrorist or me? You can't have both, and your chances of catching him are sliding away the longer it takes you to decide."

Robinson hesitated.

"Robinson, you can get me anytime. Don't let him get away."

Robinson stepped forward with handcuffs. Ian stepped back. Robinson raised his gun again.

"I'm still the only one who knows what he looks like. You need me."

Robinson stopped again. Kelly gambled the detective would see that he was right. The terrorist *was* more important.

"I can't wait for you to decide. I have to stop him. Shoot me if you want."

Ian took off for the fence. He waited for the shot to take him down, but it never came. Instead, he heard footsteps behind him. Robinson was going to try to tackle him. Ian tried to sidestep to avoid the dive. He was surprised when Robinson caught up to him, looked at him, and ran past. "Come on, if we're going to catch this guy."

He reached the corner of the fence, leaped up on the support bar, grabbed the top bar and swung both legs over like a man who had done that type of thing many times before. He landed softly on the other side and started running.

Ian caught the first bar and had to pull himself to the top. There, he put one foot on the top bar and tried to jump to the other side. His landing was far from graceful. He hit and rolled several times before pushing to his feet. Robinson was already across the clubhouse parking lot. Ian caught him at the street, but only because Robinson slowed.

"Did you see which way?" Robinson asked.

"I would think to the left. The other way would bring him back toward the police."

They ran left, but saw no one who fit the description Ian gave. The street was lined with houses on both sides. They had to slow and give a quick look at each one before moving on. Two blocks later, they crossed the street where a school's parking lot had been drafted into use for the tournament. The two men began looking inside cars.

Robinson walked ahead of Ian, his gun ready. Ian didn't want to pull his until it was absolutely necessary. Seeing a gun in his hand might spook Robinson into shooting *him*.

Ian finished checking a minivan when he saw movement in a car two spots down from where he stood. The window descended, but no one was in view. Robinson stood in front of the car with his back to it, looking across the lot. Ian started moving.

Ian saw the terrorist's head appear in the window and level a gun outside the frame. Ian increased his speed in an instant. He screamed, "Robinson!" and barreled into the man as the terrorist pulled the trigger. The force of Ian's tackle drove them both out of the bullet's path and to the ground.

Behind them, the car roared to life. Both men rolled clear of its wheels. The car shot forward and down the driveway. Robinson jumped up and sprinted across the grass to get an angle on the car, his arms pumping furiously. Ian regained his feet and pushed off in pursuit. He could feel the phone in his pocket vibrating. He wondered if it was Bonzo. Whoever it was would have to wait.

The car turned right at the street. Robinson gained ground as it crossed his path. He lifted the gun and fired until the slide locked open. Ian thought he saw the driver react as if struck by a bullet. The car lurched to the left and drove up the driveway of a large brick home across from the school. The driver struggled to turn onto the sidewalk. The car slowed. From Ian's point of view, it appeared the driver was working the wheel one-handed.

Ian raced past Robinson as the cop changed magazines. He would not let this killer get away. He pulled out the gun he had stashed behind his back.

Inside the car, Ahmed tried to swing the car onto the sidewalk with one hand. A bullet had hit him square in the right shoulder, making his arm all but useless and leaving him defenseless. He could either drive or shoot. Right now, he chose to drive. He pointed the car and drove over the grass toward the street. He looked to the right and saw the man from the clubhouse chasing him.

He slowed and tried to force his injured arm to raise the gun and get a shot off if only to hinder pursuit, but it would not respond. He could not lift the barrel high enough to shoot out the window. For the first time, Ahmed thought he might actually fail. The idea angered him. It was this man's fault. He needed to die.

Ahmed hit the gas and bounced back on the road. Instead of

trying to escape, however, he drove straight for the man with the gun.

Ian saw the car accelerate toward him. He tried to remain calm as the car closed on him. He fired twice and dove to his right. The car brushed him, sending him spinning. He hit the ground hard and rolled.

Robinson stopped when he saw the car race past Kelly. From his angle, he couldn't tell if Kelly had been hit or not. Robinson took a deep breath, lifted his gun, and pulled the trigger. The car veered toward him. One shot after another exploded from the barrel and crashed through the now-shattered windshield. He couldn't tell if the driver had been hit, but the car kept coming. Robinson turned and ran for the protection of the school's brick sign in the middle of the lawn.

As the car sped past Ian, he scrambled to his feet and went after it. His gun had gone flying, but he didn't want to spend the time looking for it. He ran hard. The driver was now targeting Robinson. Ian could do nothing to help him, but no matter what, the driver was not going to escape.

The car hit the low decorative stone wall in front of the sign and jumped into the air. Robinson dove to one side and rolled. The car crashed halfway through the sign. Glass, metal, and brick flew through the air in a dangerous shower. The chassis came down with its left rear wheel well on top of what was left of the sign. The car hung suspended and turned sideways, the driver side door in the air.

The driver tried to climb out, but his leg gave out and he fell, hitting the ground hard. He tried to rise as Ian ran closer. The terrorist's right arm hung at his side, dripping blood. More patches of blood covered the front of his shirt. Multiple cuts lined his face. The black-haired man staggered to his feet and took two steps toward Robinson. The detective had taken a brick to the head and lay stunned. The terrorist said something Ian could not make out and lifted the gun he held in his left hand at Robinson. Ian hit him from behind before he could pull the trigger. The two men went down together.

Ian's momentum took him past the killer. He did a shoulder roll and came up face-first, looking down the barrel of a gun. His heart froze. The end had finally come. His mind flashed to JT. *Sorry* was the only thought he had time for before he heard the shot. He felt no pain. Had the injured man missed? He looked up to see that half the terrorist's face was now missing. The dead man's finger jerked on the trigger, sending a round into Ian's left arm and knocking him backward. He writhed in pain.

Robinson stood up and followed his gun barrel toward the body of the terrorist. He kicked the gun free, checking to make sure the man was dead, then went to Ian.

He looked down at the man the city knew as The Vigilante. Ian looked back, gritting his teeth against the pain. A smile creased Robinson's face.

"Damn, Kelly, you've made me a hero."

He pointed his gun and pressed the phone to his ear.

57

While they waited for an ambulance, Robinson tried to stop the flow of blood by pressing Ian's own shirt against his wound.

"You'll be all right. The bullet went through. Just hold this and keep pressure on it."

He stood up, walked to the terrorist, and stooped over him. Ian couldn't see what he was doing.

"Is he dead?"

"Oh yeah."

A siren was growing closer. So far, no additional police had arrived. They were all busy with the evacuation of the golf course and the search for more bombs. Robinson didn't seem to be worried, though. Evidently, he didn't think Ian was a flight risk.

Robinson came back over and squatted next to Ian.

"You know, Kelly, I understand why you did it. I even have a respect for you. But it's still against the law. Just so you know that we were actually doing our job, we found Marcus Davis hiding in his Grandma's basement last night and arrested him. I thought you'd like to know there are no longer any loose ends."

"Thank you, Detective. I appreciate that."

"And, uh, thanks. You know, for saving my life."

"Ditto, but in retrospect, I wish you wouldn't have."

The ambulance pulled up and stopped. Two EMTs stepped out and started unloading equipment.

Ian's phone rang again. He reached for it but Robinson slapped his hand away.

"I think it's the care facility where my son is. They've been trying to reach me."

Robinson took the phone out and looked at the screen. He pressed the speaker button and put it to Ian's ear. Both men heard the excited voice from the other end.

"Ian, I mean, Mr. Kelly. It's KeKe, from the nursing home. Your son..." There was a sob. "Oh my God."

Ian felt his chest tighten and his throat go dry.

"He opened his eyes, Mr. Kelly. JT's awake. You don't need to do it anymore. Your son is asking for you. Don't throw your life away. He's going to need you now. Did you hear me, Mr. Kelly? JT's awake."

Ian couldn't answer. His throat had constricted too much. Tears rolled down his face. He swallowed hard a few times before he could get the words out. "Thank you. Tell him I love him, and…and…to forgive me."

"Mr. Kelly, you have to come and see him right now. He's your son. I know how important he is to you. I watched you with him. Mr. Kelly. Ian, please…"

Ian looked into Robinson's eyes, sending an unspoken plea. Robinson looked away.

"I'm sorry, KeKe, I don't think …" He never got to finish. Robinson's hand covered the phone. His other hand motioned the EMTs away.

"Give me your word, Kelly."

Ian sobbed. "Of course. I just want to see him once. I promise there'll be no trouble."

"We'll be there in a few minutes," Robinson said into the phone. He cut the connection and waved the techs forward.

"I need him ready to move. You can work on him in the ambulance. We need to make a stop first. I'll tell you where inside."

The men pressed a bandage against the wound and helped Ian to his feet. Inside the ambulance, one EMT worked on cleaning and assessing the wound.

"He needs to be in the hospital. He's lost a good deal of blood."

"We're aware of that, but this detour is more important to him than blood."

Ten minutes later, the ambulance pulled up in front of the nursing facility. KeKe Brogan ran outside to greet them. She was bouncing with energy. In her excitement, she almost threw her arms around Ian, but Robinson stopped her and pointed at the bandage and sling now wrapped around his neck. Her hands touched her face in exclamation. She looked from Ian to Robinson and back.

KeKe took Ian's good arm and led him to JT's room. The boy was sitting up, but had his eyes closed. He looked pale and so frail, but Ian's heart swelled to the point of bursting. The lights had been turned off to protect against the sensitivity of his long-closed eyes. A doctor stood next to the bed, checking JT over and asking questions.

Ian couldn't hold back the sob upon seeing his son awake. JT's eyes fluttered open, and in a weak voice, he cried, "Dad."

Ian stepped to his son's side and wrapped a loving arm around him, forgetting the pain that wracked his entire body. They both cried. KeKe added her tears.

The doctor said, "Why don't we leave and give the reunited father and son some time alone?"

Robinson hesitated. "Remember your promise, Kelly." He followed KeKe out the door.

Father and son tried to speak, but mostly cried. Ian pulled his wounded arm from the sling, wanting no restrictions. He needed to hug his son and no amount of pain was going to prevent that. Ten minutes later, the door opened and Robinson stood there. Ian couldn't bring himself to tell his son that this was the only chance they would ever get to see each other again.

"I love you, JT. No matter what, never forget that. I have to go now." Ian released his son, increasing the pain within him. JT didn't understand and reached for his dad, crying.

"Dad? Where-where--"

"It's okay, Jason. You get some rest now. I have to go." Ian turned to Robinson. "Thank you for this, Detective. You're a good man."

Robinson stepped into the room and Ian's heart broke, knowing his time with his son was over.

"What-what's going on, Dad? Why are the police here? Why are you bandaged like that?"

"JT, I've done some things--"

Robinson interrupted. "Your father's a hero, son. He helped me bring down a terrorist cell that has been on a killing spree." He stepped forward and patted Ian on the back. "Isn't that right, Ian?"

Ian's shocked expression made Robinson smile. Confused by his own words, he wondered what he was doing. *This man was a killer and had to be arrested, didn't he?*

The two men locked eyes and Kelly's filled with new tears. He fumbled for words but could push none out through his throat that seemed to have closed shut.

Robinson had his own trouble finding words. What the hell was he doing? He looked from the boy to Kelly and sighed. He had made a decision and only hoped he could live with it. The choice might not be right in the eyes of the law, but he knew in his heart it was the right thing to do. Hadn't Kelly suffered enough? He wasn't about to take him away after everything their family had been through. Besides, Kelly risked his own life to save his. The man deserved a second chance.

"Your father has to get to the hospital now, though. He needs to have that arm taken care of. He'll see you soon. You get stronger for when he comes back."

Ian couldn't believe his ears. He was so overwhelmed that his legs almost couldn't hold him upright. Robinson reached out a steadying hand.

"Tell your son goodbye. We'll talk about it later."

Ian went back to the bed and gave JT another hug. "I love you, JT."

"Love you, too, Dad."

Ian backed out of the room and closed the door. He turned to Robinson and saw the questions on the detective's face.

"Are you done? With the Vigilante act. Are you done?"

"Yes." Ian's voice was barely above a whisper. "There's no need anymore."

"If I find out differently, I'll take you down. That's a promise."

"No, I swear. No more. You have my word."

"Okay. Your family has been through enough. I'll cover this."

"Thank you. I can't begin to say how much this means."

"Well, don't give me all the credit. When I was in the hall, Nurse Brogan was very convincing on your behalf."

Ian looked to where Robinson motioned and saw KeKe standing ten feet away, trying to contain a bundle of nervous energy as she watched them.

"In case you haven't noticed, that's a pretty special lady there. Maybe it's time to bury the past and create second chances."

Robinson stepped back as KeKe approached. She wrapped her arms around Ian and held on while she cried into his chest.

"Thank you, KeKe," he whispered in her ear.

She broke the hold and gazed up at him. "Well, someone had to look after your sorry butt."

"We really should be getting the hero here to the hospital," said Robinson.

"Take care of my boy for me."

"I always do."

Despite his pain and his overwhelming emotions, he smiled at her. She squeezed his hand.

Ian's energy was drained. With his first step, he almost collapsed and needed assistance to get back to the ambulance. The EMTs helped him inside and strapped him to the gurney for transport.

"I guess you can handle things on your own from here," said Robinson.

Ian held out his hand. Robinson shook it.

"Don't make me regret this."

"Not a chance."

As the ambulance drove off, Robinson had one thought. *Damn! How do I get back to my car?*

4 Weeks Later

Ian waited outside while JT did his physical therapy. He stood with his eyes closed and face lifted, absorbing the warmth from the early afternoon sun. Life was better now. It would never be the same, but with time came hope.

JT was making great progress physically, but mentally, Ian wasn't sure. JT had repressed most of what had happened on the day of the murders, now more than a year past. Ian didn't push and never mentioned it. One day, when JT's mind was ready, it would come out and Ian would be there to help him through it, thanks in large part to Detective Robinson's kind heart.

Ian reflected on the days after the bombing.

In the aftermath of the attack on the golf course, Robinson had been proclaimed a hero. His fast reaction to the information he gained from an unnamed source was instrumental in the prevention of massive loss of life and the eventual take down of the terrorist cell. In all, seven people died that day, but the toll could have been so much worse.

Also pronounced heroes were three civilians: Robert "Bonzo" Bronkowski, James "Big Jim" Arbour, and Mathew "Tex" Dillon, for their invaluable assistance in subduing one terrorist and diffusing three bombs. Their heroic actions saved thousands of lives.

When Bonzo called Ian days later, he commented, "I'm not sure whether to hug you or shoot you for all the attention you brought us," he laughed, and Ian winced. "But the boys and me, well, we want you to know you have honorary membership status with us for life."

Ian wasn't sure what that meant, but he thanked him anyway.

Upon his release from the hospital, Ian led Robinson to the house and his weapons cache.

As for The Vigilante, a gun found on the golf course near one of the terrorists matched the ballistics from the weapon that killed four men in a basement in the north end a few days before. The police speculated the Vigilante was actually one of the terrorists who wanted to take advantage of the chaos in the city to do more killing.

Some of those in law enforcement and the media thought that made no sense, but since the killings had stopped, it was moot. The police were only happy to close the case. Ian never gave any thought to how his gun got there.

"So, how's he doing?"

KeKe's voice snapped him back to the present. He smiled at her. He had been doing that a lot these days; smiling.

"I think this will be his last session."

"Then what will you do?"

"I'd like to take him on a trip. Maybe go to Colorado and see the Rockies." He shrugged. "I don't know from there. We'll just wing it."

"That will be great for the two of you. You have a lot of lost time to catch up on."

They stood in a sudden, awkward silence. Although they had seen each other nearly every day since the attack, they hadn't really spoken about anything other than JT. It seemed better not to at the time. But with Ian's pending vacation, KeKe appeared ready to broach further subjects. Ian could feel it coming.

"What about us, Ian. Can there ever be an 'us'?"

Ian wondered the same thing. He couldn't deny he had feelings for her, but they had been repressed. Somehow, it didn't seem right to be contemplating replacing Margo so soon. Of course, she could never really be replaced, but maybe there would be a time down the road when it would feel right to move on. Right now, JT was the most important person in his life.

"Give it time, KeKe. I'm not quite ready yet."

"Should I wait?"

Ian turned to face her and placed a hand on each arm. "I can't ask you to do that. It's not fair to you."

"I just need to know if there's a chance for us. That you have an interest in being with me."

"Robinson spoke about second chances. In my heart, I believe you are my second chance. But it wouldn't be fair to you if my heart was still aching for Margo. She will always be a part of me. I'm not looking to replace her, but I will be looking for my second chance. Let's talk about it more when JT and I get back. Okay?"

She moved into Ian and hugged him. "Yes, that's fine."

Ian returned the hug and gave her a light kiss on her forehead. The door behind them opened and JT came out, walking with a metal cane.

"Seriously? Out in public?"

At first Ian, thought JT was upset by seeing his father in the arms of someone other than his mother. But when he released the hug and turned toward JT, he saw the sly grin on his son's face. "I mean, really. Have you thought about this?" he said to KeKe. "If you take up with this old man, you could end up with the name Kelly Kelly. Is that how you want to spend your life?"

Ian looked confused and turned to KeKe. "Oh, I guess I never told you. KeKe is a nickname I've had since I was a kid when my younger brother couldn't pronounce my name. My real name is Kelly."

The smile on Ian's face stretched wide until it broke into a hearty laugh. She wrapped an arm around JT and walked with him to the car. Seeing the two of them together and knowing how close they had become during JT's time as her patient and the weeks of therapy made things easier in Ian's mind. *Yeah,* he thought. *Kelly would be a great second chance. For both of us.*

Acknowledgments

Live to Die Again has undergone many changes on its path to publication. It started its journey as *The Vigilante*, but after realizing the title was too generic and not to mention used before, I made the switch.

Many people helped with this work. Thank you first to my original critique partner, author Shay Lacy, who finally gave me her thumbs up after many rewrites. (Her initial response had been, "Seriously, Dude?")

Thank you to my editor, JMac, Jodi McDermitt at Grammar and Tonic for her diligent work.

Thank you to Tyler Bertrand for the cover art.

Thank you to the wonderful people at Glory Days Press for bringing this project to light.

And finally, to my ever-growing readership, thanks for your continued support. Please visit my website www.raywenck.com for news and my appearance schedule.

Bio

Ray Wenck taught elementary school for 35 years. He was also the chef/owner of DeSimone's Italian restaurant for more than 25 years. After retiring, he became a lead cook for Hollywood Casinos and the kitchen manager for the Toledo Mud Hens. Now he spends most of his time writing, doing book tours, and meeting old and new fans and friends around the country.

Ray is the author of nine novels, including The Random Survival Series, the highly-acclaimed Amazon Top 20 post-apocalyptic series; the paranormal thriller, *Ghost of a Chance*; and the mystery/suspense Danny Roth Series.

His hobbies include reading, hiking, cooking, baseball and playing the harmonica.

Ray lives in the Toledo area where most of his stories are based.

Other Titles

Mystery/Suspense
The Danny Roth Series
Teammates
Teamwork
Home Team
Bottom of the Ninth (coming soon)

Post-Apocalyptic
The Random Survival Series
Random Survival
The Long Search for Home
The Endless Struggle

Paranormal Thriller
Ghost of a Chance

Young Adult Fantasy
Warriors of the Court

Made in the USA
Lexington, KY
26 March 2017